CARNIVAL

'Life is just like a carnival ride'

K.B. NELSON

DEDICATION

To my family and friends, thank you all for your patience and support. You're all extremely crazy, but I wouldn't have it any other way. To my editors Rogena and Carol, you are both rockstars and this book wouldn't have been possible without either of you. To my cover designer, Clarissa Yeo, who is an amazing and patient talent. A huge shoutout to my partner in crime, Sera Bright. You were my biggest support, and at times, my only motivation to press on. You kept me sane on this arduous journey and I'll be forever thankful.

"You never know when something is going to happen to change your life. You would expect it to arrive with fanfare, like a wedding or a birth, but instead it comes in the most ordinary of circumstances."

—Carole Radziwell, *What Remains*

CHAPTER ONE

I've got half a mind to set fire to the local news station. Why might I risk spending the rest of my life in prison for arson, you might ask? Because Jimmy Clay is a fucking liar.

I had stayed inside the past few days and needed to get out of the house. My mother was still reeling from her recent divorce from my father, so I've spent the entire summer after graduation by her side, helping her cope. At first, we just stayed at home and drank a lot, which wasn't too bad, until that one night when I awoke on the couch to her sobbing her eyes out, wondering why all men couldn't be like Ryan Gosling. I set fire to *The Notebook* the following night.

Ohio State University is calling my name, but it's a calling that's going to be left unanswered. My mom and dad don't know that, of course. They still believe they'll be waving to me as I drive off into the sunset in less than two weeks. Telling them the truth isn't a conversation I look forward to having.

The blazing hot sun beats against me like I've just walked into a cage match I didn't sign up for, causing a damp layer of sweat to swell against my hairline.

Yesterday was supposed to be the last day of the heat wave from hell. *It's going to be a cool night tonight,* the weatherman Jimmy Clay said.

Believing him was my first mistake. The most important lesson I've learned since birth is to never trust the weatherman, especially Meteorologist Jimmy Clay. I would have stayed home if I'd had the foresight to know that Mr. Clay was a lying piece of shit, but alas, my senses aren't so keen.

I slam the car door shut and take a longing glance at the county fair in front of me. It's in full swing but at the same time, running on empty. It seems that the majority of inhabitants in this small town were smart enough to avoid the heat. I take one last glance at my car, a two-year-old Civic that my dad handed me right before he dropped the divorce papers on the kitchen table. Talk about spilled Cheerios.

It's about six o'clock as I approach the gates. Most of my friends have already left for college. A few are still packing and the ones who aren't leaving are probably too drunk to tag along. If someone had told me a year ago I would be attending the county fair alone, I would have told them they were full of shit. Who knew that growing up really would suck.

I take my place in line, stuck between a rock and an overweight man who hasn't showered in a week. By the way, the *rock* is a pair of screaming children. Apparently, for them and their mother, the line isn't moving fast enough. Poor woman. I could plop my ass down on the cracked asphalt right along with them with no shame. It is nowhere near what any intelligent person would refer to as *cool*. It's at least ninety degrees. Toss in the hair-destroying humidity of Ohio and you have a clambake of hillbillies and hicks.

Forced to remain optimistic, I hand over my nine dollars to the aging man with the tickets. An accomplished businessman, I'm sure. As I stroll past him, I catch him biting into his lip, ogling my ass. He's a creep, and I instantly regret giving him a playful shake.

The scent of deep-fried obesity and tilt-a-whirl-induced vomit permeates through the air. I wish I could bottle up the wind and turn it into a perfume for that distant day when I finally leave this town behind. It would be the perfect reminder of home, or I could make a lot of cash on the side selling sniffs of it to people who wouldn't believe it existed.

From ahead of me, I hear the midway call my name. We have a special relationship, the midway and I. In the past, it has been abusive. When my ever-growing belly and the buffet of unhealthy food choices began to fight, I was a diplomat in those wars. I'm not sure my stomach ever won a single battle. So this time, I've narrowed my food choices down to deep-fried veggies or a blueberry-topped funnel cake. That's a difficult decision...

Not.

* * *

I toss my half-eaten funnel cake into the trash as I head toward the ticket booth. That's right. This bitch is riding solo. Call it juvenile or sad. Call it whatever you want. I love cheap thrills and nothing beats being thrown around in a rusted cage.

The line for the ticket booth is nonexistent. Probably because it's hotter than the asshole of Satan. "One ride stamp," I say to the woman behind the yellow caged booth. She's missing her two front teeth, and I can't help but take an extended glance. Their dental insurance must be as nonexistent as their lines.

"Just one?" she has the nerve to ask me.

"Just one." I smile as I place my hand into the lion's den.

"We've got a solo rider tonight," says a voice from behind me.

I pull my newly-stamped hand out from the booth and turn around prepared to attack with a sharp tongue. Instead, I just grin from ear to ear, looking like an idiot I'm sure. He's gorgeous, like a teenage Brad Pitt—tall, lean and muscular, wearing worn jeans and a white t-shirt that clings to the sweat on his sculpted chest. I stare into his eyes and I'm not going to lie, I can feel the sting of Cupid's arrow in my ass. Those beautiful blue eyes...

"...are beautiful," I slip.

Awkward.

He chuckles as he rubs the back of his head, his t-shirt sliding up the bulge of his biceps. "Yeah?"

"No," I say. "I mean yeah. I was just daydreaming."

Oh, my God, stop it!

"I'm just going to shut up now," I continue sheepishly.

"All right." He extends his hand. "I'm gonna introduce myself."

I don't think I've ever met someone who introduced that they were going to introduce themselves before.

"I'm Blue."

"I'm Pink," I say with a laugh as I reach out to shake his hand.

"What are the chances?"

Oh, he's serious. "I thought you were joking."

"Most people do. They're just a little more tactful about it," he says with a wink. "So, Pink–"

"Charlie," I interrupt him. "It's actually Charlie."

"So we both have boy names." His turn to joke, I guess.

I'm not sure why I can't drag my feet to walk away. My only hypothesis? Those fucking eyes.

"Who are you here with?"

"I'm actually here alone," he says, which is exactly what I want to hear. "Want to go for a ride?"

"Sure. What's the worst that could happen?" *I can't believe I just said that. Talk about stiff dialogue.*

"Want to start with the tea cups?"

"I think you should start at the ticket booth." I point to the stamp on my hand.

"Oh, I don't need a stamp. I know everybody here." He flashes a wide grin. "I'm kind of special."

Whatever. If they don't let him on the ride, I'll just have to leave his ass behind.

My new acquaintance and I make our way to the tea cups: a ride that so many times as a child had thrilled me, shook me, and at times, sent me into embarrassing fits of vomiting. I lost my first boyfriend to that damn ride. We were both seven and on the fast track to marriage. It was a love so strong that only regurgitated pizza could break it.

We take our place in line behind two gossip queens I recognize, but can't place the names to the faces. They're sophomores, I know that much, and they have about thirty-six months before they discover they'll never amount to anything. Harsh, I know, but I've been on the long tail of a dream that ends abruptly.

"What are your plans for the rest of the evening?" I ask in a bid to strike up a somewhat intelligent conversation.

"I'm staying here."

"All night?"

"All week."

"You must really love the fair," I say.

"Like it's my job."

I can't help but think that's some sort of foreshadowing, but I laugh anyway. "Are you a carnie?"

There's a short pause before he replies assuredly, "No."

The short line begins moving, and we make our way to the entrance, our feet padding along the metal floor. I've always been fond of the pink cups, but Blue has another color in mind as he leads me to the blue one. He climbs into the cup as I take a parting glance at the empty pink one behind me. Combustible laughter and excitement from teens and young children fill the air around us. They cackle and cheer. They argue over who's going to spin the wheel. The gossip queens are too busy grimacing to enjoy the magical ecstasy around them. They're the perfect reminder to use condoms until you're thirty.

Face to face, I sit across from Blue. Those damn oceanic eyes pierce my soul. The slight slant of his jawline cuts off boundaries before they even begin. Razor-edged brown hair hangs just above his eyes.

He grabs the wheel with rugged hands as the hydraulics pump and swoosh. The metal platform beneath us begins to move at a glacial pace, and I don't know what I'm more excited about—the ride or him?

Probably him.

He has a certain glow, bright enough to take you out of this world.

Definitely him.

His hands handle the wheel with force as he stretches his arm across it, spinning it to the right then repeating. His forearms tighten with every movement. He lets out the cutest little grunt as he meets resistance, but at least we're beginning to spin.

"Need some help there?" I question with a curious smile.

"It's tight," he says with his eyes focused intently on the wheel.

"Should have picked the pink one," I mumble under my breath.

We begin to spin faster and the world around us begins to blur. The force of the wheel is no match for his strength, after all. Everything escapes focus, except him. Both of us move at the same speed in the same direction. It's as if we're the only two people in the world. I want to say something, but I'm afraid how distorted my mouth will look against the wind. I'll just wait.

Blue lets go of the wheel and gravity pushes him firm against his seat. He stretches his arms out over the tip of the cup and relaxes. His shirt wrinkles in the wind—the hem rising over his bare stomach revealing a has-to-be-airbrushed set of abs.

I catch him staring at me. "You just gonna sit there and let us slow down?" he asks.

Challenge accepted.

Gravity fights me as I hunch forward and I reach my arm around the wheel, grabbing it with my sweaty palms. I pull as hard as I can, but can barely turn it. Blue bites into his lip, amused, before reaching forward and grabbing the wheel again.

"I told you it was tight," he says, his beautiful but slightly uneven teeth beaming through a grin.

Our arms cross and brush against each other. It's sensationally soft, even as we're both pulled tight fighting against the wheel. The pumping hydraulics scream as we spin in increasingly rapid circles. I thought I was the queen of the cups, but I've never gone in circles so fast.

The random people on the ground and in neighboring cups are nothing but flashes of blurred colors, all bleeding into each other. Even Blue begins to fade away until the ride comes to an abrupt end. The wheel locks up and the cup jerks. Both our arms are gripped to the top of our seats as we slow down and come back to reality. In the distance, everything becomes clear again—people, rides, and wide-striped circus tents.

Blue stands up and steps out of the cup. He's light on his feet and almost trips on the platform. Still dizzy myself, I need a second to recover. The last thing I want to do is attempt to walk in a straight line and trip. I don't need another relationship cut short at the hands of a carnival ride.

"Need a hand?" He extends his hand to assist me.

At this point, I could probably manage to walk on my own, but I'm not about to turn down an opportunity to brush my skin against his. Also, chivalry's not dead, but it's rare. I grab his hand and notice the roughness of his fingers. They've definitely been worked. He pulls me up onto the platform with one hand. The other steadies me at the waist.

"You good?"

"Yeah. Kinda hungry, though."

What the hell is wrong with me?

His lips are pursed. "I know where we can get some free grub."

My hand pats against my chest. "You're stealing my heart," I say with a smile, and I'm only half joking. My heart rate is well above a physically fit, eighteen-year-old girl's normal rate. I could blame Blue, but a doctor would probably blame the thrill ride we've just exited.

* * *

We sit on a spoiled park bench. Half of it is covered in half-eaten fries and spilled ketchup. Screams echo behind us as red cages tumble against the setting sky. The entire scene isn't as chaotic as you'd expect for a small-town carnival. I suspect that once the sun disappears to harass another continent, it'll be a different story.

"Where are you from?" I ask Blue.

"I've been a lot of places but never really been from anywhere, you know?" He wipes fry grease off his hands with a napkin.

"So you're a gypsy?"

"Something like that."

"What brings you to Lakeview?"

"I like to travel. It's a necessity of the job." He shrugs. "What about you?"

"Never been anywhere else."

"That's horrible."

"It's not so bad," I say and ball up a napkin, tossing it into the trashcan that sits beside the table.

"That's because you've never been anywhere else." His eyebrow arches.

He's right. I'd love to leave this town to find something new. I've spent the past eighteen years in this place, and every time I think about leaving, I'm reminded by the reality that I've already given up my first chance to leave it all behind.

"Someday," I say without conviction.

"Someday what?"

I look straight into his eyes. "I'll go somewhere else."

"The first step is to want something and the second is to act on it. Where you wanna go?"

An actual conversation with a handsome stranger? The kind where they ask questions and actually want answers? That shit just doesn't happen anymore. Well, it does, but the question is usually phrased as such, *my parents are out of town. Want to fuck?*

"Got a map?"

"Just a second." He slides his finger against the screen of his phone. "Right here." He pushes his phone over to me. There's a world map on the screen. "Close your eyes and point to a random place."

I close my eyes as told. A light laugh escapes my throat because I know this whole thing's kind of silly. My finger circles above the phone before pressing against the screen. I can hear his jeans brush against the bench seat as he stands up. He circles around to stand behind me and leers over my shoulder. My eyes open and he gets closer. His arm comes around me, brushing against my arm as he pinches and zooms in on the screen.

"Las Vegas," he says. "Never been there myself."

His breath smells like fair food, which is a mouth-watering scent, but it's the last thing you want to smell coming from the mouth of a gorgeous man. However, the way his breath catches my neck ignites me. The heat so close to turning into passion, I want to reach around his neck and pull him close to me. Pull him in to kiss me. Now, I don't tend to kiss strangers, but damn if I'm not about to make an exception.

"That's a long way from home," I say, resisting the urge to pull him to my mouth.

"Well, let's go there. You and me." His warm breath continues to taunt me. "Someday."

The way that word rolls off his tongue excites me. It almost sounds like a promise.

"Let's just go now," I say, fully ready to run. You can't live in the moment much more than that.

"Right now?"

"Right now. I've got a few bags packed for college, and I'm not in the mood to unpack. I can pick them up on the way out of town."

"Nothing would make me happier than to jump in a car with you, a perfect stranger, and follow the sun until it sets, but I can't right now." He stands back. "Sometime soon, though."

I swing my feet out from under the bench and stand up in front of him. "Feels like eternity."

We talk as if what we say is the truth, as if we're not aware that we've got a few good hours together and that's it. Still, playing make-believe isn't the worst thing I could be doing on this miserable Saturday afternoon—I could be working in a fried veggies concession stand like that poor Romanian behind me.

"Eternity's not so bad. Some things are worth waiting for. I've found that time goes irrationally slow for those things until one day—*bam*—you find yourself on a cross-country road trip."

"You still haven't told me what your job is. Are you a philosopher?"

"Like a *Plato?*"

"Something like that."

Blue looks down at his watch and lets out a frustrated sigh. Buzz kill.

"Need to be somewhere?"

"Unfortunately, work needs me for a few hours."

"You could blow them off."

He laughs and it's contagious. "I would love to, but they'll know I'm blowing them off to spend the evening with a beautiful girl."

"How would they know that? Do you work for the NSA?"

"They've got eyes everywhere," he says, nodding his head.

"Are you a spy?"

"Would I be able to tell you if I were?"

"You were doing so well until you hit that cliché—" Then, like running into a brick wall, "You said I was beautiful."

"Huh?" he asks with a raised brow.

"You called me beautiful." My heel digs into the dirt.

He shakes his head. "Don't act like it's uncommon."

I push my hair behind my ear. It's a nervous thing. "I've been called beautiful my whole life—"

"For a reason."

"But sometimes, it's just unexpected. Like the rest of the world is just lying or something."

I've spent the entire afternoon staring at him like some kind of an obsessed creep, and it never really crossed my mind that he was thinking the same things about me.

Blue reaches around me and grabs his phone off the table. "Here, give me your number, and we'll hang later."

Maybe I'll tease him. Now entering child mode...

"Who says I want to do that?"

"Playing hard to get?"

"I'm certainly not easy." That's definitely not the way I intended that to roll off my tongue.

"Good. I'm not a fan of easy." He grins, nodding his head.

"How do you like crazy?" I bite into my lip.

"Oh." He puts his hand to his chest. "I love crazy."

I reach for his phone, taking it out of his hands without express permission. I dial my number and put it into his contacts under the name *Crazy*. I hand the phone back to him. "Don't keep me waiting."

"Never." There's sincerity in his voice even as his eyes are glued to his watch. "I'm running late though, so..."

"Goodbye, Blue."

His face lights up and he presses his lips against my cheek. Unlike his hands, they're soft. "Not goodbye, Charlie," he whispers in my ear, and then pulls back and turns around to walk away. He doesn't need confirmation because he knows he's got me exactly where he wants me. *Wanting more.*

He walks away as the sun sets behind us. The light shines in between food trucks, casting shadows onto the midway. He has my number, but that doesn't mean I'll ever see him again. The unknown can't wipe this smile off my face, though. I'm not in love—that would be stupid—but I've got that feeling in my gut that you get when you meet someone and somehow know they're going to change your life forever.

Also, the way his ass moves in those jeans certainly doesn't hurt.

CHAPTER TWO

It's been a few hours since Blue went off to work. I've spent the previous hour strolling through the animal barns, petting horses, and plotting to steal a donkey. I wasn't sure which animals were going to be slaughtered for food, and which were going to go on to live long, happy lives, so there was a brief moment spent pondering a life of veganism followed by a long, drawn-out affair with a cheeseburger.

It's a quarter till ten and my phone has yet to ring. I would settle for a text. A young carnie, maybe seventeen years old, hollers at me to come win a bear. In my experience, I would have better luck winning a marathon. And those odds aren't great, either. He's running that game where you have to throw the ball and knock over three canisters. I lie to him and tell him I'll come back after I find my boyfriend. That's a lie on two levels. I don't have a boyfriend, and I'm definitely not coming back. I'll make it a point to avoid Game Street for the rest of the evening.

The crowd grows thicker as the heat finally comes down to habitable levels. Most everyone has long forgotten the war from earlier when the sun was leading a full on assault. I haven't forgotten. The damage has already been done to my hair and clammy skin.

The screams of ride-goers and the sound of questionably assembled carnival rides boom through the fairgrounds. A big-footed clown walks past me with a fistful of balloons and a wide smile of sadism.

A clown called IT.

Another glance at my phone and my stomach sinks. Should have known better, I guess. I decide to return to my initial premise of being a solo riding bitch. The bumper cars are out of the question—I couldn't steer one of those bastards if my life depended on it. And let's be real, in that magnetic arena, it's always life or death. The cages are also out of the question. They're basically just an inferior version of the Zipper, built for those who feel the need to always be in control. The last time I rode one of those things, I felt the furthest thing from control as a bolt ricocheted off the metal cage with every flip.

The Zipper is something special. It's basically the closest you can get to the thrill of riding a roller coaster without setting foot in an amusement park, even if the only thing it and roller coasters have in common is the total forfeiture of control. In the cages, you have that bar that sometimes tells the damn thing to stop flipping. No such thing exists when you're in the trenches of the Zipper.

So just when I've decided to make my way to the Zipper, it seems fate has other plans.

"Charlie!" a familiar voice calls out.

We all have those moments where our head is telling us *Don't turn around*, but nobody ever listens because we always fucking turn around.

"Hey, Dylan," I say, feigning enthusiasm. It's not like I'm on bad terms with my ex, but we're definitely in the awkward post-breakup stage. He was going to stay here, and I was going to college. We decided it was best to end things because of the distance. Neither of us knew at the time that I wouldn't actually be going anywhere. That was well before I became the parent in the household.

Dylan stands about eight inches taller than me—seven if he ever took off those damn heeled boots. He's a classic case of a small-town guy—the kind you could live next door to anywhere. Out there in the real world, in that mythical place called a big city, he would probably be a seven out of ten. Here in our own little world, he's an eleven. Getting lost in those emerald-green eyes and unkempt hair has never been difficult. I loved him for many reasons, but I see no point in lying—I was pulled in for the shallowest of reasons.

He's standing in front of the Ferris wheel. His friends, Joey and Tyson, stand beside him drinking whiskey out of lemonade cups. They're all practically wearing the same outfit, which is to say their wardrobes don't extend beyond jeans, plaid shirts and plain tees. They're all brown-haired, Midwest country boys. Dylan is the tallest of the bunch. Joey and Tyson stand a few inches shorter than him. Dylan wears a green plaid shirt, rolled up to the crook of his elbow. The other two boys have theirs thrown over their shoulders. Why they even brought them on an evening this hot is a question for which there are no logical answers.

And then Dylan comes running up to me.

"Hey," he pants. "I haven't seen you since Summer's graduation party."

"I've been busy." A total lie. Lucky for me he never caught on to that thing I do when I lie. *Running my hand through my hair as we speak.*

"How's your mom?" He's always been sincere and polite, unless he's drunk.

"She's better. I'm hoping she goes back to work soon."

"That's good. She was always my favorite teacher."

I laugh, not because it's funny, but because he's also always been a suck up. Everybody in a twenty mile radius knows his actual favorite teacher was Mrs. Berry, who doesn't teach anymore after being caught screwing the running back. She was young, beautiful, and stupid. But weren't we all?

"Yeah, whatever," I say. "How are you doing?"

"Baby, you know I'm always good." The edges of his lips pinch. "Been working at Pete's shop."

Dylan has always been good with cars, which from personal experience, was no surprise because he was always good with his hands.

He stands on the tip of his boots and peers behind me, then to the side. "I see you're here by yourself."

"Thanks for the reminder." I punch him lightly above his pecs. They're firmer than the last time I noticed them—which was in his parents' barn right after we had broken up. "I see you've been working out."

He flexes his arms and a mountain of red plaid forms where his biceps should be. "I try."

"That's good, but—"

"Let's ride the Ferris wheel."

I could slap the shit out of him. "Have you lost your damn mind?" I already know the answer. He obviously has.

He grabs me by the arm and pulls me toward the line. And I use the word *line* sparingly, since there are a whopping four people in it.

"Absolutely not." I stand firm on my decision.

"Come on. For old times' sake?"

His grip loosens on my arm and I break free from him. "It'll be a cold day in hell before I get on that God-forsaken thing."

* * *

Don't ask me to explain it, because I probably can't, but I'll try anyway. The Ferris wheel is the scariest fucking ride in the world. For one, you're not strapped in. For two, God forbid you adjust any part of your body to get comfortable because you then face five-to-one odds of smashing your brains against the ground. Gruesome image? Consider it my obligatory public service announcement.

But here I am, on top of this death trap for the first time in two years. Coincidentally, it's only the second time in my life I've been up here. Both times sitting beside Dylan. I'm not sure if he wants to reminisce or revel in my agony. Both are torture. Even though I'm not going away to college as planned, there won't be a reconnecting. Not right now at least. As much as I love him, I need to experience something new. Something dangerous.

Something like Blue.

I try not to look down, but it's a natural reflex. My stomach instantly turns. Staring danger in the face isn't something we ever intend to do. It just happens. The neon glow from the Zipper across the midway taunts me.

Dylan looks at me with his amused face—a devious, judging smile telling me I should just man up. Unfortunately for him, that would involve growing balls. I bet that would knock that smile right off his smug face.

"You're an ass," I scold him.

He shrugs his shoulder. "You miss it, don't ya?" He looks out into the distance.

I see an opening, a fleeting chance for confirmation that we couldn't get back together. I'm not leaving on schedule, but someday, I'll get away from this place. "Would you ever leave this town, Dylan?"

"Why would I ever wanna leave?" He shakes his head. "It's got everything I'll ever need in life. I've got friends, family, and enough booze to last a lifetime."

"Well, you know me. I couldn't live in this town forever."

"Sure you could."

No, I really couldn't.

He scoots closer, wrapping his arm around my back. See? He's smug, and I bet he thinks I wouldn't notice. Never mind we spent four years together.

"What are you doing?" I ask. My palm tightens around the safety bar as the seat rocks to his adjustment.

He pulls me closer with his arm. "Getting comfortable."

"Well, don't get too comfortable."

Then it begins. The wheel is fully loaded, like a twenty shot revolver, and we begin cycling around the circle of death. Each bullet is ready to fire, sending us all to our deaths. I grip the bar tighter. As our seat comes around to the bottom of the wheel, I catch Joey and Tyson drunkenly cheering us on.

"Kiss her!" Joey screams out.

From the corner of my eye, I see Dylan give them a thumbs up. "Don't even think about it," I say, hopefully putting that situation to rest.

Or so I thought.

His palm massages my side. "Relax," he says, followed by a sly grin.

I look him dead in the eye. "No."

"What's wrong?"

"Near certain death has a way of making me sweat."

"That's probably the heat," he points out, resting his hand on my leg. "I like it when you sweat."

"Shut up, Dylan."

He bites into his lip. *Shit*. That was always the last straw before I was lying on my back on his parents' basement couch.

"Wanna make me?"

I don't respond. Then, without warning, his lips are pressed to mine with the speed of Clark Kent. Yeah, it feels good but our seat begins rocking like a boat in

Jaws. I push him off me, which doesn't help our life-threatening situation.

"What are you doing?"

He shrugs his shoulders again. "Just saying goodbye."

"Most people say goodbye with their mouths."

His eyes roll toward the top of his head, then he lights up with that damn smile. "That's what I was doing."

I throw my hands up. "You know what I mean."

"Yeah, yeah." He lowers his hand to his jeans and begins to adjust himself.

Oh, my God.

We're close to the bottom of the wheel again and from behind us, Tyson yells, "Rock that boat! Rock it!"

I throw my middle finger up at him. It's a sign of love. Dylan's still adjusting himself, and at this point, I'm not sure if he's doing it for pleasure or comfort.

"Could you quit playing with yourself?"

The ride comes to a halt. It's time to get off this damn spinning wheel of hell. I crane my head and look behind us to see that they're unloading backward. A mother and son hop out of their seats and exit. And we're next.

I look back to Dylan and mercilessly slap his dick.

"Ow," he yelps. "What the hell?"

"Put that thing away before you end up in prison."

"I'm trying. Why don't you try having a dick?"

"Oh, I would love to have one."

If I did have a penis, I'm almost positive my list of sexual partners would be more than one.

It's our turn to exit the ride. I raise the bar and hop off onto the platform, leaving Dylan behind. I have no intention of going down with his sinking ship. But he's the worst ship captain in the world because he jumps off and wraps his arm around me. His erection is pressed against my back. He's a fugitive taking refuge behind me and using my body as a human shield.

So romantic, just like the old times. Joey and Tyson look on in amusement, sipping away at their whiskey. They're not bright enough to know what's really going on and probably assume that Dylan and I have hitched our wagons back together.

My ex-boyfriend and I push through the metal gate. Once we're back on solid ground, I pull away from him, leaving the tent in his pants wide open. Joey throws his fist to his mouth and his face turns cherry red as he fights to hold back the laughter.

"Dickzilla!" Tyson yells as he mimics the famed reptile. "Argh."

I turn around and step toward Dylan, getting close enough so the heat of my body teases him. I look into his eyes and go in for a kiss—on his right cheek.

"You're teasin' me," he says through gritted teeth.

"Something like that," I say and turn to walk away, making the most of the way my jean shorts curve around my ass.

"Someday," he hollers, "you'll be mine again."

Someday. I've heard that a lot today.

CHAPTER THREE

Fifteen minutes before the fair is set to close, I find myself standing in line for the Zipper. In front of me are about ten teens, presumably out well past their curfew. The sign on the gate reads 'No Singel Riders,' misspelled and all. And here I am alone and ready to wrestle my single riding ass into one of those cages. I'm the last person in line so I'm hoping to get a free pass.

The line begins moving as they load the delinquents into the cages two by two. Two carnies—one on the left and one on the right, each doing their job of latching their respective cages shut. The carnie who stands the furthest away from me has a nice little bubble butt. Can't say much for the rest of the package as his back is turned to me. Certainly couldn't be worse than the toothless meth head on my side. I consider switching lines out of concern that he would incompetently secure me in his allegedly high state. But, hey, danger's part of the game.

It's my turn. I push the gate open and dart for the cage without making eye contact with the carnie. I multitask between shutting the cage myself and grabbing my seat belt. It would seem that I've succeeded in averting that stupid rule.

"No single riders," I hear him say.

I try to think quickly for an appropriate response as the rugged carnie opens my cage and gives me a disapproving glare.

"Nobody has to know," I say with a toss of my shoulder.

"I could lose my job," he huffs.

"Well," I say and rub the back of my neck. "Why don't you ride with me?" My hand caresses the seat beside me, inviting him in. And yes, I'm embarrassed by my own behavior.

"No, ma'am." His hand grabs the cage and rattles it. "Don't trust these things."

That's promising. I purse my lips. "Please?"

"Fine." He turns around and calls out to the other carnie. "Hey, get your ass over here. Got a pretty little thing that needs a partner."

Correct. In life, and in this damn cage. The other carnie latches his cage shut then turns around and—

It's Blue. How sweet of him to volunteer his time for the county fair. I wonder when he got off work. Why didn't he call me? Oh, my God... Is he still at work?

After that internal debate in my head, it hits me like a semi full of *No shit*. This is his work. He's a carnie. Many things speed through my mind—*My life has come to this; Even Chelsea Handler wouldn't sink this low; What will I tell my mother?; I've never seen such beautiful blue eyes.*

So yeah, once again those fucking eyes have become decision-making factors. The mental battle is over, but I still haven't snapped out of it.

The steel cage door slamming shut and being locked into place pulls me back to reality—a universe where I'm now closer than I've ever been to this beautiful stranger. We sit shoulder to shoulder, our arms rubbing against each other.

His lips rest on his teeth, grinning from ear to ear. He obviously isn't aware of the thoughts writing themselves in my mind, and he's definitely not ashamed of his profession.

"I lost my phone," he says to me.

"Why did you lie when I asked if you worked here?"

"I didn't want to scare you away," he says nonchalantly.

That was probably smart of him, but I'm not sure what difference a few hours could make. I'm torn though—one part of me wants to do the dangerous thing and fuck him in the house of mirrors. The other part of me wants to throw open the cage and run because I'm better than that. I couldn't be with Dylan because I wanted something different, something a little dangerous. But is Blue a little bit too much of both?

All night I've been enamored with this perfect stranger, then a switch flips, and I'm torn between playful flirting and messy seduction. I don't know if he actually wants either but since he's a guy, I assume he's at least down for the latter.

"You wouldn't have scared me away." Fifty percent chance that's a lie, fifty percent it's not. Not even I am in the loop of what I want. It's only been about three months since high school graduation and a little longer than that since my dad tore my family apart. In that space of unquestioned dreams and paralyzing fears, I've lost the person I was so sure I wanted to be. That uncertainty has carried over into the rest of my decisions like the nosy bitch that lives next door. *Can I have a cup of sugar?*

"Is that right?" He lets out a relieved chuckle. "You must be a carnie chaser then."

"Yeah, they're hard to resist."

"You know what I think, Charlie?"

I turn to him. "What do you think, Blue?"

He has a face full of intent, like he's about to say something caught between sweet and philosophic. "I think the ride's about to start." His palms push against the roof. "No hands?"

I get what he's going for—that unrivaled thrill of riding a roller coaster with your hands in the air. That feeling when your innards float in all the wrong places. This isn't exactly that, and it certainly isn't no hands, but it's a petty exchange of semantics that I'm not about to get into. I just put my palms to the roof and we're off.

* * *

Blue's hollering echoes everything I'm feeling on the inside. We flip forward and backward. For all intents and purposes, we flip sideways too—a physical impossibility without crashing to the ground, but sideways we go.

One, two, three flips in a row. Reaching the top of the rotating axis, we're flung upside down. It's the moment where thrills reach the point of climax. The point in the ride when everything has lined up perfectly—the cage, the axis, and the chains. If that happens at the tip of the axis, then it feels as if you are being thrown into another world. At the very least, it feels like you've been thrown from the chains.

Two minutes in this cage feels like a lifetime in seconds. Two minutes in this cage with Blue feels like being swamped by a thousand migrating butterflies. The childish grin on his face, in between shouts of ecstasy, argues with his strong, muscular body as we flip.

We could lose a bolt with every flip and I probably wouldn't notice. We could be one bolt away from breaking news and I wouldn't be any the wiser. The cage could fly open, and I wouldn't even know it until I woke up in hell.

Blue turns to me with his palms still pressed against the roof. It's magnetic, and I have no choice but to look right back. Neon lights swirl behind him, illuminating half his face at once. He's just as perfect in the shadows as he is in the light. There's something in those eyes—a lifetime of stories and I want nothing more than to go down the rabbit hole.

Engines roar from the derby in the distance and just like the crashed-up cars there, I know what it feels like to be wrecked. This ride won't last forever, and when it comes to a stop, I need to have made a decision.

* * *

He's right behind me. I'm not running, but I'm not walking either. If I really wanted to, I could get away from him with ease. The fact that I haven't means I'm still contemplating an illicit one night stand.

We're outside the fairgrounds and in the first of two fields. There are still hundreds of cars even though the fair has technically shut down—blame the congestion on the derby that is now well into overtime.

"Charlie," he yells. "Wait up."

The sound of his brisk footsteps against the dry grass morphs into a sprint as he runs to the front of me and turns around to face me. Walking backward while talking isn't something I would attempt, especially not at the pace he's maintaining.

"I have to get home."

"Let me take you," he says between ragged breaths.

"I'm illegally parked."

"But you're walking toward the field."

"That's where my car is..."

His head tilts as if he's confused. "How can you illegally park in a field?"

That stops me dead in my lying tracks. My fingers run through my hair. "You caught me."

"I get the feeling that you're trying to avoid me." He shakes his head and gestures with his hand. "I can leave you alone if you want."

"You're a great guy and you're adorable," I say. "And by adorable I mean hotter than Mars."

His cheeks blush and he grabs the back of his head. "So what's the problem, then?"

"I don't know." I swallow a breath. "We're from two different worlds."

"I'm not trying to marry you..."

"That's good. You couldn't afford a ring," I say, cracking a grin.

"You sure? I got a nice little savings account." He moves in closer. "One of the perks of living out of a camper for nine months out of the year."

"A camper?" I say and push my body against him.

"Yeah. It's real comfortable."

I bite into my lip. "I bet."

And just like that, I'm sucked back in. I can't control myself when it comes to him, and that's not normal for two reasons—I'm always in control and hello, *Don't talk to strangers*. It's as if I can't think rationally and it's liberating.

"I'd give you a tour, but it's getting late and I've got a roommate." His hand brushes against my waist. My tongue rolls across the inside of my lip.

"I have to go home," I blurt out and turn to walk away. I wipe the dampness off my forehead. Blue grabs me by the arm and spins me back around.

"I want you to stay," he says sternly. "I've never met anyone like you."

"Do you say that to all the girls?"

"No," he says. "I usually avoid all the other girls. They tend to be crazy, and not in a cute way."

I gaze into his eyes, trying to read him under the starlit sky. "Who are you?"

"I'm Blue, remember? We met earlier today."

I can't help but smile. He cups my chin with his palm, raising me up so that he can peek into my soul with his eyes. He comes in slow and presses his lips against mine. They're even softer than I remember.

He's rough in places and smooth in others. Everything about him is a contradiction.

Both his hands move to my cheeks, caressing them as we kiss. I grab him by the waist, pulling him closer to me. My hands rise to his chest, pushing him back so I can breathe.

"Let's go somewhere a little more private," I say and grab his hand.

I lead him through the field by his hand. We pass the last row of parked cars and cross into the second field. The field is mostly empty, and I can spot my car from a distance. It sits alone by a solitary tree.

"Where are we going?" he asks.

"To my illegally parked car."

CHAPTER FOUR

Blue's palms hold firm against my cheeks as we glide backward, our feet cycling through damp grass. His lips massage mine as we fumble through the dark, and I can't help but think this would be the worst time in the history of my life to trip. My back meets the warm metal of the car door, and Blue pushes himself into me, pinning me to the Civic. My head tilts back as his head drops to my neck, mouthing a path to the bone in my chin.

My back arches to the firm grip of his hand wrapping around me. His warm breath brushes against my ear, sending stray strands of hair into the darkness. I dig into his back, grabbing a fistful of damp, thin fabric. I push myself into him, craving the heat of his body on this humid night.

The hardness in his jeans rubs against me.

This has to be the quickest way to start a fire.

His lips swell against my neck and the scent of musk and sweat is all too much. I sway my hips and grind against him, causing his whole body to tense up. His hand rolls into a fist against the glass of the car as if he's trying to hold himself back.

"Charlie," he rasps. "I want you."

My hands fold against his chest, and I push him back so our eyes can tangle. He can say it all he wants, but I need to see that want in his eyes. Those blue beauties swarm with lust like the rolling clouds in the sky that have overtaken the starry night. There's no use pretending anymore. No more pretending that I'm someone or something else, like I'm not about to be that girl who fucks a perfect stranger—*a carnie*—in the grass outside of a carnival.

I give him a nod of assurance, but his entire body rests in place, his chest heaving. He's not exactly taking the hint. "You can have me," I say firmly.

There's a short pause before his lips are pressed against mine. It's slow, gentle, and passionate. Then it's quick and rough, and his tongue parts my lips. One hand crawls under my neon tank, navigating its way to my breasts.

"You're hot. We should get you out of these clothes."

A light chuckle rests in my throat.

He stands back and grabs the bottom of my tank and in one lightning motion, rips it over my head and tosses it to the ground. I reach behind myself and unhook my bra. It rolls down my arms and drops to the ground. I catch his eyes on my breasts, and then, like a perfect gentleman, he looks away for a split second before facing me again.

His eyes fill with desire and lock with mine as his arms cross each other, and he tugs his shirt from the hem and pulls it over his sculpted torso, then his head, cutting off my line of sight to his eyes. His slim, rock-hard abs are like Mount Rushmore with six presidents instead of four. He closes the distance between us, and my hands knead against the ridges in his stomach, feeling every dip and groove on his damp body. My head tilts forward, resting on his pulsing chest as his lips caress the top of my head.

I prop my head up and shake my hair to the side before kissing him again. His fingers fumble with the button on my frayed jean shorts. Once the button has popped, my shorts slide down my legs and form a puddle on the ground. His muscular arms wrap around me and pick me up, wrapping my legs around his back and pushing me against the car. My breasts smash against his firm pecs as he heaves against me. His hardness pulses through his jeans, past ready for release.

"I've never met anyone like you." His warm breath fills the air around us. "I've never wanted someone the way I want you right now."

An arrow of lightning lights up the sky, turning everything around us blue.

"Then what are you waiting for?"

He takes a moment, nods, and in slow motion, we fall to the ground as a violent burst of thunder explodes in the near distance. The trodden grass is cool and damp against my back and I know there are two storms brewing—one in the sky and the other somewhere deep inside.

Blue plants kisses down a path on my bare stomach as his fingers curl around the fabric of my panties, pulling them down my thighs and off my legs. My chest heaves as I look down to find him staring back at me. He keeps eye contact as he lowers his mouth against me. My body instantly stiffens, and my head is thrown backward against the grass.

His tongue dances around the edge of me before driving in. My toes curl. My palms dig into the grass, grabbing a handful of dirt. Behind me, the last neon lights of the carnival power off.

The heavy weight of his muscular body crawls over me, but he has one hand still running against me. He presses his lips to mine, but instead of a kiss, I give him a command. "Fuck me."

"Are you sure you wanna—"

"Do you want me to change my mind?"

He pulls himself onto his knees and unbuckles the brown leather belt around his jeans. A slick hand pulls a condom out of his pocket. He tears it with his teeth and pops a row of buttons, pulling the denim down his hips. The same for his stark black boxers, causing the full length of his cock to spring free.

Another streak of lightning and another explosion of thunder booms as he rolls the condom onto himself.

His body lowers onto me and one hand travels to his length, guiding himself in gently. My back arches as he begins to fill me slowly and painfully. I hook my legs around him, firm against his ass as he sinks all the way in. Once he's filled me entirely, we couldn't possibly be any more connected, he kisses me softly, and I don't need anything else.

There's a pained look on his face as he draws out slowly. My fingers dig into his back as he tortuously steals himself away from me. Once he's at the edge of undoing me, he pauses and swivels on his knees. His breath is ragged as his body shakes. I sweep my palm against his flushed cheek.

"Okay?" he asks under his breath.

I nod.

And he drives into me, filling me to the hilt. My vision goes black. An entire galaxy exploding is painted before my eyes. I pull him closer to me as he begins thrusting erratically. He's not making love to me—he's fucking me. And that's exactly what I want. It's what I've wanted even when I've been unable to say it.

His breath quickens, and when I finally reclaim my vision, the only thing I see is his beautiful face full of ecstasy. Once he catches my eyes, his pace slows. He begins to sync to a more natural rhythm. Inch by devastating inch, with measured thrusts, he pulls every part of me to the surface. I'm turned inside out, and I wonder if he even notices.

This right here is vulnerability. The way his body begins to quake, I imagine it's the same for the both of us. His eyes pull tight, his mouth circles into a familiar shape. He's close to the edge, and I'm not ready for this to be finished.

His mouth lowers to me, the warmth of his ragged breaths brushing against my lips. "Come for me."

That's new. I mean to nod, but I don't think it comes across that way. I'm too busy holding onto his back, trying not to break. In order to save himself, he must switch tempo. I feel every changing beat as his rhythmic thrusts become drawn out. An inch becomes a mile. His cock pulls back, tight like a bow, and then slams back in. It's fast and it's slow. It is torture and pleasure beyond compare.

My entire body cries out for release, perfectly timed with the earthquake beginning to rumble above me. I wonder if this is how Californians feel right before the plates shift. Helpless.

"Yeah?" he asks through shallow breaths. He wants to know if I'm ready, but it comes off more like begging, as if release could save his life.

"Yeah," I choke on my own words as I forfeit my entire being to the rupture within. My fingers curl against his back. My heels dig into the curves of his ass, pulling him fully into me. Just when I think he can't go any further, he pulls himself onto his elbows and slams into me, furthering his strokes by another intoxicating inch.

He fucks me through my orgasm, the stars in the night unable to compare to the stars beneath my eyes. My arms fall to my sides, unable to hold onto him any longer. I see the explosion from light years away. His entire body shudders, rattling me to my core before he drives in one final time, slamming me to the hilt and threatening to send me into an immediate relapse.

When he collapses onto me, I swear I can hear our hearts gearing up for war. Un-poetically, a drum of thunder roars through the sky about ten seconds too late.

"Amazing," he says, then laughs nervously.

I'm still trying to catch my breath, but I'm sure he can see the agreement in my eyes. He brushes a curl of hair away from my face and lowers himself to kiss me softly.

My phone vibrates against the ground, so I reach over and grab it. It's too late to answer, but there's a voice-mail waiting for me from my mom. Blue crawls off me, grabs his jeans, and takes a seat against my car. I slide my finger across the screen of the phone, loading up the camera.

"Hey," I smile, catching his attention. "Smile."

"What for?"

The flash illuminates the scene. Captured on my phone is a gorgeous, candid photo of Blue.

His lips purse.

"It's okay. I took it above the waist."

"It wouldn't bother me if you didn't," he says with a wink and stretches out, placing his entire weight on one arm. He'd do great in porn.

I click the camera icon again, capturing another memory. This one in its entirety—his naked, suntanned body contrasting against the slick grass.

* * *

I'm fully dressed now. Blue wears nothing but his jeans as we both sit flush against the car. I pull my hair through my hands, trying to make myself presentable for when I walk through the door of my house. There's a good chance my mom will be wide awake on the couch, lost in a rented copy of a certain Nicholas Sparks movie.

"It sucks that I'll probably never see you again," I say, fully aware that I couldn't sound any more unaffected.

He pops one palm against my knee. "I wouldn't say that."

"You're leaving town tomorrow."

"I didn't tell you?" He tosses his shoulder, his trademark. "I think I'm gonna be sticking around for a while."

"What are you talking about?" There's gravel in my throat.

"I've spent my entire life dreaming of going home, but I've never had a home to go home to. I've decided to give life away from the carnival a shot. Most people run away to the carnival. Well, I'm running away from it."

There's no point in lying. That scares the hell out of me. Him staying here would mean that this is no longer an isolated moment in time. People in this town, like any other small town, talk. It's not even that I'm ashamed of what they'd say. It's just that this was all supposed to be dangerous, random and done.

I shake my head in disbelief. "How are you going to afford to live?"

"I've got enough money to last a few months. I guess I'll have to find a job or something, which shouldn't be too hard, since I've been working since I was twelve."

My brow arches. "Twelve?"

"I spent my youth robbing civilians of their hard-earned coins, working the game booths with my mother."

I'm sure he's a walking storybook, every page filled with a lifetime's worth of magical text, but I still can't get past the fact that he's planning on calling my home his home. "Not to badger you with an exhausting game of twenty questions, but where will you stay?"

"My uncle has an empty apartment above his barn."

"I didn't know you had family here."

He laughs. "Charlie, there's a lot you don't know about me."

Isn't that the truth. "And there's a lot you don't know about me."

"Touché." His abs fold as he leans across me. One hand brushes against my cheek. "I wanna know things about you, though. Your favorite movie, your favorite song, your favorite color—"

"It's Blue."

"I know." He smiles and it lights up the dark, though that could be the lightning.

The other half of me, the half that's not scared shitless, wants nothing more than to see him again.

"Will I see you again?" he asks, but he doesn't wait for an answer before he's kissing me, cupping me at the chin. My body shifts so that I can embrace him in return as he says goodbye with his mouth.

When it's over and he pulls back, I have an answer. "Call me."

* * *

The skies are in full-on downpour mode and I'm parked on the side of the road. For a car that's only two years old, my windshield wipers are far too inadequate. I hope Blue was able to get to shelter before the torrential rain began, but it's mostly a false hope. The storm began moments after I pulled onto the pavement.

I sit here contemplating several things, but at the forefront of my mind are two things in particular. I would like to thank Jimmy Clay for being an uneducated meteorologist, because if it weren't for him, I never would have met this mysterious, sexy, charming man.

I would also like to not-thank Jimmy Clay for the same reason, because thanks to him, I'm torn—torn between wanting to see Blue again and wanting to keep tonight as nothing more than a snapshot of a memory in time.

CHAPTER FIVE

The sun shines through my window, setting my skin on fire. It's the first of September and a thin layer of sweat coats my body. While I was asleep, I dreamed that I told my mother I wasn't going to college. I was prepared to face the scorn, but she embraced me instead. She followed that up with the promise that I had made the right decision.

In reality, I'm sure that conversation is going to go slightly different than I optimistically dreamed.

* * *

"You're doing *what*?" my mother screams as she paces back and forth, her recently cut bob-do bouncing against her neck. I don't know what it says about me that my eyes are focused on her bare feet padding against the soft carpet. From the television, there's a familiar mating call, the atrocious sound of Sarah Palin thinking out loud.

"I know the timing's bad, but you know I can't leave you right now." There really has to be another reason I'm staying. Sure, she's heartbroken, but I shouldn't be putting my life on hold for her, especially since she hasn't asked me to. There's something else holding me back, and I just wish I knew what it was.

"You don't need to worry about me." She motions with her hands. "Go finish packing your things."

I sigh. "I'm not going, Mom."

"Why?"

"I don't know, maybe I'm not college material." Then again, that nut-bag on TV graduated college. What does that say about me?

She's waving her hands again. We all have that one annoying thing we do, and that's her nervous tic. Personally, I'm a *run my hands through my hair* kind of girl, but to each their own. "Don't be stupid. You're not stupid."

"Of course, I'm not stupid, Mom."

She quits pacing and her green eyes focus on me. It's like looking in a mirror, well except for the fact that she's a blonde and I'm a brunette. And I've moved on from the nineties. She's definitely my mother and I imagine I'll look just like her, when I'm her age. "Then how could you do something so stupid?" she snarls at me.

That was a quick turnaround. "My life doesn't end today because I'm not starting school tomorrow." I'm on cracked ice, and I really need to be careful with my choice of words. She could go into melodramatics at any moment.

"Oh, my God," she cries and brings her hand to her mouth. She sits on the edge of the loveseat and shakes her head. "This is all my fault. I should have been a better parent."

My eyes somersault backward. She's ridiculous. "You were a perfect mom." It's not exactly the truth, but she was no Mommie Dearest either. I mean, there were no wire hangers to be found in this house, but I'd chalk that up to the changing times.

Her attention snaps toward me. Her brow furrows, and I know things are about to go south. "Are you on drugs?"

"No." I let out an exasperated sigh that fades into a moan. "But I should be."

Her chest sinks and I suddenly remember she's not one of my friends and will expect me to pee on a stick within the end of the hour. "I let you watch too much television." She's really gunning toward an Oscar nomination.

"Good God, would you get a grip?" My turn to snap, I guess.

She throws herself onto her feet. "Get a grip?"

"Yes, get a grip. You're acting like it's the end of the world. It's not. Whatever my reasons are, they're my reasons. If I leave and go to school now, I'll fail. Not because I'm stupid, but because I don't want to be there. I'm not saying I'm never going, but I am telling you that I'm not going right now." I say this in one breath, and I suddenly feel like a smoker unable to catch my next breath. "It's my decision. So find a way to deal with it."

A little overboard, Charlie...

She doesn't say a word. She's stunned, sad, angry, or all of the above but definitely over-sensitive. I could try to make things better, but I don't think it would make a difference what I say next. She walks past me, brushing her shoulder against mine, and exits the room.

Not able to take the rambling of *Fox and Friends* anymore, I whisk the remote off the coffee table and flick the television off. The front door slams shut, and I hear something hit the ground. Could be a family photo, or it could be the foundation of the house cracking. But there it was—her Oscar-winning breakdown. I hope she comes home later tonight cooled down and able to talk about this rationally. Maybe I could even snag an Oscar of my own—in the supporting actress category—as I bring my mother back to the realm of reality.

* * *

Summer isn't exactly happy with me, but who is these days. We're in her bedroom folding clothes and packing them into boxes that were stolen from the trash behind the local supermarket. We've been best friends since kindergarten, and up until about five minutes ago, we were supposed to be roommates at Ohio State. I'm supposed to leave tomorrow for an early start, but she's not leaving until next Saturday. In retrospect, I probably should have given her more warning, but on the bright side, my dad still doesn't know. And he won't be finding out anytime soon.

"I can't believe you're leaving me." She shakes her head and throws a pair of jeans into a box.

It's only semantics, I know, but she's the one who's actually doing the leaving.

"You could have told me earlier. Like, at least a month ago," she says. "You do know that I'm going to be the only girl on campus living solo in a double, right?"

That sounds awesome to me.

She grabs a pile of shirts and stuffs them into another box. "I can hear the whispers now. *Who's that loser bitch with no friends in room 23?*" She throws her hands in the air. "*I bet she smells funny,* they'll say."

She's always had a flair for the dramatic and I can't help but laugh. "You'll be fine."

She looks at me with a huge grin. "I'll just have to find someone to replace you."

"Bitch, I'm irreplaceable," I say and push her lightly.

"Speaking of irreplaceable..." She grabs me and throws me onto the bed. Her legs straddle me as she pokes at my forehead with her finger. "Since you just dropped out of the rest of your life and doomed yourself to forever live in this town—"

"Thanks..."

"Does this mean you're going to get back with Mr. Plaid? The love of your life, Dylan fucking Parker?"

"Doubtful." I grab her by the waist and roll her off me and onto a pile of *not going with her to college* clothes. I scoot off the bed and hop over a pile of shoes, before standing in front of the body mirror that hangs off her bedroom door.

"Something's off," she says. "Wasn't college the reason you broke up with him?"

"I thought so." But I'm not so sure anymore. The girl looking back at me has the same flowing brown hair as me. The same burnt green eyes, and she even dresses like me. But she doesn't feel like me. I wonder if that girl on the other side of the mirror understands me better than I understand myself. If she does, then this would turn into a fantasy, so it's best if my mirror self doesn't start talking to me—though I'm sure it'd be an interesting conversation.

Summer approaches me from the back. She's taller than I am so I can see the top of her head in the mirror as she draws in closer. Not many girls can pull off red hair quite like she can. She makes it look effortless and beautiful and somehow gives off the illusion that she actually has a soul. "I wish you would have given me more notice," she tilts her head sideways and flips her hair, "cause I would've fucked him."

"He's not into gingers."

"Everybody's into gingers. It's just not something you say out loud."

I turn to her. "They might want to get in your pants, I'll give you that." I sit back down on her bed. "But really, who could ever really love a redhead?"

Her shoulders brush against her chin. "Your dad."

If anybody else said that to me, they'd probably end up face down in a pool of blood. At the very least, I'd block them on Facebook, but Summer and I have known each other since we were four. We've been ride-or-die ever since and we can say the bitchiest things to each other without a hint of resentment.

"Yeah, well, there's no accounting for my dad's bad taste."

"He's kind of hot."

She's had a thing for my dad since we were in high school. Since she also wants Dylan, I'd say she has a rabid taste for my leftovers. And just to be clear, Dylan is the leftovers, not my dad. "Can you at least wait until the divorce papers are dry?"

"Can't wait," she says, rolling her tongue between clenched lips. If she ever actually fucked my dad, I wouldn't care. He's been around town like a straight inmate on early release after five months of imprisonment. Calling him a father at this point is a joke anyway. He can be her daddy because I don't need him anymore.

Summer resumes folding a pile of jeans that lay on the bed. "How was the Lakeview family reunion, otherwise known as the county fair?"

My body tenses and my fingers dig into the mattress.

"Charlie?"

"Summer?"

"Come on. How was it?"

"Hot." I shrug.

Her eyebrow cocks.

"It was fine," I say exasperated. "It's the same fair as every other year, with the same people, same rides, same food, and same stench."

She tosses a stack of jeans in a cardboard box and grabs another pair to fold. "You're being mysterious."

"I'm not. I just—there's nothing to say." My hand glides through my hair, and she knows me well enough to know what that means.

She tosses the denim in her hands to the floor and springs to life, pushing me onto my back and straddling me again. She grabs my arms and throws them above my head, pinning me down. "I've known you my entire life, so I know when you're full of shit. And right now, you're full of it."

"You're not as light as you used to be. Can you get off me?"

"Not until you talk."

My eyes roll. I contemplate telling her the truth, but a modified version of it. She'd get all the gruesome details, right down to the size of his dick, but I'd conveniently leave out his profession. We may love each other like sisters and never fight, but there's still plenty of room for judging, like the time she got chlamydia from some—admittedly cute—guy at a college party.

"I've got shit to pack, but I'm really not letting you go until you spill."

"Fine," I yell. "I met a boy."

"My God. I want all the details. Height, weight, eye color, and dick size."

"The fact that you think I know how big his dick is makes me question what you really think of me."

"The world, Charlie. That's what I think of you. The world."

"He *was* gorgeous."

"On a scale of one-to-Dylan, how gorgeous?"

"Well... He wasn't wearing plaid."

"Sounds like a downgrade," she says. "I wouldn't waste my time."

Once again, I push her off me and sit up on the edge of the bed. "I'm not sure there's anything to waste. It was a one-night-only kind of thing."

She jumps onto her feet. "So you did fuck him!"

I give her a simple smile because I don't need to say anything else.

"What's his name?" she asks in her best detective voice, trying to discern whether or not she knows him.

"Blue."

Her nose rumples and her smile fades into a grimace. "Like the color? That's a thing?"

"It's a thing."

"Well, he's obviously not from around here, is he?"

"I actually don't know where he's from, but apparently, he's sticking around."

"Oh, no," she says perturbed. "He's obsessed with you."

"You're so dramatic."

"You're obsessed with him, too." She nods her head accusingly.

"Shut up. I'm not obsessed with a carnie..." It's like my brain just ran out of brake fluid.

Her eyes widen and her smile fades into a frown. "You fucked a carnie!?"

I look around the room nervously. "Would you be quiet?"

"Okay. Whew." She runs her hand through her ginger hair, and then glides down onto her knees so that she's kneeling in front of me. "Intervention time."

"What the hell are you doing?"

"I'm intervening. You can't go around fucking carnies. For one, they're gross. For another? Eww."

"First of all, I can do whatever the hell I want. It's America. Secondly, it wasn't exactly intentional. And besides, he's different from the others."

"I'm going to give your judgmental statement a pass—"

That's ironic.

"—but nothing good will come from fucking a carnie. Do you remember Rebecca Ross?"

"I don't."

"That's because she dropped out of school in the ninth grade after getting knocked up by Bigfoot the clown."

I grab her by the arms and force her onto her feet. "She was in ninth grade and Bigfoot was obviously a pedophile." My hand digs into the pocket of my jeans and I grab my phone. "Besides, did Bigfoot look like this?"

She takes a fleeting glance at the picture on my phone—the snapshot of Blue the night of the fair. "No, because Bigfoot was a clown. What part of that—" She rips the phone out of my hand. Her eyes light up and her jaw drops. "God spent a little more time and all that hocus-pocus on this man. Those beautiful eyes…"

Being a bit too possessive, I wrestle the phone from her hands. "Tell me about it."

"Please tell me that he's coming to my party Saturday."

I just shrug because I couldn't tell you what's happening tomorrow, let alone what's happening in six days.

CHAPTER SIX

It's the night of Summer's party, and I still haven't heard from Blue. It dawned on me Tuesday that he had lost his phone. My best guess is that he's not in a rush to run out and get a new phone, as that would take a dent out of his mysteriousness, and we just couldn't have that.

I stand in front of the mirror in my bathroom, running a brush through my hair and considering a color change. Red's out of the question, but I've had blonde on my mind for a while now. I'll see how the night turns out and make a decision in the morning. We always make the best decisions when we're drunk or hung over.

The heat wave is now a thing of the past, so this is the first time in weeks I'm able to straighten my hair without the paralyzing fear of humidity. My faith in Jimmy Clay is slowly being restored. The jeans that I'm wearing, paired with a red plaid top, are counting on honesty. If a temperature spike occurs, then I'm going to roast.

I sit down on my bed and kick off a pair of heels I've been wearing around the house for the past hour. You never know what life is going to throw at you or when you're going to need to strap on a pair of pumps. In small-town Ohio, where girls don't wear heels, this is how we practice. I slide into a pair of comfortable sneakers then make my way down the carpeted stairs.

If all goes well, I'll spend the night on Summer's couch. Or her bed, if I'm feeling an abrupt need to jump start the rumor train one last time before she goes away to college. It was the same year Rebecca Ross went into hiding that the initial rumors began. Summer was having a slumber party and I wasn't about to sleep on the cold floor in the middle of winter. When everyone awoke, Summer and I were tangled together like Rapunzel's hair during an F4 tornado. I'd wager to say the *Are they or are they not scissoring?* scandal was directly responsible for nobody noticing the disappearance of Rebecca Ross, myself included.

My mom said she would drive me to the party, so I began drinking early. She understands about this sort of thing, that I'm going to drink no matter what. She blames MTV, but I blame my drinking on the lack of family dinners. Both are bullshit excuses. I'm young and I'm going to drink and anybody who doesn't needs therapy.

Three shot glasses sit on the counter, two empty and one full. I grab the one full of Jameson—my favorite drink—and throw it back. The shot burns as it rushes down the back of my throat. It's a wonderful explosion of sensation—taste, touch, and aroma. Reminds me of Ireland, somewhere I've never been, but hope to go someday.

I glance up to one of the hundred clocks in my mom's house. This particular one sits above the kitchen sink. Reading this particular clock has always been a chore. It has two forks for hands that are exactly the same length. When I came down the steps, the clock on the wall said it was ten-fifteen, so I guess the fork poking at the six is the minute hand. Ten-thirty it is, then, and my mom still isn't home from doing what the hell ever it was that she said she was doing. I'm not about to get in my car and drive as I've never driven drunk and have no intention to ever do so. It's something I've promised to nobody but myself. Sometimes I may be *stoopid* but I'm not stupid.

I could wait for her to get home, but I'm feeling a little antsy to get to the party because this could be the last time I see Summer for a while. Also, if I wait for Mom to return home before I go to the party, I'll have this bottle finished, and it's not a good look to show up to a party completely blitzed. It is, however, perfectly acceptable, and a display of good manners, to show up buzzed.

* * *

It's about ten degrees cooler than Jimmy predicted. For him, that's probably a record, but still, the difference between sixty and fifty degrees is no minor infraction. Especially, in a state like Ohio. In the fall, and before the first snowfall, fifty degrees feels like thirty. In the spring, fifty feels like eighty.

I walk briskly along the cracked sidewalk but not fast enough to break a sweat. In the midst of taking shots while showering, I forgot to apply deodorant. If the situation gets too dire, I'll stumble up to Summer's bathroom and apply when necessary.

Dylan's supposed to be there, so I'm a little worried about that, after our run-in at the fair. Drunk Dylan is kind of like sober Dylan, except more intense and hornier. If you're having a party, and he's on the guest list, it's best to have a shock collar on hand for when he inevitably starts humping anything remotely humpable. In a house like Summer's, there's a very real possibility that she could spend the following morning cleaning up his army of *little dills* as he likes to call them.

I come to a rest outside Summer's home. Music blares from within but the porch is deserted, which is unusual, as the wrap around porch that folds around their beautiful Victorian home always seems to be the hot spot.

I knock on the wooden door once and then open it, wondering why I even bothered since we were well past knocking years ago.

The door swings open and it's an unusual sight. Just like the porch, the inside is mostly devoid of human life. Four teens dressed in cut-offs and basketball shorts play beer pong on the dining room table to the left—a formal dining room that has never seen formality. The carpet beneath the teens is soaked with spilled beer. Or urine.

"Summer," I call out and the four players turn and look at me like I'm stupid.

"In the kitchen," Summer calls from the back of the house.

I give the teens a smirk before making my way through the very basic living room. There's a flat screen hanging on the wall and a vintage couch sitting in front of it. Once Summer's gone, this place will be the perfect bachelor pad. The openness is perfect for throwing parties but not so good for hosting responsible adult company.

I make my way down a short hallway lined with pictures of Summer, her dad, and her mother who had passed five years ago from breast cancer. At the end of the path comes the cherry-coated kitchen. Summer lunges at me, greeting me with a hug. Based on the strength of said hug, I'd say she's five shots deep, because the drunker she gets, the stronger she becomes. I sit my half-empty bottle on the counter beside a tray of dark-colored Jell-O shots and a bottle of Jager.

"Where the hell is everyone?"

"They should be coming. And don't even ask who those boys are out front because I have no idea. But I've been here alone, and I wasn't going to confront them." She wraps her mouth tight around her finger and sucks Jell-O off it.

"They're cute." I lean my head around the corner, peering down the hallway and into the living area where they're still playing. "But they look kind of young. Are you sure your dad's okay with this?"

She waves her hand. "Yeah, it's cool. He said he might stop by to grab some clothes after work, though."

Her dad used to scare me. Before I knew him as Mr. Daniels, I knew him as Officer Daniels, the mean ol' bastard who pulled my mom over for going sixty in a thirty-five. It was a few months later that I ran into him again at Summer's house. Gone was his uniform, and ever since then, he's been like a second father to me, albeit a better one than the first.

Summer reaches for one of the dark-colored Jell-O shots and asks if I want one. The answer should be obvious. I grab one of the plastic cups and we each tongue the Jell-O, loosening it up before swallowing. I gag as the blob slides down my throat. It's the most disgusting thing I've ever tasted.

"What did you make these with?" I shake off my disgust.

"Jager," she smiles. "Don't like it?"

"What the hell is wrong with you?"

"Party's here," Dylan yells. I pivot to see him and Tyson standing in the doorway to the kitchen, each holding a cheap case of beer. "Room in the fridge?"

"You know there's never room in the fridge." Summer points to the kitchen sink, which is full of ice. "Put it in the cooler."

"Nice." Dylan grabs the beer out of Tyson's hand and makes his way to the sink to begin unloading beer into the ice.

Tyson reaches past me and grabs the bottle of Jager. He smells like a potent combination of wood and musk—must be trying out some new cologne. He twists the cap off the bottle and throws his head back, chugging the thick black liquor.

Summer darts from the other side of the island and snatches the bottle out of his hand, then smacks the back of his head. "Go stand in a corner."

"Easy, babe," he says coolly.

"Don't call me babe." She steps close to him, invading his personal space. "I'm not drunk enough yet." She throws her head back and takes a long swig. Once finished, she savors the thick taste of black licorice with a wincing mouth.

When Dylan's done filling the improvised cooler, he turns around and braces his hands against the sink. "Is this gonna be one of your lame parties where it's just the four of us? Plus those four losers playing pong?"

"People are coming. And if they don't, then the four of us will finish everything in this kitchen."

Tyson, assuming he is out of the doghouse, wraps his arms around Summer and me. "You guys are gonna miss us," he says.

I'm not going anywhere.

"Probably not. Those city people are more my kind," Summer says through a smile.

My eyes roll. "Shut up. You're the trashiest person in this kitchen. You were born for the sticks."

Summer grabs Tyson's arm and throws it off her. "Whatever. I'll send you pics from the top of the world."

"The top of the world?" asks Dylan.

"Yep. The dorm is right beside the stadium."

"Shut the fuck up," Dylan says, springing to life. "Your room overlooks the stadium?"

"That's right. I'll be cheering on the Buckeyes from my bedroom."

"O-H," Dylan yells.

"I-O!" The rest of us yell in unity. Say what you want about Ohio, but we've got the Buckeyes and you don't.

It's the one thing that connects all of us Ohioans. We would steal, maim, and murder in the name of Brutus.

Dylan turns to me with a sly grin. "I'll be your boyfriend again if you let me stay with you on Saturdays."

I'm not sure what I'm supposed to get out of that deal. And he still doesn't know I'm not going and won't be sharing a room with the thousand dollar view. "Sounds like a terrible plan to me."

He glides across the hardwood floor, spins around, and grabs me by the waist. "Please." He nuzzles his nose against my neck.

My hips swivel against his groin. "Sure."

He pulls back, his eyes wide in excitement. "Really?"

"No." I break away from his grip and grab a Jell-O shot.

"Where's Joey?" Summer leans against the granite counter.

"He'll be here in a little bit. He's bringing his cousin," Tyson says.

I turn to him, my finger coated in Jell-O. "I didn't know he had a cousin."

"That's silly. Everybody has cousins."

I swallow the disgusting chunk of Jell-O and raise my hand. "I don't."

"That's unfortunate," says Dylan. "I'd love to meet up with a cousin of yours."

"If I had a cousin, he'd probably be a boy."

"Hey, get me drunk enough..." He bites his lip and pumps his hips forward. His hands cradle an imaginary ass while moans purr out of his throat.

Remember what I said about the humping? It's time to start hiding shit.

* * *

Summer and I walk into the living room, leaving the two boys in the kitchen. Summer grinds her heels into the carpet. "Where did all these people come from?" she asks, referring to the crowded living room.

Don't ask me how we failed to detect the entrance of well over twenty people into the house. I see a lot of familiar faces in the crowd. Most of them are still in high school. Like spotting Waldo in a collage of cowboys, my eyes dart straight to Cassadee James. The mere presence of her stupid ass almost makes me want to leave or go back into the kitchen with the boys.

Cassadee James is your basic fake bitch. Two-faced and she has the laugh of a donkey crossbred with a goat. Mentally, she never progressed past knock-knock jokes and basic algebra. Physically, she's been carrying around love potions shaped like tits since the sixth grade. And don't think for a minute they weren't battle tested, because those headlights have blinded more horny teenagers than it would take to fill a football field.

She flashes me a smile, and I immediately need a drink. *If she comes within five feet seven inches of me, I'm going to Caty with a 'D' her ass.* That's a *Mean Girls* reference, by the way. I twist toward Summer, but she's gone. I spot her, the life of the party, in the middle of the room with her hands up, dancing to Usher's latest jam. I'm seven shots deep, but I'm not drunk enough to join her and make an ass out of myself.

Now, seven might sound like a lot, but I was blessed with a man's tolerance for alcohol. Sometimes that's a great thing, but mostly, it's a bank account burning disaster, since I wouldn't get drunk as quick as the other girls and sometimes the men. Then I would overcompensate and drink too much, too fast, just to catch up. The catch was, by the time I actually caught up, my system was at least five shots behind.

I stroll back into the kitchen to find Dylan and Tyson arm wrestling on the island. I lean against the doorframe and look on in amusement. No way is Tyson going to win this. He's not a wimp, but Dylan spent the last year working on what he calls his *beach bod*. We had all planned to get into tip-top shape for our senior trip to Florida, but Dylan was the only one who followed through. It's not like any of us are out of shape though. You could certainly do body shots off Tyson's stiff abs.

If they were having a grunting match, Tyson would definitely be winning. Alas, this isn't that kind of war and Dylan slams Tyson's arm down hard against the granite, knocking a shot glass onto the wooden floor where it shatters.

"I'm not drinking that," Tyson declares.

"Yeah, you are." Dylan grabs a drink that appears to be a combination of tar and cream soda and pushes it into Tyson's hand.

"Gross. What the fuck is that?" I ask.

Tyson peers into the glass and grimaces.

"Something we invented. We're gonna call it the toilet bowl. Want a taste?" Dylan extends a glass to me.

"Does it taste like a toilet?"

His eyes narrow in confusion. "Why would it taste like a toilet?"

Tyson slams the empty glass onto the counter and spits up all over Dylan's shirt. I laugh and Dylan moans, "Oh, man..."

Tyson rushes to the sink, grabs a Natty Light, and pops it open.

"Didn't you just throw up?" I ask.

"Need a chaser," he says in between gulps.

He's always had this thing where he gargles with beer to rinse vomit out of his mouth. He'll probably forget the sink is being used as a cooler, and then spit the improvised mouthwash onto the ice. I decide to take my chances with Cassadee rather than watch.

Prepared for the worst, I walk back into the living room and notice a crowd has gathered around the dining table. The vixen is propped against a window on the other side of the room, mingling with her latest victim—a young man with a chinstrap and a Tapout hat. If anybody deserves her herpes, it's probably him.

I find and stand behind Summer as she loudly chants for Joey, who must be at the opposite end of the table playing pong. From the battle cries of the drunks, it must be a close game. If God had made me three inches taller, I'd probably be able to see the game in all its glory. I tap on Summer's shoulder. "Why the hell is Cassadee here?"

She turns to me. "It's my party and I can invite whoever I want."

"Sorry. I thought you hated her," I say sheepishly.

"I do hate her. I don't know why the fuck she's here," she says and turns back to the table. "Go throw her through a window."

That's the best idea I've heard all night. I turn and glance at the temptress. I don't have the strength to pick her up. Her tits alone have to weigh thirty pounds, but she's positioned perfectly against that window for me to rush her. The visual of a scale pops into my head. On one side is an unconscious Cassadee and on the other, me behind prison bars. That side of the scale is practically glued to the ground. In an effort to stay out of prison, I begin to push through the dense crowd.

"Checkmate!" I hear Joey scream.

Now, I know they're not playing chess because this isn't a grade school party. I assume checkmate means that he's won, so I squeeze between two stoners to be sure. I don't have a good view, but I can make out Joey tearing his shirt off and bumping his chest against his partner. Yep, they've won.

Someone bumps into me, almost pushing me to the ground.

"Sorry," I hear Summer say. "But do you see Joey's cousin? Total babe."

That piques my interest. I shove my way past the two stoners and freeze in place. Everybody's calling him Joey's cousin, but from where I'm standing, I simply call him Blue. Of course, it's fucking Blue.

CHAPTER SEVEN

Fight or flight is totally a real thing, but even with that basic high school health class knowledge, I can't help but stand and stare at him. My brain goes through the motions of thought so fast that my body can't keep up. Brain says turn around, but eyes say *Just give me a damn minute.*

Blue cracks open a beer and chugs it. In beer pong, the loser is the one who's supposed to drink. But since beer pong is a drinking game, win or lose, the game has evolved into a way to pass the time while you drink.

Blue wipes beer off his mouth with the back of his hand. There's a visible trail of spilled beer rolling down the front of his white tee. Then it happens, as it inevitably always does, his eyes meet mine. His lips, very slowly, form into a huge, brimming smile. He's definitely a grower and not a shower—I'm referring to his smile, by the way. He always seems to be smiling. That's one of the key components of my inexplicable lust for him, but boy, he really can charm the panties off a girl with that smile.

We're shooting lasers at each other, unable to turn away. Will people notice? Would people notice two elephants locked in a loving embrace in the middle of flat field? Probably. The elephant in the fucking room's about a millisecond away from being the talk of the party, and I'm not about to allow it.

With a tilt of my head, a little shake, and a few fingers through my hair, I tell him to follow me. But he's obviously not fluent in my body language, because he just stands there, frozen. I wave my hand at him, hoping to get his attention and mouth the words, *Come on*. His brows perk up, and I'm positive he thinks we're about to have a repeat performance. He's wrong.

He makes his way through the crowd and over to me, but I turn and lead him out of the living room before he comes into contact with me. We make our way to the bathroom and he rushes inside. I slam the door shut and pivot to face him.

He grabs me by the waist and zooms in for a kiss, but I arch back. "No. We're not having sex in the bathroom."

"Oh?"

"I brought you in here to talk away from prying ears."

He rolls his head and moans. "Are we just gonna talk? Can I at least go get a beer?"

My eyes squint. "Are you serious?"

"That depends on how long we're gonna be in here," he chuckles.

"Not long enough for you to sober up."

"Good."

I glare at him. "Why didn't you tell me you were Joey's cousin?"

"I didn't know you knew him." He shrugs roughly and bumps his shoulder into his chin. "Ow."

"We're the same age in the same small town. *Of course* I know him."

"I guess I just didn't think about it. I thought you were older."

"How old do I look?"

"Twenty-five?"

My lips pull tight.

"I'm kidding."

The night at the fair, he was sweet and genuine. Now he's making jokes about my age. That's obviously the quickest way to a girl's heart. I punch him in the chest.

"Ow," he whines, rubbing his chest. "I'm gonna need medical attention by the time we get out of here."

"The point is that I know him. I know him very well, and not to scare you away, but his best friend is my ex-boyfriend," I say. "And do I really look twenty-five?"

He shakes his head, smiles and runs his palm against my face. "No. You look beautiful."

Every damn time he says that, I lose track of my inner monologue. "Stop..."

"No," he says firmly and lowers his hands to my waist.

I don't stop him this time but lean in instead. "Not to sound like a creep, but I've kind of missed you."

"It's okay. I like creeps and I've missed you, too."

His eyes ask for permission before he leans in and kisses me. It's everything I remembered, plus his intoxicating beer breath. His fingers dance on my hip as he draws me in closer. There's a pulse in his jeans, and I pull back.

"When we leave this bathroom, don't go around blabbing about how you just kissed the prettiest girl at the party, because then everyone will know it was me," I say. "Except Cassadee. She'll probably think it was her."

"Who's that?"

"Some bitch."

"She easy?" he asks with a smirk.

"Like reading a how-to manual."

"Wow. Looks like I'm barking up the wrong tree."

I push my thigh into his groin, pushing him back against the pristine pedestal sink. "Shut up."

"Okay."

And it's me kissing him this time. More passionately than I should if I ever had any intention of playing coy. I think it's crystal clear there won't be any playing hard-to-get in whatever this is between the two of us. I bring one hand to his chest, stopping him from diving into my mouth. "Don't take this the wrong way—"

His breath is sharp and ragged. "I don't think there's room to take this the wrong way. Unless that knee of yours should jerk into my—"

"Not that." I stand back. "I like you, and I'm glad you came tonight, but right now, we need to keep this private."

He leans in and whispers, "Isn't that why we're in the bathroom?"

"I'm talking about everything. I don't think my ex is over me, and I haven't even told him I'm not going to college, which is the entire reason we broke up in the first place."

He sucks on his lip and folds his arms as he leans against the sink. "He's your ex, and I'm sure it's for a reason, but do you really owe him that?"

"I just need to talk to him first."

"I guess I understand." He nods and stands up straight. "But I'm ready to drink."

I grab him by his arm as he walks past me and opens the door. "Blue?"

He twists on his heel. "Yeah?"

And I kiss him again.

* * *

Cassadee's all up in my face. I wish she were fighting me, but she's doing far worse. She's talking to me. Grunts and moans would probably pass for intelligent conversation with this imbecile. But I accidentally bumped into her in my race out of the bathroom and was forced to stick around after apologizing.

"Oh, my God. Sarah Palin is such a twat," she says to me. I definitely agree with her there, but I don't know where Cassadee's sudden passion for years-old politics is coming from. *Saturday Night Live* reruns, perhaps? "She's the reason I got into politics. Somebody has to stand up to her."

Stand up to her? She's as irrelevant as tartar sauce at Taco Bell.

"Totally agree." I'm regretting not staying locked away with Blue. I could be getting fucked on a bathroom sink, but instead I'm being sprayed with the spit of a wilder beast.

"I never saw you as the brainy type."

Excuse me? I wasn't the valedictorian, but I'm pretty sure a three-point-four beats a one-point-zero. The former is about a B and the latter is about a D. I think those are pretty accurate digits in multiple facets of our lives, including our breasts, which is the only thing she'll ever have on me.

"Excuse me for a moment," I say and reach into my pocket for my phone that isn't ringing. I put one finger up to her. "My mom's calling. I'll be right back."

I walk away in a hurry with my phone pressed against my ear. Too occupied conversing with Casper the Friendly Ghost, I stumble into Joey and Blue. "Hi," I say enthusiastically.

"Are you talking to us or your phone?" Joey asks.

"You. There's nobody on the phone." I lower my phone and push it into my pocket.

"Hi," Blue says, reaching out a friendly hand to me. "Nice to meet you."

He's definitely overplaying the *We haven't met before* card, but it impresses me that he took the initiative. His grip is tight as I shake his hand. "Hi, Blue."

Shit. I'm not supposed to know him.

Joey zeroes in on me. "Do you know my cousin?"

My instincts scream three words: deny, deny, and deny.

"I've met him before," says not-my-gut.

He laughs. "Are you the girl from the carnival?"

Huh? What? Who? The Girl? From the carnival? My eyes shift to Blue, rubbing the back of his head, looking not at me, but past me. *I'll deal with him later.* "Not there." I shake my head.

"Fender bender," Blue blurts out.

"Huh?" I say. Blue's eyes beam toward me. "Yeah... he hit me. I was sitting at a green light and up he came and bumped right into me."

"The light was green." Blue motions with a flat hand. "And I yelled *Green means go.*"

"That's not how it—"

"So then I rammed her in the ass." He shrugs. "But we're cool now."

"Yeah. We're cool. He agreed to pay me five hundred dollars for damages if I didn't get the police involved."

"But I already paid her. So we're cool."

"Actually, I haven't received a penny yet."

"Well, it's in the mail."

Well, this cover up is certainly escalating to absurd levels of stupidity, but don't think I'm not going to get my money's worth. "Oh, I forgot to give you my address. That's probably why I haven't received it yet."

It's becoming a game to the both of us, and I have to admit, it's kind of fun. Every time we say something, Joey's head shifts toward whoever is lying at that moment. He can't be stupid enough to believe either of us, but I guess we'll find out.

"Of course you did. You probably don't remember because you were drinking," Blue says and bumps Joey with his elbow. He has a winning smile, and I could smack the shit out of him.

"*You* were drinking and driving?" Joey asks with his mouth agape. I've always been *that friend* who lectures others on the dangers of driving drunk.

"Before noon," Blue adds while shaking his head in disapproval.

"Of course I wasn't drinking and driving." I'm now faced with a decision. I can continue along with this ridiculous charade and enroll myself in a string of lectures from concerned friends, or I could out myself as the whore of the county fair. "For fuck's sake. I met him at the carnival!"

Joey's head sinks, his mouth dropping in shock. He's either surprised his cousin could get someone like me or flabbergasted that I would sleep with a carnie. I don't know how much Blue told him, but I guess it was too fucking much.

"I told you she was pretty," Blue says to Joey with the widest, most innocent grin.

CHAPTER EIGHT

I walk by Joey, who is passed out on the couch on my way to the kitchen. I'm not going to come out and say that I got him as drunk as possible so that he would forget that I was the girl in the grass outside the carnival. I will admit that, against my own better judgment, I encouraged him to bong a half bottle of Jack, however.

He's lying on his stomach, so on the off chance he upchucks while he sleeps I think he'll be safe. Since I'll probably be up all night, I can keep a close eye on him. That's what friends do. Get each other blackout drunk, and then babysit them until sunrise.

The kitchen is a mess, much like the rest of the house. The floor is soaked with beer, whiskey and over by the sink, a small puddle of vomit. During parties, Summer attempts to keep a clean house but the higher her blood alcohol content, the more trashed the house becomes. At this rate, she'll still be drunk when driving to State tomorrow.

There is no ice left in the makeshift cooler in the sink. All that's left are two bottles of beer. I grab them both. On my way back outside, I make a pit stop in the bathroom. As I swing the door open, I see Dylan lying on the floor with his head propped against the toilet. He's asleep, so it's best that I don't bother him. I do have to pee, though. Quite the conundrum.

I pull the front door shut behind me and toss a beer to Blue, who's sitting on an antique wooden porch swing. "Be right back," I say and gallop down the steps.

"Where you going?"

"Please don't make me shatter all illusion of mystery."

Once I get to the side of the house and behind a thick bush, I pull my jeans down and take care of business. Like a horror movie, I hear a twig snap and leaves rustle. My head jerks and I grab hold of my jeans, prepared to run.

"I knew it!" Blue shouts accusingly through the darkness.

"Yeah, you caught me, but I'm telling you right now that I don't poop because girls don't do that. Now turn around."

He does as told. I pull my jeans back up and stand. "Where's my beer?" *Oh, there it is.* Lying sideways in a puddle of piss. "Shit."

"It's okay, I'll share mine." Blue grabs my hand. "Come on."

* * *

Four in the morning and we are the only ones still awake. The bench rocks back and forth gently. Swaying. It's as if we're at sea. There's a calmness in the way the morning air tangles around us. It's not like the afternoon or evening air when it all feels so thick and dense. I can't be the only one who notices the quiet beauty in it. Billions of people are awake in this world at any given second, but here in Lakeview, it's as if we have the city to ourselves.

Blue takes a swig of beer and the world is quiet enough that I hear it rush down the back of his throat. "It's quiet," he says.

"It's four in the morning."

"I'm used to it. Being the only person in the world awake." His body shifts on the swing, making himself more comfortable. "I could never really sleep at night."

"But you worked during the day."

"I wasn't the most responsible worker." He laughs and brings his arm behind me, gripping the back of the swing and causing us to jolt before settling back into a rhythmic swinging pattern.

"You really should find some time to sleep. It's kind of important, since you can't live without it."

"What you can't really live without is dreaming."

"How drunk are you? You dream when you sleep."

"Not if you're doing it right. There's nothing in the world comparable to dreaming when you're wide awake."

"I don't know about that. I believe your subconscious can tap into your wants and desires more than you ever could. It's like everything is locked deep somewhere inside, and the only way to retrieve it is to fall asleep. Then you drift away and find everything you never even knew you wanted."

Or you find Freddy Krueger.

"I don't know about you, but I don't need my subconscious to tell me what I want. I dream with my eyes wide open, and right now, I'm dreaming about you." He sets the bottle of beer on the railing beside him, then straightens himself out and turns his gaze to me. "I've thought about you every moment of every day since that night we met."

"I don't know if I should be flattered or creeped out."

"A little bit of both, perhaps?"

"Let's stick with flattered."

"I was hoping you would say that." He rubs his palms against his jeans, stands up, and offers me his hand. "Come?"

"That depends on where we're going."

"It's a surprise."

"There's something you should know about me, Blue." I stand up and take his hand. "I'm not big on surprises."

"Then why did you take my hand?"

"Because I'm drunk and not in control of my actions."

"Is that right?" he asks through thin lips. He pulls me by the hand, down the antique steps and into the center of the road where we come to an abrupt stop. He pivots on his feet and grabs my free hand, locking us together at the fingers. "Will you dance with me, Charlie Brown?"

I throw my head back, laughing. "Charlie Brown?"

"I'm just making assumptions since you never told me your last name."

"It's Scott," I say as we begin dancing in a slow circle. "And yours?"

His lips crumple contemplatively. "You know? I haven't decided that yet."

My eyes narrow on him. "What do you mean?"

"You don't need to look at me that way. I'm not crazy. I swear. I've just decided that I'd rather be anyone else than who my parents wanted me to be. Including my name."

"Are you saying that Blue isn't your real name?"

"I'm saying that someone would have to be pretty different to name their child that."

"Well, if it's any consolation, I like it. It has a unique ring to it."

"Does it, Pink?"

"Definitely."

One hand lets go of me as he spins back, expecting me to roll into his arms like we're on *Dancing with the Stars*. I relax my chest before giving it a whirl but end up twisting my ankle. The only thing that saves me from the asphalt is the quickness of his hand as he catches my fall.

"Let me take you on a real date." His strong grip holds me by the small of my back. If I say no, he could drop me against the cracked pavement. "It won't be anywhere fancy because I'm not that kind of guy. We won't go to a five-star or even a four-star restaurant, but I'll take you somewhere you'll never forget."

I lift myself up and grab him by the waist as we resume dancing in circles. "It's okay. I'm not into fancy anyway."

"So why don't you give me your address, and I'll pick you up Monday at noon?"

"How are you going to write down my number if you don't even have a phone?"

"I've got an excellent memory. You know people were able to manage their lives perfectly fine without phones, right?"

"I wouldn't remember that dark time in history."

"My parents would never let me forget it." He lets go of me and reaches into his pocket and pulls out a Sharpie marker.

"Handy," I say, impressed. "Got any other tools in there?"

"Nothing you haven't seen." He winks. "Give me your arm."

I do as told and he scribbles a permanent message on my arm: *You have a date Monday with your favorite carnie, Blue.*

"Definitely won't forget about it now." I grab the marker out of his hand and pull his arm to me. "Do you have any idea how many showers I'm going to have to take to wash this off?" I ask as I scribble my own message on his arm—my address. I'm drunk so I hope I don't flub the house number, or worse—like accidentally give him my dad's address. That would be a disaster.

I push the marker into his pocket and fold my hands into his again. We resume dancing, and I secretly hope the sun never comes up. I could stay here forever, or at least until I pass out.

CHAPTER NINE

My head thumps before I've even opened my eyes. The back of my throat is dry with the aftertaste of binge drinking. When my eyes blink open, everything's a blur. Must be Sunday. I wonder what time it is—it has to be at least noon.

The alarm clock next to my bed is lying because it says it's three. Did I miss the rollback of the clocks? God, I hope not, because then it would actually be four. I think. I need a glass of water, but the bathroom is what seems like miles away. I'm going to die in this bed. It'd probably be more enjoyable than Sunday dinner with dad.

Shit!

I throw my comforter off my body, prepared to jump out of bed, but my legs don't cooperate. I could miss one dinner. No biggie. He thinks I'm visiting from college since I still haven't told him yet. Theoretically, I could tell him that I can't make it because of schoolwork. On the other hand, if I do go, I could guilt trip him into giving me money for books. Could I go that far down the rabbit hole?

You betcha.

Last night feels like a dream in the sense that pieces are missing. The last thing I remember is dancing in the street with Blue. I'm sure the walk home was full of adventures that I wish I could remember.

I could definitely get used to Blue sticking around. Our elders have always lectured us youngins' about the dangers of drinking, but they never really talk about all the good things. For example, how getting drunk is the quickest way to open doors to the mind and soul of a stranger. Before last night, Blue was just a guy I had met at the carnival. Last night, he became a fully realized person. More than a gorgeous face on an incredible body, there's depth behind those dangerously blue eyes—dreams, fears, and hints of heartbreak.

Somehow, I finagle my way out of bed and onto my feet. My arms rise over my head as I force out an obnoxious yawn that threatens to knock my light-headed ass to the floor. Good thing I've decided against visiting my lawyer father, because I'd probably get a DUI on my short, five-minute drive.

* * *

I hold onto the stair railing for dear life as I descend the steps into the living room. It's unusually quiet for a Sunday afternoon. So quiet that I wonder if my mom ever made it home.

I find her in the surprisingly pristine kitchen with a cup of coffee in her hand and a bright smile on her glowing face.

"What's wrong with you?"

Her hand swings to the side, almost spilling her Folgers. "Nothing, why?"

I'm not buying it, but I'm too hung over to dig into her issues. "I'm not going to Dad's today."

"I already told him. I saw you lying in bed about an hour ago, looking like death, and I knew you wouldn't be in the mood to put up with his bullshit," she says with glee. "Mom of the Year right here."

"Wait a minute, *you* talked to him? Note the emphasis on *you*."

She shrugs. "You know, we can be civil."

"Seriously, what the hell is up with you?"

"I don't know what you're talking about." Steam rolls off her chin as she takes a drawn out sip of coffee.

"You're happy, perky, and you've cleaned the entire house. You're not on the couch watching some crappy love story, sobbing your eyes out. And you're not reprimanding me for not going to college tomorrow." I lean against the counter for support. "You're acting like an adult and it's freaking me out."

She brushes me off and walks past me, toward the living room. "Why does anything have to be going on?"

"Because people don't just wake up being happy after spending months on the couch moping." I give her chase. "I'm really hung over, so please... don't make me follow you around this entire house."

She spins around, cradling her cup with both hands. "I just woke up today in a better mood."

"Whatever," I groan and fall backward into the cushiest loveseat in the world. Time for a nap. I rest my eyes and fold my hands against my chest.

"You really want to know?"

Now you start talking...

I throw myself up in the chair and push myself back against it. She sits her cup on the table—on a coaster, even. Who is this woman? "I had a business meeting last night."

"Sounds like a blast. Am I missing something here?"

"Well." She sits on the edge of the couch. "Business turned to pleasure," she says with a shrug.

My eyes widen. "Please spare me the details."

She frowns. "Nothing like that, but I did manage to get a job—"

"Congrats," I say, deadpan, fully aware my enthusiasm is lacking. It's there, even if I'm unable to show it.

"And a date."

Under normal circumstances, I'd be proud of her for moving on, but— "You can't date your boss before you've even started working. You're going to be one bad date away from a spoiled résumé."

"Charlie, it's not like that. I'm not going to be dating my boss," she says and rubs her palm nervously across the arm of the couch. "I'm going on a date with his son."

My mouth sinks further and I spring to action, almost vomiting on the freshly steamed carpet. "I'd almost prefer if you'd go back to dating Ryan Gosling, to be quite honest."

She rolls her eyes. "Don't you even want to know what my job is?"

"Other than being a cougar?"

"Charlie," she laughs. "I'm going to be working in insurance–"

You know nothing about insurance. You're a high school teacher.

"–training new employees. There's a lot of travel—"

I really should have gone to college.

"–and his son is very handsome."

"All right, I've heard enough. I'm going back to bed, and I'm hoping I'll wake up somewhere other than Bizzaro World." I stroll past her and grab onto the stair railing.

"Don't stray too far from Bizzaro World, or you might wake up to find your carnie boyfriend doesn't exist."

I turn around ominously slow. She's wearing the wickedest smile this side of Halloween. "I haven't the slightest clue what you're talking about." Then I turn and walk up the stairs, knowing full well that someone has spilled the gossip-flavored jelly beans.

"I'm thinking of painting the house blue," I hear her say as I ascend the steps. I happen to catch, for the first time since I awoke, Blue's scribbling's on my arm.

Good grief. Do I need a drink.

CHAPTER TEN

September is the first bipolar month in a typical year. Temperatures can rise and fall like a roller coaster hitting the highs of heaven and the lows of hell. Today is one of those days in heaven. There's a light breeze blowing against Blue's Jeep as we travel down a dirt road. Dust billows behind us forming clouds. Straight out of a *Toy Story* movie, the sky is painted in shades of blue beauty.

I don't have a clue where we're going. He says it's a surprise and I'm excited. I've had too many curve balls in my life, so I normally hate surprises, but everything is different with Blue.

I've been down this road many times before. Just up ahead, to the right, is Pine Ridge Road. Dylan's road. I've spent so much time on that road. In that house. In those woods. From when we were still too young to understand love to a few months ago when we still believed it was enough.

Those days are in the past, and now so is that road. Both are close enough to turn around. I stare into the passenger side mirror, watching Pine Ridge fade into the distance.

"You're being quiet," Blue says to me.

I look over with a smile. "I'm being contemplative."

"Do you ever not think?"

"I don't think it's possible to turn your brain off."

"You're telling me that you've never shut it all down?" he asks, one hand on the wheel, the other on the gearshift. "No dreaming, no thinking. Just nothing."

I shake my head. That doesn't make sense to me.

"You should try it sometime. It's peaceful."

"Is that what you're doing now?"

"No," he says. "I'm driving." He turns his head and looks at me. I want to tell him to focus on the road, but it's impossible for me to tell him to turn away.

Then I get an idea. "Pull over."

* * *

The grass is warm against our backs, scratching against cotton and denim. About twenty feet away, the Jeep sits against a guardrail.

"What are we doing?" Blue asks.

"Hypothesizing," I reply. "Trying to turn it all off."

"Oh," he grumbles. "I thought we were gonna do it in the grass."

I'm not disgusted, but I look it. "Where any Billy Bob or Sally can see? No, I don't think so."

"Does anybody even drive down this road?" He rises up slightly, resting his body on his elbows as he takes a survey of our surroundings. "I don't think anybody's gonna see us."

"You're right, because we're not doing anything."

"Yeah, yeah," he mumbles again.

I ignore him and close my eyes. The leaves on the trees rustle in the wind. An annoying yacking bird circles the sky. The sun must be coming out from behind the clouds as I begin to see a thick, blinding shade of red. It's hard to focus on not focusing when I can feel the heat burning against my eyes.

I'm not tired, but I force out a yawn. If I fall asleep, does that count? I think back to our conversation on the porch. According to Blue, and maybe basic science, the answer would be no.

When I first told him to pull over, I thought it would be a cute and quirky side adventure. Maybe even romantic. I was devastatingly wrong. It's just awkward and pointless. I've mucked up our first date.

"Not to ruin the moment—" Blue's voice punctures through the silence.

"Too late."

"—but this wouldn't be the first time you've had sex in the grass."

"How could I forget? I was living in the moment."

"Yes, you were," he says, his voice slowly trailing off.

"Well, my concentration is effectively shattered, thanks to you." I'll just pretend this whole failure is his fault. "Let's go."

As I stand up, I see a speeding car in the distance. As it draws closer, I can faintly hear the gears shifting.

"What's that?" Blue asks.

"That's the sound of nobody driving down the road."

He stands up beside me and smirks. "Good thing you didn't drop your pants then, huh?"

I pay no attention to him as the car speeds past us. It's Dylan's car. Of course it is. I'd recognize that Lancer anywhere. He's been working on it for a while and says he's going to start drag racing. I've always believed he was full of the usual shit, but that thing is flying, leaving bombs of dust behind him. He's heading south, so he must be racing home.

"Earth to Charlie." Blue waves his hand in my face.

I snap out of a daze that I didn't even know I was in. Dylan and his car are long gone, out of sight and out of hearing range. "Sorry. I must have dazed out." I turn to him. "No thinking, no dreaming. Just nothing." I finish with a smile.

"Well, it's a good thing we stopped for a few minutes. Wouldn't wanna be on the road with that douchebag."

"Why is he a douchebag?" I ask with a light chuckle.

"Because who drives like that on a dirt road?" He shrugs. "Also, douchiest car ever."

If he only knew.

* * *

If it were one week later, I'd think we were heading to the Founders Carnival. An annual event much like a county fair, but with a purpose and more booze. Our fairs and festivals are dry, as in no alcohol permitted. Ten miles over, across county lines, and their carnivals, festivals, and fairs are medieval exercises in alcohol consumption.

So, yeah, welcome to Ale County. I grow more excited but mostly more anxious. Where is he taking me? What if everything leading up to this point in time has been an act, and he's actually a madman driving me to my final resting place? For it being such a small town, people have a way of turning up dead.

Blue flashes his blinkers and then turns right. My anxiety grows to confusion. There aren't too many roads in this five-stoplight town, and Poplar Street dead-ends at the fairgrounds.

Inside the gates, trucks are scattered about. Concession stands line both sides of a paved path that runs horizontally across the entirety of the grounds. Long trailers attached to transport trucks, with unassembled rides on the back of each, are spread out across the grounds. *If this is Blue's idea of a date, then you can go ahead and find me on christianmingle dot com.*

"You know the carnival doesn't start for another week, right?" I turn to him.

He nods. "I know."

Of course he knows. This was probably one of the last stops on the circuit. I've been to this place many times. The same for the fairgrounds back home, but can't recall seeing Blue before. I'm sure he's been in the background all these years and I just never noticed.

"I just need to stop here for a few minutes and pick something up."

"What's that?"

We come to a stop and he pulls the brake. "Don't worry about it." He turns to me. "It's a surprise."

"Two surprises in a day? I think I'm going to explode."

He shakes his head, grinning. "You're so weird."

"Thanks."

"It's a good thing." He brushes his hand across my cheek. "Do you wanna wait in the car?"

I peer out the window. Beside us is a parked camper that's rocking violently. Could be a washing machine for all I know. Most likely, though, it's the conceiving of next generations Blue. "No. I'll go with you."

"All right," he says and pulls the key from the ignition.

* * *

We walk past four men assembling the teacups, and I have an instant flashback to the county fair. The night I met Blue. Two stocky, sweaty men are in the process of bolting down our blue cup. I watch in equal parts wonder and horror, questioning if I'll ever ride a carnival ride again. I guess it never occurred to me how quickly they put them together. How have I survived all these years?

A middle-aged man yells for Blue, asking for his help in assembling the ride, and I think he's only half joking. It seems Blue is the most popular kid in the carnival world. If they had a prom, he'd be a shoe-in for king. If I had it my way, I'd be his queen. From another school, of course.

Blue informs the man that he's under strict doctor's orders to not lift anything over twenty pounds. Arthritis or something. The man chuckles and begins to scoot a cup onto the platform, fully aware that Blue's full of shit.

As we approach an old rickety camper that sits on the edge of the grounds against a chain-link fence that wraps around the entire perimeter, Blue turns to me. "Can you wait outside?"

I give him a simple nod.

"All right." He glances behind him at the camper, then back to me contemplatively. "If I'm not out of there in five minutes, call the police."

I jerk. "Call the police? What the hell for?"

He flashes a grin. "Don't worry about it."

"Don't worry—"

He cuts me off with his finger against my mouth. "Don't freak out. I was mostly kidding."

"Whatever." My arms fold against my chest. "Don't be long."

"I won't, but if you get too bored, you can talk to Marvin."

"Who's Marvin?"

Blue points to a man sitting on a milk crate outside the camper beside us. He has a familiar, unshaven face. He could definitely use a shower. I lean into Blue and whisper in his ear, "Is he a meth head?"

"I don't know," he whispers back. "Why don't you ask him?"

"Absolutely not."

He whistles and Marvin looks to us. "Take care of my girl, all right?"

Marvin nods and stands up with a lit cigarette hanging on the edge of his mouth. I grab Blue's arm as he approaches the camper. "It's fine," he says with a smile. "I'll be right back."

I let out a frustrated sigh as the older man approaches me. "Want one?" He grabs at the pack of cigarettes in his flannel pocket.

I shake my head. "I'm good."

"Suit yourself." He leans against the camper and shakes his cigarette at me. "Do I know you?"

It takes a moment but it hits me quick. He's the guy who loaded me into the Zipper. "We met once in Lakeview," I say, nodding my head.

"That's right. Can't forget a pretty face like that, I guess."

"Thanks."

He draws his hand to his mouth and takes a hit. "How is he?"

"Good," I say proudly.

He exhales and the breeze pushes a cloud of smoke toward me. I gently wave the smoke away from my face.

"Sorry about that." He throws his cigarette on the ground. "You know something? I didn't even know the boy was leaving." He grinds the butt into the ground with his unlaced boot. "That night he met you," he says, and I perk up, "he came into the camper and said he was leaving the circuit. Said he was gonna be sticking around." He looks me directly in the eye. "He didn't even tell his dad he was leaving. Although it shouldn't have been that surprising, seeing how they barely talk these days."

"His dad is here?"

Marvin points with his thumb at the camper behind us. The one Blue walked into.

"He's here, in the camper?"

"Might have to call the police," he says.

"Blue mentioned that, but I didn't think he was serious."

He lets out an amused sigh. "We don't know things till they happen."

I take a pained look at the camper and want to ask so many questions, but it would feel like a betrayal to dig into Blue's past without his permission. The issue has already been raised, though, and I'm a naturally curious person. "Why don't they talk? Blue and his dad."

"They've got a hell of a relationship. He was twelve, maybe thirteen, when his mother ran away. I guess it was just never the same after that. I think they reminded each other of the woman they had lost. One lost a wife and the other lost a mother."

"That's sad." I don't know what else to say. It's not my place to keep this conversation going and I would be content if it would end.

"I think you're good for him." He grabs the pack of cigarettes out of his pocket and pulls one into his mouth. As he's about to light it, he glances at me. "Sorry."

"It's fine." Sure, they bother me, but I'm on his turf.

The end of the stick burns bright. "I think he deserves someone like you." He slips the Zippo lighter into his pocket. "God knows the kid's got his fair share of problems, but maybe you can be the one to help him," he says, pointing a finger squarely at me.

"Problems?" As soon as it comes out of my mouth, I regret it.

He rubs a thumb across his bottom lip and peeks behind him, as if he's making sure nobody's there. He turns back and scoots closer to me. "He's a good kid. He really is, but a few years ago, I noticed a change in him. We were over in Indiana and he disappeared one night. When he came back the next morning, he was still rolling."

"Drugs?" I ask, unconvinced.

He nods. "He got into some trouble about a year ago. Apparently, he owed some guy in Junction City thousands. That guy came to the carnival looking for trouble. Blue had been saving up money since he was fifteen, so he could settle down. You know, find a home somewhere. He had to give it all up. Come to find out—"

The camper door swings open and slams against metal panels. "Let's go!" Blue huffs and rushes past me, toward the Jeep. He's burning red and filled with anger.

I look to Marvin one last time and he nods. "He's a good kid," he says as softly as a lie, but I know that he means it.

I jog to catch up to Blue. The first thing I notice is his hand balled into a fist. I grab his shoulder and he stops. "Are you okay?"

He places both hands on my cheeks. "I'm fine," he says with a forced smile. I want nothing more than to believe him, but I know better. I want to know what happened between him and his father in the camper but asking him is out of the question.

"You wanna get out of here?"

"Yeah," I nod. "Let's go."

* * *

Blue's in the Jeep and has it started before I've even opened the car door. I climb into my seat and his head spins around to look behind us as we back out. There's a loud thud against the driver's side window and we come to a full, jerking stop. Standing outside is a young man in a worn gray hoodie. I don't know him, but it's obvious Blue does.

A huge grin flashes across Blue's face, an instant change from anger. He throws the parking brake into place and bursts out the door. "Cookie!" he yells and embraces the man with a bear hug. "How have you been?"

"Almost got fired the day after you left, so things are ace." He laughs. "How the hell are you?"

Blue pushes his hands into his pockets. "I'm a civilian now, haven't you heard?"

"Living the dream, huh?"

"Something like that."

Cookie grabs Blue's arm, pulling him further away from the Jeep. They begin talking again, but I can no longer hear what they're saying.

He has a family here. Biological family, like his dad, but also the family he has chosen for himself—Cookie and Marvin. I'm sure he has more than that, too, but I don't know any of them. I can't shake my ill-conceived notions of who these people are. There's a tinge of guilt rising in my stomach. Even if it was only a passing thought in my head, I had written Marvin off as a drug addicted loser. It wasn't until we had an actual conversation, and he really spoke to me, from the heart, that I realized how deeply I was wrong.

Blue reaches into his pocket and grabs his wallet. My view is obfuscated by his back as he hands Cookie something. I have no idea what's being said or what's going on, but I begin thinking the worst. Something Blue said that night in the grass comes rushing back to me. He said he had saved up enough money to live off of for a while, which is how he was able to quit his job in the first place. But Marvin told me that he gave it all up to the man in Junction City.

There has to be more to that story.

Blue climbs back into the Jeep, happier and more alive than he was just a few short minutes ago. We begin backing up, and I watch Cookie walk across the green and toward the horse barn.

As the fairgrounds fade into the distance, a stray thought crosses my mind, and it's a question I must have an answer to. "Do you miss it?"

"The carnival?" He pauses, processing the question with a blank face followed by a shrug. "It's the only home I've ever had."

We drive away from his home, and to me—it's no longer a place. It's an idea or a group of people or something else entirely. It's the first time for me that 'home' becomes a concept instead of a place. Like it can exist anywhere, with the right person.

Home.

CHAPTER ELEVEN

The sun streams through trees, casting ray-filled spotlights onto the gravel littered path. We ditched the car about ten minutes ago, after we drove up to a rusted gate. The path we now walk on has all the remnants of a forgotten gravel road. Patches of grass have sprouted up through the rocks, and it's clear that nobody's driven on this road in years.

Blue's hand is laced with mine. His firm grasp, as so many other things, betray his easy-going demeanor. I'm still unsure of where exactly we're going or what we're doing, but no matter how ridiculous a thought it is, a fraction of my being still believes he's taking me out into the middle of nowhere to murder me.

"Are you going to let me in on the secret?"

"Well." He scratches his head. "There's a nice little watering hole just up ahead. About eighty feet deep, I'm told it's a great place to ditch a body."

My feet glue themselves to the rocks beneath me. He's a mind reader, cracking a joke about my hysterically insane inner-monologue. "That's what I was afraid of."

"It *is* pretty creepy out here." He looks to his left and takes in the sights. A dense forest lines the road on one side and on the other, there's a sparse sprinkling of trees. "I was definitely kidding, but I'm kind of getting a *Deliverance*-y vibe. I hope the quarry isn't as terrifying."

"That's the big secret? A quarry?"

His hand breaks free from mine and he thumps himself on the head. "Dammit!"

The truth is out. We're going to have our first non-whorey date swimming in a terrifying quarry that's eighty feet deep and the perfect spot for an afternoon murder. Truly touching. I grab his hand again.

"Just a thought that's running through my head," I say, "but what would you have done if I told you I couldn't swim?"

"Dump you, probably."

"We're not even dating."

He nods his head, a smile on his face. "Sure we are."

My eyebrow arches. "You think?"

"Well, you're holding my hand right now, and our first date was the carnival." He clicks his tongue against his cheek. "That was my favorite," he says with a wink.

"Oh, my God!" I break free from his grip and playfully push his chest.

"Our second date was in the grass, earlier today." He puts up his quotation fingers. "With your science experiment—that was pretty much a bust, but a date nonetheless."

I shake my head at him but am unable to refrain from smiling.

"And now we're on our third date," he continues. "At the quarry."

"Which, if I weren't able to swim, would've been our second bust of the day."

"I don't think it's possible to have a bad date with you."

"Charming."

"Besides, Joey told me you've always loved swimming."

My feet dig into the gravel again, and I whip around to face him. "Joey knows?"

"Yeah, he's the one that told me about this place."

My hands rub against my face. "That's the reason I got him drunk, to make him forget."

"You're still ashamed of me," he accuses but not too seriously.

I don't respond. Not saying it's true but also not saying it's not. A part of me believes it is. The other parts know better. It has nothing to do with me... and everything to do with Dylan. Now that I'm not going to college, he's expecting that we're going to get back together. He doesn't have to say it for me to know it's true. Dylan's a very strong guy, but he would be hurt if he found out the reason we broke up wasn't the reason keeping us apart. It'd be worse still if I weren't able to come up with a reason other than *maybe it's Blue.*

"I'm not ashamed of you. It's just complicated."

"What is?"

"Whatever we are, I'm not ashamed of it," I say and grab his arm for reassurance. "I just don't want Dylan knowing. Not right now. There are some loose ends that I need to figure out."

"Relax, Charlie. He said he's not gonna tell anyone."

"Joey's got a big mouth."

Blue laughs. "One of my only memories of him growing up was this one time that his big mouth got us grounded from the jungle gym during a family reunion."

"I take it you haven't spent too much time with him since then?"

"I see him about once a year at the county fair." His face begins to glow, and I'm not exactly sure why.

"You look mysteriously happy all of a sudden."

"Behind you." He grabs me by the shoulder and turns me around. I don't know where the fuck it came from, but we've entered Wonderland, Oz, or Narnia. The sun reflects off beautiful blue water, completely out of place along this long forgotten road.

"Wow. It's beautiful," I say, somewhat stunned.

"Just like he said it was."

That causes me to chuckle. "*Joey* said something was beautiful?"

"Shocking, right?"

We step down onto a narrow path between the trees. Standing before the quarry, where the water hugs the land, it has become even more beautiful than from just twenty feet back. It's astounding that something like this exists so close to the place where I grew up, and I've never heard about it. It's out of place. It belongs in paradise.

Blue tugs the bottom of his shirt, pulling it over his head. He tosses the shirt to the side and my eyes soak in the sight of his chest. The sunlight that glistens off the thin layer of sweat trailing down his body almost blinds me.

I grab my shirt and begin to pull it off. As it passes over my head, it occurs to me that I'm not wearing a bikini. Thankfully, I have a bra on, so it's not a total disaster. I drape my shirt over a low hanging tree branch.

Blue grabs the button of his jeans and unsnaps it. With an inquisitive look, he peers down at his lower half, and I know exactly what he's thinking, because I've already beat him to the punch. "I've made a huge mistake," he says.

"Yeah?" I laugh softly. "What mistake would that be?"

"I got so excited about the date and the secrecy of it all," he says. "I'm not wearing swimming trunks."

I shrug my shoulders and state the obvious. "We'll just have to go in our underwear. Or we could just go in bare?"

His entire body perks up, including his brow. "I like that idea."

Of course he does.

The water appears clean and to be honest, it sounds like a great idea, but I'm really trying this *no sex on the first date* thing. And no, I don't have a selective memory. I remember the carnival all too well. Every sweat-dripping moment and every slippery movement. I remember every micro sensation of the grass on my back. That wasn't a date though, and despite what Blue says, it certainly doesn't count as one.

I slide my jeans down my legs with a sincere attempt at being sexy, but as the denim bunches at the calf, it comes off clumsy. I kick my shoes off and pull my jeans the rest of the way off. They are thrown alongside my shirt on the branch.

Blue's turn to stare, apparently. I believe, more so now than ever, that he fantasizes about me the same way I do him. "Don't just stand there and drool. Drop 'em, boy."

He tosses his shoes behind him and smiles. His teeth bite into his lip as he pushes his jeans down to the ground—

And that's how you undress sexily.

His bleach-white boxers are almost see-through and they compliment the dark tone of his tan skin in a sexually compromising fashion.

"Now who's drooling?" he asks smugly.

"Shut up and let me enjoy my moment."

He reaches down and adjusts himself, and I know exactly what he's doing. The proper part of me wants to tell him to do it in private, just as I told Dylan. The other part of me, the one keen on sinning, says we should just gloss over the swimming portion of our date and fuck against the tree.

Must.

Be.

Good.

His smile and his gaze remain locked on me for a second more before he's rushing into the water. It's shallow at first. The crystal-clear water splashes around him, soaking his bottom half. The outline of his equally cute and sexy bubble butt is visible for a few seconds before he hits a drop-off and dips beneath the surface.

He comes back up almost instantly, shaking water off his face and pushing his hair out of his eyes. "Are you coming, or are you just gonna stand there and watch?"

I immediately run toward the water. Instinct tells me I should dive, but I know better. Still, if he hadn't gone first, there's a good chance I'd be suffering a broken neck. I glide into the water, slow at first. It should be chilly, but it's comfortably warm. Like paradise without the price or the hassle. The trees that line the quarry on both sides block the cool breeze that was so prominent in the earlier hours of our date.

I make my way to Blue. We're both wading in the water when something hits my leg, causing me to freak out before realizing that it's just Blue's foot. While it's perfectly clear on top, by the time you reach our feet the water becomes hazy. Still, it's clear enough to make out the outline in his boxers.

"So I still haven't told you about our date?"

I laugh at that odd statement. What's to tell?

"I'm serious. I didn't bring you here to swim."

"Are you still on the sex kick?"

"Always," he blushes. "See that cliff behind me?"

I saw it when we first came to a stop on the path, but I check it out again. It looks taller from our current location.

"We're gonna jump off it," he says seriously, not realizing how dead wrong he is. If he thinks I'm going anywhere near the top of that cliff, then his date will end in massive disappointment. And then jump off it? Absolutely not.

"I think you have me confused with some other girl."

"I've already told you, there are no other girls."

I caress his cheek. "That's so sweet of you, but I'm still not going anywhere near that thing."

"I know you, Charlie. Not as well as I would like to, but enough to know that you love thrills."

"In controlled environments."

"Do you really think those carnival rides are safe? You should see how we put them together, especially when we're tired, hung over, or drunk. Mostly drunk."

My shoulders rise. "Sorry, I can't do it. It's not in my blood." I eye the cliff again because I really want to do this for him. "You saw me on the Zipper. I love that thing, probably a little too much for a grown ass woman, but you haven't seen me on the Ferris wheel."

"That scares you? It's just a tall kiddie ride."

I frown. "It's terrifying."

"Why don't we just go to the top and check it out. If you chicken out, we can just climb back down the rocks."

That's fair enough, I guess. "Race you to the top?"

His head wobbles in thought. Then I'm blinded by a violent splash of lake water to the face. Once I've wiped the water out of my eyes, I can see he's already racing toward the cliff. "Cheaters never win!"

"We'll see about that," he turns and hollers back.

* * *

Blue beats me to the cliff by about thirty seconds. He beats me to the top by about two minutes. It was a rugged climb and I almost lost my footing a few times. We both stand over the edge of the drop-off. He's excited, ready for the thrill, but I could lose my lunch any second.

From the bottom of the cliff, it looks about thirty feet high. From the top of the cliff, it looks like a hundred. I was always terrible with math, but Blue seems to have it figured out. "It's about fifty feet."

"Is that all?" Just looking over the edge makes me want to vomit, or pass out. Maybe both.

"It's not that bad," he says. "The Zipper is about a hundred feet in the air."

"Except that you're not falling for a hundred feet to the ground. Cages, remember?"

"It's practically the same thing."

Nope. "I wish I had some liquor."

"I could just push you off," he suggests.

I turn to him. "You wouldn't."

Blue arches his eyebrow. "No?"

I look back down. I know many people who have jumped into water from much higher cliffs and bridges, and they're still alive. Still, I can't shake the looming danger of death. I'm not twenty-seven and I'm not ready to die.

Then I'm in the air. Barreling toward the water and screaming like a banshee. I can feel Blue's arms around me. He's hollering in ecstasy and I'm going to kick his—

We slam into the water, sinking a distance equal to the distance we fell—if my memory of basic high school physics is correct. Blue lets go of me, and I kick to the surface. It's darker down here, far from the clear waters of the surface.

I rise above the surface and take in an extended breath. Blue comes up beside me laughing.

"I'm going to kill you."

"At least I'll die happy," he says.

His wet hair sticks to his face. I move closer and push his hair back—nice, neat and out of the way. I take a sideways glance and rub my palm through his hair, roughing it up. "You're much hotter with messy hair."

"Then you'll never see it combed."

"I want to jump without your helpful assistance." I don't know where the hell that came from but it's too late to take it back.

"If I hadn't pushed you, you never would have jumped to begin with," he says. "Trust me. The longer you stand there, the less likely you are to jump. Sometimes you just gotta make the move."

I can't help but think he's talking about something else entirely. He wades closer to me, his eyes dancing with mine. "You've done this before?" I ask.

"Other places. Bridges mostly." He's now within an inch of me, and he gently grabs me at the waist, pulling me close.

"My own personal daredevil."

"Something like that," he says quietly. I can feel the seduction in the words. He's going to kiss me—I know it. He gets closer still and I'm about to pucker my lips.

I jump out of the water, bringing both my hands down on his shoulders and push him under. Little does he know we're about to have another race. By the time he resurfaces, I already have a comfortable lead.

I look back and he's racing toward me. I don't know when he found time to train for aquatic Olympics while working the carnival circuit, but he's quickly catching up. My arms are worn out by the time I get cliff-side. With one last feat of strength, I pull myself up onto the rocks.

I clench my fists and throw them into the air, celebrating my win. When I turn around, I notice Blue isn't moving. Instead, he wades in the water, watching me intently. *Sore loser*.

"I'll just watch you," he says.

"You don't think I'll do it?"

"Eighty-twenty. And the odds are not in your favor."

Really? I pull up my big girl panties and begin the long climb to the top. It doesn't take as long as the first time to scale the cliff, but it's just as difficult. I grab onto branches of trees that sit awkwardly on the side of the rocks.

Once I'm at the top, I don't go to the edge. Looking down will only scare me. If I'm going to do this, I can't see where I'm going. Blue's expecting me to take a walk of shame down the rocks or is waiting for his opportunity to rescue the damsel in distress. Neither is going to happen.

I breathe in and breathe out before sealing my eyes shut. Then I run and find myself flying. My eyes open mid-air and at the moment, I love the lack of control. The thrill of falling.

My body darts against the water, causing waves of commotion above me as I sink. I hold my breath for as long as I can. Slowly, I rise to the top. When I surface, sight and sounds are blurred. I spit water off the edge of my mouth, pull my hair out of my face and see Blue right in front of me. Even with blurred vision, he's gorgeous.

He grabs me by the waist again, pulling me close to him. He doesn't hesitate. It's quick and it's heaven. His lips are on mine. I wrap my arms around his neck and sink deeper into his mouth. This is as close as we've been since the night we met. And I'm wishing we could stay locked like this forever.

Then he pulls away but still holds me. "I think I really like you," he says. "Like, I think I'm in like with you."

"In like with me?" I ask, pushing him away, playfully and not serious. "What the hell does that even mean?"

He shrugs his shoulders. "It means that I'm not in love with you, but I could be someday."

There's that word again. Someday. "Well, then, I think I'm in like with you, too."

It sounds stupid. Maybe it is, maybe it's not. But it feels right. Whatever it is, it's ours.

I embrace him one more time, and behind me, I can feel the coolness of the sun beginning to set.

* * *

We're back on top of the cliff. Blue sits with his back against a rock formation. My head rests on his lap, on the thin fabric of his damp boxers. I'm looking out into the distance, not thinking about anything in particular. Not even dreaming.

Like Blue, I'm almost naked, but I don't feel like it. When you're naked, you feel exposed and vulnerable. Neither of those is true at this moment. I feel safe and free.

I turn my head gently and peer up at him. He's looking out into the distance, across the quarry and into the forest. "You've got something on your mind."

"I do," he replies without breaking focus. "Just thinking about earlier."

I haven't thought about our pit stop at the carnival for hours. It's been the furthest thing from my mind. Now, it all comes back to me. The Blue that Marvin told me about isn't the same Blue that I'm lying on. He's not the same Blue that I'm falling in love with.

"Can I tell you something?" he asks.

"Anything."

He bites into his lip and pulls a finger to his mouth, just on the edge of chewing on it. "Earlier, at the carnival, I was angry. I felt like I could have punched my fist through a brick wall." He stops, contemplating. "There are things in my past that I've tried to get past, and in that camper, it all came flooding back to me." His voice is shaky, as if he's on the verge of some revelation.

"You don't have to talk about if you don't want to."

"Thank you," he says softly and combs his hand through my hair.

I rise up and sit beside him. He grabs my hand with his and I lean in and kiss him on the lips. It's not passionate. Just soft and comforting.

No matter where he's been or what he's done. It's in the past and it doesn't matter.

CHAPTER TWELVE

Blue says it's our third date. Summer says it's our second. I say we're still at one. Going to a bar with four other people is not a date, unless it's a group date, which is an interesting thought. I'm with Blue, Summer's flirting with the bartender, and Tyson rubs his junk all over Joey's ass, which is extremely homoerotic. They're just too drunk to know that, let alone care.

The four of us drove up to Columbus earlier to surprise Summer. In typical Summer fashion, she was the one to surprise us. Joey brought balloons painted with scary clowns, Tyson brought a vibrator, and I brought a bottle of whiskey. Call us the three wise men. We walked down the narrow hallway of her dorm, and when we came to her room, we busted through the door to surprise her. Blue waited in the hallway—which, in hindsight, was the smart thing to do.

The bottle of whiskey dropped to the ground and shattered. Joey retreated and Tyson looked on like a natural voyeur as Summer was being double teamed by twins. My first thought was to intervene, but it quickly became apparent that she was a willing participant.

Then she noticed us and screamed. She knocked the two guys off the bed, one on each side, and then wrapped the sheet around her. "Just a moment."

I exited the room, shaking off a laugh. Tyson was still watching, though I'm not sure what for. It's not like he's into redheads. That was when I first became suspicious.

The way he moves against Joey now? I sense a closet door creaking open in the very near future. Blue is off in the bathroom or something; I couldn't really hear where he said he was going. It's my first time at a club and it's overwhelmingly loud. The bass thumps off the walls in perfect sync with the laser lights scanning the crowd.

It's just Summer and me at the bar. We're waiting on our shots, some mysterious drink called a pancake. It's the house special and I'm eager to see what it is.

"Do you do this every night?" I can barely hear myself over the music.

She nods. "Just on Fridays and Saturdays," she says. "Sometimes Wednesdays. It's where I picked up the twins."

"That was two days ago."

She shrugs and grins wickedly. "I've been very busy."

The hunky bartender, Jayson, pushes four shot glasses toward us. Alcohol in two, orange juice in the others.

"What's in it?" I ask Jayson, taking notice of the tribal tattoos painted on his bulging biceps.

"Jameson and Butterscotch." He leans in. "Tastes like breakfast in your mouth."

"Are these on the house?" Summer asks, puckering her lips.

Jayson leans in and gives her a peck on the cheek. "No."

Summer frowns.

"Instead of pouting, you should be thankful that I'm letting you drink." There's cockiness in his voice, and he certainly carries it well.

"Just put it on my tab," I say and hand him my dad's card.

"Cheers to college." Summer bumps her shot with mine.

I take the pancake in one go and slam the glass down on the slippery bar. I turn around, grimacing on the inside, smiling on the outside. It tastes exactly like breakfast. Blue emerges from the darkness of the dance floor. "Where have you been?" I ask him as he wraps his arms around me.

"I've been looking for you."

"I've been at the bar all night."

"Yeah, I noticed. We should dance." He grabs my hand and pulls me toward the dance floor. His hand is sweaty and clammy. I pull back.

"Why are you so sweaty?" I notice a thick sheen of sweat smeared across the top of his face, dousing his hair.

He shrugs and smiles. "I get really hot, really easy." Then his hand is on mine again as he attempts to pull me to the floor. I push my feet against the floor, resisting. "What's the matter? Can't dance?"

"I'll make an ass out of myself."

He points to Joey, who is now bumping and grinding all over a short-haired blonde girl. He has the rhythm of a legless socialite. "You couldn't possibly look any worse than him. Besides, everyone's too drunk to pay attention. I'm definitely drunk, and I like to dance when I'm drunk."

"Well, if you promise not to be embarrassed by me, then I'll oblige."

"That word isn't in my vocabulary, so I'm a little unsure if that was a yes."

"It was a yes," I say and take charge, leading him past Joey and his tramp, and into the center of the floor. I turn on my heel and push my back against him. He grabs me by the hips, pushing me into effortless sync with the music.

The way he moves is slow and sensual. Every move choreographed to the slowed down beat, a far cry from the dance anthems of the past hour.

His palm runs against the fabric of my jeans, down toward my crotch. I don't want to stop him, but I look to make sure no one is watching too closely. The last thing I need is to become an internet sensation. When I'm sure nobody's watching, I lean my neck against his shoulder and he presses his lip to my collarbone, sending endless vibrations through my bones.

I can feel him growing against the small of my back. With one of his hands still against me, the other rises under my shirt, caressing my stomach. I'm being touched in four different places, a sensual assault on my entire body.

"I want you," he huffs into my ear. The warmth of his breath going in one end and out the other. "Right here on the dance floor, and I don't care who is watching." His hand rubs against me, pushing against me through the thick denim of my jeans. And I'm two seconds away from public indecency charges on my rap sheet.

I break away, glancing back at him with a knowing look. He gives chase and we weave through the crowds and find the stairway to the second level. We fumble up the steps to find a door at the top. When I give the knob a forceful pull, the door stays in place, locked.

"I've got this," Blue says and pushes past me in the narrow hallway. He retrieves a card from his wallet and slides it between the crack of the door, against the locking mechanism. After a few tries, his criminal skills allow him to pull the door open. I rush past him and he shuts the door behind us.

Blue hops across the counter of an unmanned bar, scavenging for free alcohol. I make my way to the edge of the second floor to a railing that overlooks the rest of the club. You can see everyone and everything from up here, including Summer, who is flirting with the bartender. And I think, *This is what I gave up. The college experience. The big city life that I've always wanted.*

Blue's warm hands brush against my skin, right above my hips. "Jack or Jose?" he breathes against my neck.

"Neither."

Two full bottles clatter, and then roll against the ground. "What about some Blue?"

A light chuckle. "That's more like it."

He pushes himself tight against me, mouthing kisses against my neck. It feels so—

"Dylan," I say.

"Huh?" Blue asks, pulling away from me.

"Dylan's here."

He maneuvers through the crowd with his head held high, looking for any of us. He's completely out of his element here in this club, in the city, dressed in his country-boy attire. The entire club goes black and the music cuts to an abrupt stop. The crowd is torn between panicked cries and loud *boo's*.

Then, like serendipity, the lights flash on from directly behind us. The club is lit up as the lights cast our silhouettes onto the crowd. Dylan looks up, blinded, with one hand over his eyes. I push Blue backward, out of sight, as dance music begins to blare.

"Do you think he saw us?"

"Who cares," he says with a smile.

"I'm going to have to take a rain check on this public act of depravity." I pat him on his chest and head for the door.

* * *

We find Dylan at the bar, pushing two empty shot glasses toward Jayson. I approach him slowly, unsure if he saw me and Blue in the loft. I grab him at the shoulder. "Hey," I say. He doesn't budge to my touch. "I thought you weren't coming."

He holds up two fingers to Jayson, who begins pouring two shots. Then he turns to me, gripping himself against the bar. "I said I had to work. Now I'm off." He scratches at the mold above his lip, glaring at Blue. "Something going on with the two of you?"

"We were just dancing."

"Really?" He points to the loft. "You call that dancing? It looked like foreplay to me."

"We're just having fun."

"You can stop being coy and just tell me what's going on."

"I think we're dating."

He laughs drunkenly. "You're dating a carnie. Awesome." He turns back around and grabs the two shots, offering one up to me. I shake my head, fearful of an escalation that could cause a scene. He pushes the shot toward Blue.

"No thanks, man."

Dylan huffs. "Don't act like I'm your friend." He throws back one shot and slams the glass down on the counter. It's a welcome surprise when it doesn't shatter. Then he shoots the other shot, this time slamming it harder against the counter. Broken glass slides against the bar.

Jayson motions toward the muscular bouncer standing in a corner nearby. I grab at Dylan's arm, attempting to get him out of the club with dignity. He jerks back and falls against the bar.

"Dylan, come on."

"You're out of here," the bouncer says sternly, grabbing Dylan forcibly by the arm. Dylan pulls himself away, and the bouncer pushes him in the back, guiding him toward the exit. Blue waits behind as I follow them out of the bar and into the alley. "Don't come back for at least six months," the bouncer says as he pushes Dylan into the road. "You're banned."

"You've had too much to drink," I say softly.

He collects himself, shrugging his shoulders and straightening his clothes. "I know, right?" He laughs. "I'm just gonna go sleep in my truck. Go back inside."

"Dylan..."

"Just go," he says with his back facing me as he walks down the dark alley toward the parking lot.

* * *

I find Summer at the bar getting Jayson's number. I find Tyson in the stairwell half asleep on his back. And I find Joey in the girls' restroom having a little too much fun with the short-haired blonde girl, but Blue is nowhere to be found.

I push through the waning crowds, seemingly going in circles around the entire club infinite times until I finally spot him running down the same steps where I had found Tyson, and the same steps that lead to the loft.

"I've been looking everywhere for you. Where have you been?"

"Nowhere."

I give him The Look.

"Fine. I was upstairs drinking for free."

"Whatever. I've managed to round up everyone. We need to go out to Dylan's truck, pick him up, and take him back to Summer's dorm with us. He's too drunk to be driving anywhere."

"All right, that's fine."

The closing-time lights all flick on, illuminating the darkness, including many things that are best left in the dark. There's visible shame on many faces, drunken wonderment on many others. But the thing that strikes me the most is the way they illuminate Blue's eyes, pulling something into focus I thought I had seen earlier. They're like cop sirens, white, blue, and bloodshot red.

"Are you high?"

"No." He practically jumps. "Just really drunk." His teeth sink into his jaw.

"Don't lie to me," I say gravely.

He turns away, unable to look me in the eyes.

"We need to go." I turn and walk toward the exit, not caring if he keeps up with me or not. If he wants to do drugs, that's on him, but I'm not about to be lied to.

CHAPTER THIRTEEN

I'm the first to wake up, and I bet Summer and Blue weren't expecting that. They lie beside me in bed, wrapped around each other, cuddling. Other girls might automatically jump to conclusions, but I've been there myself; when you're drunk, it's easy to end up in compromising positions while you sleep. On the bed across from us, the three other boys are all spooned together. They're tight against each other, with Joey perilously close to the edge. If my phone wasn't dead and I hadn't forgotten my charger in Lakeview, this would be quite the blackmail opportunity.

I roll out of bed, feeling fresh and instantly awake. I step to the window and pull the shades, taking in the view of the empty football stadium, and then the cityscape beyond that. I should be waking up to this view every morning with a cup of coffee in my hand.

Joey's body thumps against the carpet as he rolls off the bed. He turns onto his side, seemingly unaffected by the fall. Summer throws herself up in bed, her hair frazzled and her makeup smudged. She looks like she's just survived a nightmare, but I'm sure it's just a nasty hangover. She rubs her face and grumbles.

* * *

Summer and I walk along a brick path leading to a cross section in what seems to be the center of this sprawling campus. We've left the boys behind to sleep off the alcohol in the dorm room. They're not in the business of waking up at nine in the morning. It amazes me how many students are out and about this early on a Sunday. I mean, where could they possibly be going?

The morning air is refreshing, but it feels different from home. Instead of a few thousand people breathing it in, there's half a million. I think about every student we pass and try to read into them and understand their lives. What makes them tick? What's their major? What's their family like? They're all strangers, but I feel like I know each and every one of them.

A starry-eyed brunette, an education major, walks hand in hand with a tall geek, a computer science major, from the previous decade. Their relationship is new, untested, and beautiful. They probably met during the unofficial freshman orientation, the one where they hid away from the noise and the parties within the safe walls of the multiple-floor library. They both come from nice families, but her parents are on the verge of a divorce. See? I know them. The only real question is, why the hell is there a four-story library?

"Earth to Charlie." Summer waves a hand in my face.

"What?"

"Did you hear anything I just said to you?"

"Uhm…"

She rolls her eyes, then grabs me by the arm, pulling me down onto the seat of a fountain. "I saw the two of you last night on the dance floor," she says, and I perk up. "The sparks lit up the entire room—figuratively, of course. So my question is, for the third time, how much do you like him?"

"Blue?" I ask rhetorically. "Too much for barely knowing him."

"And where does that leave Dylan?"

My palms press against the damp rocks of the fountain. "Friends?"

"You would give up Dylan for Blue? I'm not judging, just assessing the situation."

"We haven't been together for months, and there's no doubt that I still love him. I probably always will, but with Blue, I'm just falling so quickly, and I'm not really giving myself time to think things through."

She turns to me. "Then don't think. Just keep falling."

"I want to," I say, running fingers through my hair. "But I think he was on drugs last night."

"Oh, he was definitely rolling on Molly last night," she says without thought.

I burn a hole through her with my glare. "How would you know?"

Her smile fades. "Just a guess," she says nervously, her palm running against the rocks.

"So he *was* on drugs?"

She glares at me, her eyes lining up twelve jurors. "What's the big deal?"

The big deal?

Her shoulders rise and fall. "We're young and stupid, and drug use doesn't always mean drug abuse."

I bite into my cheek. "I guess."

"Don't *guess* me. If you like him as much as you say you do, then you're stupid if you give him up over some minor drug use."

"Thanks," I say. "You may not always be the most tactful, but you always steer toward being right."

She grins. "I guess that's why I'm in college and you're not."

I push her above her breast. She falters backward, almost landing in the fountain before grabbing onto the rocks to break her fall.

"Oops," I say. "I guess I can't control myself, probably because I'm an uneducated bitch."

"Just remember that you're the one who said it."

We both stand up. "What should I do?" I ask.

"Just keep on doing what you've been doing."

"We're supposed to go to the Founders Carnival tomorrow."

"Then do that," she says pointedly.

"Should I at least confront him?"

"No, you should lighten up and take a hit." Her eyes flicker and she tosses a shoulder. "It's fun."

"And how would you know that?"

"I took some ecstasy last week."

Good grief. I really should have gone to college, if for no other reason than to watch after her. She obviously needs adult supervision.

* * *

When I dropped Dylan off at his pick-up, which was left in the seedy parking lot of the club, Tyson and Joey decided to ride home with him. I'm sure I was the talk of the truck.

Blue and I decided to get ice cream as we crossed county lines, back into Lakeview. I put my car in park, prepared to walk into Burger Shack for the first time since I was fired. It was the day after I turned seventeen. I knew I had to work the following morning, so I had a birthday night planned that involved sobriety. That plan was shattered thanks to a surprise party thrown by Summer at the request of Dylan, which resulted in the loss of my job due to a hangover. That's the day I first began to hate surprises.

I pull the glass door open, hanging my head in shame. Blue walks behind me, shades covering his eyes—a different kind of shame.

"Hey," Cassadee James screeches at me from across the counter. Automatically, a hand clasps around my ear, a defense mechanism. I bite into my cheek and raise my head, forcing a smile. "Welcome to Burger Shack, can I get you a triple stack—"

"No."

"Okay..." she says, her hands folding against the counter.

"I just want a triple thick, blueberry, strawberry, chocolate shake." I turn to Blue. "What do you want?"

"Whatever you just said, I'll take that."

I turn back to Cassadee. "Did you hear that?"

She nods. The tip of her ridiculous Burger Shack hat tilts as she fumbles for the correct keys on the register. "Your total comes to seven eighty-eight."

I grab for my purse but, unfortunately, my arm isn't long enough to reach my car. Blue smacks a twenty against the counter. "Keep the change," he smiles at the temptress. I can't see through his shades, but I can read his poker face. He has to be joking.

I pull him aside. "What do you think you're doing?"

"That girl's not going to last here. I give her a week before she's unemployed again."

"So?"

"I'm a charitable guy." He flips his shades up and grins, his eyes reminiscent of glass.

"Well, aren't you a prince." I grab his shades and pull them back down.

"Order's ready!" Cassadee yells, followed by a slap of a bell that makes my ears bleed.

I step to the counter and grab our shakes, one in each hand. I pass one off to Blue as we exit through the glass doors with no intention of coming back for another year, or until she's fired.

"We're going to need to set ground rules," I say wryly.

He laughs. "Seriously?"

"You don't know—" I come to an immediate halt that causes Blue to bump into me. I almost drop my shake when I see my dad leaning against the hood of my car. "What are you doing here?"

"I was in the drive-thru getting a triple stacker when I saw your car. Thought I'd come say hi."

"That's unfortunate, because I'm actually in a hurry."

He stands up straight, but I push past him and open the car door.

"You can't spare a few minutes for your dad?"

Blue perks up and turns on one foot to size him up.

"You want to tell me who this gentleman is, at least?"

I have no current plans to do so.

"I'm Blue." He extends his hand.

My dad hesitates before giving him a disturbingly firm shake. "I know you from somewhere, don't I?"

"No, sir," Blue says through gritted teeth, playing it smart, using the respect card.

"If you're done murdering my boyfriend, can I go?" I ask dryly.

"Boyfriend?" He turns to me, freeing Blue of his grip.

Blue flexes his hand, shaking the cramps off, while mouthing to me, *Ow!*

My eyes roll. "This isn't a conversation we're going to have." I take a seat in the car and shut the door.

"You can't stay mad at me forever, Char-Bear."

I glare at him. "Don't call me that."

He laughs nervously as he scratches the side of his head.

"Blue, get in the car."

He does as he's told, but moves much slower than I'd like. Damn hangover.

"I know that kid from somewhere," my dad says quietly, then leans against my window, resting his elbows on the seal. "Since I'm a lawyer, you know what that probably means."

"That you're a liar?" I smile broadly, though he probably has a point, I'm not going to give him that kind of power over me—the kind where he's right and I'm wrong.

Blue shuts the door as he scoots into his seat. My dad's eyes focus intently on the side of Blue's face.

"Be careful," my dad says as I pull the car into reverse, prepared to run over his foot if I have to.

* * *

I pull the car into the supermarket parking lot, right beside Blue's Jeep. "Do you know my dad?" I ask as the car comes to a stop.

He shakes his head. "Not that I'm aware of. Maybe I just have a familiar face."

"You've got many things going for you, but a common face isn't one of them," I say, taking in the view of his gorgeousness and paying close attention to the edge of his jaw, where his boyish features blend into a masculine physique. "Trust me, I would know."

"Are you saying I'm cute?"

"I'm saying there aren't enough words."

"I'd kiss you, but I haven't brushed my teeth since last night."

"Thank you for caring. You can just make it up with me tomorrow with two kisses."

"Right, then." He pops his door open. "I'll pick you up then." He hops out of the car, and then shuts the door gently, peering inside before he leaves. "By the way, what does your dad do?"

"He's made a career out of lying," I huff. "He's a lawyer. Trust me. I'm used to getting the third degree."

His throat pulls tight, his fingers dancing along the edge of the window. "Awesome."

I sense it in his voice and it's something else we have in common—we both hate lawyers.

CHAPTER FOURTEEN

My favorite part of the Founders Carnival is the Metallic Monster. It's a roller coaster that's only a fraction of the size of thrill rides at amusement parks, but it gets the job done. It sits at the front of the carnival and promises an adventure much more thrilling than it actually is. Behind that beautiful monster is just another mundane carnival.

We arrived about an hour before sunset. Blue was hesitant at first, wanting to avoid another confrontation with his father, I assume. He doesn't know anything Marvin told me or even that he told me anything at all, and I want to keep it that way—even if part of me wants him to open up and fully let me in. It's still the beginning of our relationship and I figure in time he'll trust me enough with his past.

I don't blame him for withholding. There are things in my past that I'm not sharing, and it would be hypocritical to demand to know all his darkest secrets when I'm still carrying my own cheetah-print baggage.

We've been treated like royalty from the time we hit the front gate. Not only did we get free admission, score, but Blue promised we would be treated to free food and front-of-the-line admissions. You already know how much I love thrill rides—especially hastily-put-together roller coasters. And I definitely love fair food even if I hate the extra hours in the gym the following week. It can take up to twenty hours on the treadmill to burn the extra calories, but it's more than a fair—get it?—tradeoff.

"You know I'm eying the Metallic Monster," I say to Blue.

"That thing?" He points to the coaster. "You don't wanna ride that."

"I've been riding it since I was six."

"I'm surprised you're still alive."

"I've cheated death more than my fair share of times," I say. "When I was three years old, I was playing with my baby doll, Lilly, in the road. A trucker was speeding down the road and didn't see me. So my dad ran into the road, pushed me into the grass, and saved me." I shrug my shoulders. "At least that's what he says. I don't remember it."

"Didn't you say your dad was a liar?"

"Yeah," I say, mildly offended. It's different when it's someone else pointing out my dad's flaws, and there are plenty of them. "But that was before we had contempt for each other."

"I shouldn't have said that." He shakes his head. "I'm sorry."

And that's why our relationship works. He can sense when I'm upset without needing signs or without me spelling it out for him with my words. "It's all right." I see an opening and take it. "What about your dad?"

He bites into his cheek, uncomfortable. "What about him?"

My hands rub against each other, unsure if I should press on. "What's he like?"

"I don't really know him." His words come out slow and sheepish.

Liar! It angers me, saddens me. This is the second time in three days that he's lied to me. Why doesn't he just say *We don't talk* or *I wish I didn't.* I can't say anything to him without admitting my own guilt of peeking into his past. We're going to have a good night, even if it means saving all the bullshit for later.

"I'm riding the Metallic Monster with or without you," I say, putting an end to the conversation.

"Fine. We'll ride the monster. But if we start to derail, I expect a kiss before we die."

"Oh." I smile. "I'll be holding you the entire way down."

"Then I hope we go off the rails."

My smile turns to a frown. "Why would you say that?"

"Isn't it obvious? I wanna hold you."

"I'll tell you what. If you're that afraid of a simple carnival ride, you can hold onto me the entire time, whether or not we're on our way to our deathbeds."

"I think we're gonna have a good night." He nods.

"Going to be a great night," I add.

He grabs my hand and we begin walking toward the line for the monster. "I wanna talk to you about something later," he says with a hint of trouble vibrating in his voice. "It's our fourth date and I have something I wanna show you."

By his count, it's four. By mine, it's two.

* * *

The worst part of cutting a line is looking at the faces on all of the children. Blue and I make our way to the front of the line and stand against the gate. Blue shakes hands with the carnie and makes light conversation. I'm too busy scanning the crowd to listen to what they're saying. In the back of the line, I spot Dylan and Tyson. If Blue and I are going to have a good night, avoiding Dylan is a necessity.

I turn around to shield my face from them, hoping they didn't see me. Dylan would give me a lecture about how we should be together again. Tyson would want to follow us around, cutting all the lines. I just want to be alone with Blue all evening.

"Roger's gonna let us get on next," Blue says, talking about the ginger carnie.

"Is he one of your friends?"

"No." He shakes his head. "We hate each other, but he owes me."

"C'mon, asshole!" Roger yells. I turn toward him in shock. There are kids in this line, and then I take a short glance at those kids that we're ditching. Blue grabs my hand and pulls me through the gate.

I get into the train and pull the harness down over my head, and then look up to see Blue pat Roger on the shoulder. "Thanks, buddy," he says condescendingly.

Roger gives Blue the finger. Blue responds with a light chuckle.

The chains below us pull tight, causing our car to jerk. Blue's face goes stiff. Knowing that he loves the thrill of roller coasters gives me reason to worry. He knows this ride better than I do. He's assembled it countless times, so I probably should have listened to his reasonable wisdom earlier.

The train cranks its way up the incline, maybe a hundred feet in the air. We're in the second seat of the second train, so we'll have the best of both worlds. At the tip of the ride, you can see everything for miles. It's a reminder how terribly boring and flat the world around us really is. Above us, storm clouds race against the clock of the setting sun, and I'm hoping the rain holds off for the next minute and thirty seconds.

Blue takes in a deep breath as the car in front of us peeks over the edge and I know we're at the point of no return. This is it.

The sudden drop is equally terrifying and euphoric. The metal of the train grinding against the metal of the track is reminiscent of a certain horror film involving final destinations. Blue's hand falls into mine and grasps it as tight as a woman giving birth.

I scream into the wind, my hair blowing in a million directions. This right here is freedom. It's ecstasy. It's a drug. Everything inside me floats over the second hill, like an out-of-body experience. I'm far from my own body. Tears begin to well up in my eyes as the wind lashes against us.

There's a jarring jerk as we come to a winding curve. The train turns onto its side, circling around the track. Angled just enough so that you could fall out, but you won't. I swear I can hear the hydraulic fluid shooting out the side as the brakes screech against steel. My ecstatic glee is threatened by impending death.

Blue screams, finally letting go and throwing worry away at the most worrisome time. His hands rise into the air, clapping at the peak of the third hill. He tangles one hand with mine, the force of the strong wind unable to break us.

When the ride comes to a sudden halt, the revolutionary idea that we survived is a well-earned relief.

* * *

The rain came about three minutes after we stepped off the roller coaster. We were standing in line waiting for our fries when it hit. I was forced to forego the vinegar as we made a mad dash to the arcade for shelter.

It came fast and hard, like so many other things lately. We barely made it under the thick vinyl tent in time. The rain could be seen racing toward the ground at a pace of about a thousand miles per hour, but the only sounds powerful enough to overtake the noise of the arcade was thunder. And it roared.

"I hope the storm goes away soon, I don't wanna spend all night in here," Blue says, leaning against a coin machine.

"Jimmy Clay said on the news this morning that there was a ten percent chance of rain showers," I say, straightening out a dollar bill on the corner of the machine. "But that was the forecast for this morning. Typical," I huff.

"Who's Jimmy Clay?"

"My worst enemy."

Four golden coins shoot out the bottom of the machine, each engraved with the face of a clown. Traumatizing.

I give him a nod and he follows me to an old-school zombie shooter. If I had to pick a favorite arcade game, this would be it. Nothing like an old-school shoot 'em up. I load the coins, grab a gun, and prepare for war. Of course, his gun is blue.

He's much better at this game than I am. I haven't spent more than thirty seconds in an arcade since I was a teenager. He's probably spent his lunch breaks for the past ten years in this very tent. There are so many things I want to know about him and I'm getting tired of waiting.

"Blue," I scream, directing him toward a creeping zombie hiding behind a wine barrel.

"I think you've got bigger brains to fry."

Huh? I look back to my half of the screen to see two zombies throwing axes at me, both connecting with my electronic, first-person point-of-view face. A gruesome image flashes on my screen, rubbing my incompetence in my face: *You Died!*

"Dammit!" I force the gun into the metal holster. On one side of me, Blue annihilates an onslaught of undead mutants. On the other side, the setting sun peeks from behind the clouds, blinding the entire tent.

It's arbitrary, but I decide this is the perfect moment to question him about what happened in the club. "Can I ask you something without you getting defensive?"

"Sure." He squints, taking aim at targets on the screen. "What's up?"

"It's about the other night, when I found you on the stairs."

His eyes level to the side. He adjusts his arm and sinks closer to the screen. "What about it?"

"I don't like being lied to." Much more straight to the point than I anticipated. My fingers curl into my palm, nervous about what comes next.

He bites into his lip, non-responsive.

"I just want to know the truth," I say.

"Fine." He slams the gun into its resting place. Zombies flood the screen and move in on him. He grabs me by the arm and pulls me out of the tent. I know he doesn't mean to be aggressive, but the way he's handling the situation is bothersome.

A shadow hangs over us—the last remnants of the fading sun. The carnival lights all begin to flicker on, seemingly in purposeful succession. I break away from his grip and take a step back.

"I don't know what you want me to say," he says rigidly. "But I'm not gonna talk about it in there, in front of the rest of the world."

"As if anyone would be interested in our conversation."

"That's not the point." He scratches his head. "Do you want me to tell you that I lied? Would that make you feel better?"

"Well, the first step to sobriety is acceptance," I say with sarcasm, then immediately straighten myself out. "Sorry."

"Yeah." He shrugs and chews on his cheek. "I was high. I went upstairs and did a line of Molly."

My body shifts, my feet search for friction. "See, that wasn't so difficult."

He angles his eyes at me. "You're not mad?"

"I was, but not because of the drugs. There's a long list of things I can take, but the last thing I'll deal with is a liar."

"You have nothing to worry about with me. I'm not a liar."

My lips purse. "Really?" I ask, with no need to present further evidence.

"I don't mean to lie, but when you ask me these questions, I feel like you won't like the answers. And I like you too much to lose you over something so stupid," he says. "So how about we don't call them lies? Let's just say I have a tendency to stretch the truth."

"I think that's kind of the same thing."

"No more lies then." He steps closer. "I promise."

Let's test that out. "How well do you know your dad?"

"Where did that come from?"

This whole *no lies* thing should probably apply to me as well. I hesitate, fearing his reaction. "You remember our first date?"

"Our second date?" he corrects me, smiling.

"When we stopped here before and we went to the quarry?"

"I remember."

"Marvin told me some things about your family and about your past."

"That stupid mother—"

I hold my hand up to him. "Don't be mad at him. He was concerned for you."

His face tightens. "What did he tell you?"

My turn to stretch the truth. "He just said you and your dad weren't that close."

"You know, earlier today I thought you were upset and I guess now I know why. It's because you knew I wasn't telling you the truth about my dad, wasn't it?"

"There are a million and one things that I still don't know about you, but I want to know everything, and it's frustrating because you're the furthest thing from an open book."

He huffs, but it's more of a chuckle. "We have the rest of our lives for all that. Can't we just take things page by page?"

"That depends on how many more pages we have."

"An infinite amount, I hope." He leans in and kisses me softly. The noise of the carnival fades away. The only sound left is of some lucky gamer hitting the ticket jackpot. If they don't snatch up the life-size giraffe, then they're an idiot. "Any more questions that need to be immediately addressed?"

"Just one," I say. "During your time on the circuit, did you ever run the game booths?"

"The worst four years of my life."

"Would you mind putting those skills to use? I've been lusting after an oversized stuffed animal since I was four, but the odds were never in my favor."

He shakes his head. "The odds aren't in anyone's favor. Those games are rigged more than a Vegas casino."

"Tell me something I don't know."

"All right." He pushes my hair behind my ear. "I think you're a little too old for a stuffed animal." I push his chest. He laughs and grabs my hand. "C'mon. Let's go make your childhood dreams come true."

They kind of already are.

We come out of hiding, out from behind the tent, and merge into the midway crowds. Across the way, carnival rides are in full swing, their lights blurring against the sky. It reminds me of a beautiful puzzle nobody has thought to cut up yet.

* * *

This carnie has no idea what's about to hit him. Blue says he must be a local because he's never met him before. Poor sap.

"I don't think this game is winnable," Blue tells the carnie, tapping his fingers against the booth.

"Here," the carnie says. "I'll show you that it is." The carnie moves to grab a ball, knocking over the three old-school milk bottles in the process. "Shit."

Blue turns to me with a winning smirk as the carnie reassembles the bottles into a three-piece pyramid. With the ball in hand, the carnie approaches us, prepared to jump over the counter and prove just how winnable the rigged game is.

"You know what," Blue says amusedly. "Never mind. We're in a hurry, so I'll just throw the ball."

The carnie jerks back. "It's okay, man. I'll just show you real quick."

Blue nods, then wrestles the ball out of the carnie's hand as he hops the counter. He quickly squares his shoulders with his feet and throws the ball with force, knocking all three bottles off the stand and onto the

137

ground. A little too excited, I jump up and down, clapping.

"We want the pink bear." Blue points to a thirty-pound stuffed bear. The carnie grimaces, knowing full-well he just got played.

"Fine," he huffs and hops back over the counter.

"I really don't feel like carrying that thing around all night," I say to Blue quietly.

"Actually, can we just pick that up later?" Blue asks the poor sap.

"I don't know—"

"Thanks, buddy." Blue smiles, and then grabs my hand and we walk away.

We travel down the midway, past an assortment of mouth-watering concession stands. From behind the cotton candy booth, the stench of weed billows out. Probably not the smartest place to indulge, with cops regularly patrolling the midway. I shake my head at the ignorance and Blue's grip tightens around my fingers.

"Something wrong?" I ask.

"I don't know. Are you sure you're okay with the Molly thing?"

"Where did that come from?" I stop and face him. "I'm sure."

"Absolutely sure? Because I'll stop."

My tongue swishes against my cheek. "Is it a problem? Like an addiction?"

"No," he says firmly. "It's just recreational."

"Then I'm not going to judge you for something I've never tried, as long as it doesn't become a problem."

He nods and his entire face goes blank. His eyes shift back and forth, scanning mine. I can't read what he's feeling. "You really are the perfect woman."

Hyperbole. "Look, we've all got our vices, Blue. You've got your Molly and I've got you." I place a hand on his chest, wanting to be close to him, but not expecting to feel his heart. Not like this. It's fast and furious, like it could beat out of his chest.

"If we're counting each other, then I've got two vices."

"What if I want two?" I ask, unable to draw my eyes away from my own hand, so close to his heart. Only skin separates us.

"Then pick up smoking," he suggests, jokingly.

"I'm serious." I pull away and peer into his eyes. I say nothing more, hoping he'll get the hint so that I don't have to say it out loud.

"I don't understand what you're trying to say." He smiles, but I know that he's confused.

"I want to go to the edge with you."

His face distorts, the realization sinking in. "I'm not gonna force you—"

"No force necessary."

CHAPTER FIFTEEN

His arm passes over my shoulder, his palm pressed against the tree. Behind us, the carnival is in full, chaotic swing. He takes an extended glance over his shoulder, then back to me. "Are you sure you want to do this?"

"I'm not one hundred percent sure, no, but I'm sure enough that I won't accuse you of drugging me if things go south." I smile.

He scratches his neck nervously. "I just don't want this to change things between us."

"You know what changes *things* between people? Sex. And we've been there, done that, and I'm still falling head over heels for you. It's fine. I'm young and stupid, and I want to try new things."

"Like Molly?"

I shrug my shoulders. "Everybody else is doing it." I can't help but grin. I've never been one to blame peer pressure for anything, but in the worst case scenario, I could easily blame my peers.

Blue reaches into his pocket and pulls out a baggie. The sight of the packed white powder makes me nervous at first, paranoia follows within seconds. My eyes dart between everything behind Blue, and then to my side as I scan for signs of wandering life.

"Are you sure you want—"

I cut him off. "If you ask me that one more time, I'm going to kick your ass. But I don't feel comfortable doing it here. Let's go somewhere else."

* * *

If you had asked me when I was younger, say thirteen years old, where I would be the first time I tried drugs, the answer wouldn't have been in a carnival bathroom. A friend's house, probably in their basement, would have been my first choice. The school bathroom? You do stupid things like that when you're young, so why not.

Even though we're not in a stall, it's still gross. It reeks, as you would expect a communal toilet to smell. Blue's emptied the baggie full of Molly onto his driver's license, which looks nothing like him, and uses my debit card to separate the drug into two lines. I'm really about to pass go and keep going, skipping right over marijuana and straight into the hard stuff.

Two bubbly teenagers—probably the same ones who boarded the tea cups with us all those weeks ago—walk into the bathroom. Blue pushes me into the stall and shuts the door gently before they have the opportunity to spot us. I bring a fist to my nose, trying to block the smell of an unflushed toilet.

"Can you believe that weirdo?" one girl asks the other.

"There's a reason he's a carnie. He's gross and weird, probably can't get a job anywhere else," the other girl replies, followed by a smack of her gum so loud that I could fly out of this stall and smack her upside her head. Blue stands in front of me, blocking my exit, so that fantasy most likely will not come to pass.

"Gimme a dollar," Blue whispers.

"For what? I'm not paying you."

His eyes lock with mine. "To snort it." He grimaces. "That sounds so stupid. I hate that word."

"Yeah, me, too." I dig into my pocket and pull out a wad of cash. There's no dollar bills, just twenties. "This is all I've got."

"That'll work." He rips the twenty out of my hand.

"No," I protest, a little too loud. Blue puts his hand up to me, the one holding the currency.

"Is somebody in here?" one of the pubescent teens calls out.

"No," I yell back and snatch the twenty out of Blue's hand. "I need this."

"You can still use it. Molly residue doesn't make it worthless."

"No, it just makes it paraphernalia."

"You need to relax." He steals the bill from my fingers again.

"I think there's a boy in there, too," one of the girls says from right on the other side of the door.

Blue's face grows rowdy. "Yeah, can we get some privacy? We're about to have sex."

The stall door bounces against the lock and they scatter away, their shoes pattering against the concrete. "Perverts!"

I frown. "Was that necessary?'

"It was funny." He wipes his finger against his nose. "You ready?"

I bite into my lip. "You go first."

He shrugs and brings the license covered in powder to his nose. He places the twenty that's rolled up like a straw into his nose and pinches the other nostril with his pointer finger. He breathes in sharply and moves the bill across the line, sucking up the Molly like a vacuum. He then hands me the card with the other line on it.

He pinches his nose and continues to snort. I peer down at the license—down at the drug. This is the point of no return. I'm anxious, nervous, and a little sick to my stomach. Blue locks his eyes with mine while pinching at his nose, nods, and I know it's okay.

Slowly, I bring the card to my nose and line up the bill. I breathe in hard and take the entire line in one hit. I feel an odd burning sensation full of excitement that I've never experienced before.

And then it hits my throat, leaving the most vulgar taste as it makes its way down the lining of my esophagus, sticking to the walls of my throat. My nose feels full and it feels empty, and I begin to snort uncontrollably. With every breath, drainage slides down my throat. I could really use a glass of water. Or vodka.

"Okay?" he asks quietly, his palm on my shoulder.

I rub a hand across my face. "I'm good."

"You want your money back?" He smiles.

"You hold onto it."

"All right," he says, pushing the bill into his pocket and retrieving a piece of gum. "Here, chew this."

"No, thanks." Gum is one of the most disgusting things in the world. If I wanted to chew on a ball of spit, I would just kiss someone with overactive salivary glands.

"Chew it. You don't want your jaw to lock up."

My entire body tenses. A herd of deer charge against my eyes, headlight style. "Why would my jaw lock up?"

"If you don't chew this, you're just going to chew on what's available. Like your cheek."

"Fine," I huff as I unwrap the gum and toss it in my mouth.

Yum, grape.

* * *

Hand in hand, we walk down the dark midway. The full effect of the drug has yet to hit, but it's become increasingly difficult to dodge other carnival-goers. For the second time tonight, I spot Dylan. He walks alone with one hand in the pocket of his jeans, casually strolling down the cracked path. His eyes are angled down, staring at his phone. The way he maneuvers around pedestrians that are out of his sight is admirable.

Instinct tells me I should run up to him and start a conversation. Just talk to him like I used to, back before things got so complicated. He lifts his head and instinct turns to panic. I can't bear to look at him, any more than I want him to see me like this. I jerk on Blue's hand and pull him to the left, past a concession stand that sells cheap beer.

We land on a field of grass and mud, and just up ahead sits the Zipper. I stop to breathe, but Blue has another idea, this time pulling me toward the ride. I'm sure it would be thrilling in my high state, but it could also be nauseating. I push my feet into the mud, bringing him to a halt as his arm breaks away from me. "Not right now," I say, the words coming out slow.

His palms slide down the side of his cheeks, a rambunctious smile snaps across his face. "We're not going to the Zipper." He points to the house of mirrors, which sits right beside the neon-lit axis of the thrill ride. "We're going in there."

I like the sound of that.

"Charlie," Dylan calls out from behind me.

Shit.

"Come on." Blue grabs my hand again. We run toward the attraction, away from Dylan. My legs fatigue instantly, like we're running toward the strong winds of a twister. I look back, and Dylan's a blur. Three bodies trying to escape each other.

The next thing I know, we're jogging up the steps to the entrance of the house of mirrors. Coming to a stop at the top of the platform, Blue digs the twenty-dollar bill out of his pocket and hands it to the carnie. It takes a moment, but I recognize him as Cookie, Blue's friend from a week before.

"Just keep everyone out for twenty minutes," Blue says, patting him on the chest. "Love ya, man."

"Yeah, yeah. I love your hokey ass, too," Cookie replies, and then proceeds to wink at me. "Have a great time."

The entrance is dark, with the promise of bright lights peeking between the cracks in the wall ahead.

"Thanks for saving me," I say, relieved I avoided a run-in with Dylan.

Blue shakes his head. "I don't know what you're talking about."

"Dylan was just outside, then you grabbed my hand, and we ran into here."

"I didn't save you from anyone. I didn't even know he was out there, and it's not like you need to be saved from him anyway."

I'm sure he was there, though it's possible I was hallucinating. I'm not exactly an expert on drug use. And who does drugs without researching anyway? Stupid people do. I did. Then the second thing Blue said resonates with me. It's true. I don't need to be saved from Dylan. That's ridiculous.

My thoughts bleed into each other, so I shut it all off. My focus scatters as we press further toward the end of the hallway, toward the lights. Blue pushes a floor-to-ceiling black curtain out of the way, revealing a large room lined with mirrors on all sides. This is not the carnival attraction I remember from my childhood. Another curtain hangs on the opposite side of the room. Neon lights flash across the space, reflecting endlessly from mirror to mirror to mirror.

It's beautiful and it's blinding. My head grows heavy. My entire body sinks into the depths of the floor. I catch Blue in the corner of my eye. His head droops and I think he's feeling the same way. We quickly make our way to the other end of the room, push the curtain aside, and step into the maze of mirrors. The intoxicating blue, green, and red colors bleed against the mirrors ahead of us, and as the curtain falls back into its resting place, they disappear.

It's much darker in the maze, lit only with black lights that are embedded in the ceiling. My chest tightens as I take a breath. My head bobbles weightlessly from side to side and I press a palm against a mirror to steady myself. Behind me, I notice Blue's wide-eyed gaze rested upon me.

"You good?" his reflection asks.

I nod, paying close attention to the girl in the mirror. Her smile's never been more infectious.

"And how do you feel?"

"Feel?" I question, searching for the right word. I feel something between ecstasy and anxiety, or a potent combination of both. "Free. I feel free." I'm a million miles away from my body, unable to control it. My fingers trace a path along the mirror, the sensation of the glass electrifying me. The desire to touch and be touched blurs into a need.

I turn and rest my back against the mirror. His eyes catch mine. "It's hot in here."

His hands fall to my cheeks, sending shots of ecstasy through me. When he moves in to kiss me, I expect it on the lips and not the neck. His lips run across the second most sensitive part of my body. His tongue taunts me further, running from the base of my neck all the way to my ear. His tongue circles my ear before nibbling.

I claw into his back, clenching his shirt and pulling it tight. When I close my eyes, everything intensifies. Another nibble against my skin and I might explode. With every moan that escapes my lips, I grow more thankful that nobody can hear or see us. His breath burns hot against my flesh as sweat begins to trickle down my face.

He gently nibbles my ear once more, and then pulls back, his own face covered in a thin veneer of sweat. One hand still holds me by the cheek, his eyes focused intently on me. "Too damn hot," he breathes frantically.

I simply nod.

In a fury, his hands grab the hem of his shirt and he rips it over his head. This is going to be a night not easily forgotten. His glistening chest shines like a mirror of its own. The way the lights paint his bare skin blinds me. I grab him, pulling him close, and I press my lips against his, tasting every atom of his grape-flavored gum.

My fingers trace across his damp back and he pushes into me. His lips are off my own and back at my neck, this time with urgency. A trail of slickness is left behind and is being warmed by every strong breath.

I can feel the thickness in his jeans with every push against me. I dig into the back of his denim and discover he's not wearing anything under them as I collect a mound of ass in my hand. Firm and smooth. It's my favorite part of his tremendous body.

He lifts my shirt as he bends to his knees, kissing every inch of my stomach on the way down. The button on my shorts popping open seems to echo in the tight space. I feel my shorts, and then my panties fall down the length of my legs.

He holds me by the hips as he plants kisses across my thighs, ending with a soft lap against my mound. I press my palms against his shoulders to steady myself. One look in the mirror behind us, and it's a sight so perfect that I know there's no turning back. The top of his ass peeks above loose jeans while he's on bended knee.

He stands up and brings one hand against me, and the other across my shoulder, holding himself firm against the mirror. "Do you get it now?"

"Get what?"

"Why I do it. Why I take this drug?" He drags his palm against my opening, and I can't even respond. "I can't quit it, just like I don't think I'll ever be able to quit you."

I moan, unable to do much else.

"You've made me wait," he says with a rough smile. "And I've been patient, but I need to hear two words before we begin."

"Free me, Blue."

His tongue rolls across his lips. "I was thinking *fuck me*, but that'll work."

I'm not used to this—these words coming out of his mouth. He can go from one extreme to the next, from cute and gentle all the way to this. But this—

A finger pushes into me and I swear I can feel his heartbeat pulsing through it.

"Blue," I moan.

"This isn't gonna be like last time." He pulls back, unbuckling his jeans. He steps out of them as they form a puddle on the floor. "You asked me to take you to the edge." He lifts me up, pulling my legs around him so that I sit between his hips and the mirror. His hardness pushes against me, promising an unforgettable journey. "Are you ready?"

I hesitate, not because I don't have an answer, but because speaking is a chore when my entire body is being held hostage. "I'm ready," I whimper.

A slow, wanting smile begins on one side of his face, hitching all the way across. Then he pushes himself slowly into me, and my legs pull tight around him. He's gentle, but I know it won't last. The careful thrusts will soon turn into something else—something stronger, more intense.

Every time he pulls back, I'm terrified he'll leave, that this will all end. Only dreams are this perfect. I pull against his neck, already feeling the impossible. There's a surge rising in me, and I'm begging him to fuck me faster, harder, but slow he goes.

Across the way, I can see what I'd call the porn-view. His ass pulls tight with every thrust, my mouth held agape. More than feeling it, I can see it, as my innards are turned inside out. I come against his pulsing flesh, tightening around him.

"Shit," he breathes, his fingers digging into my side and my ass. I lean my head back, throwing it against the glass as he continues to fuck me raw. Every time I think he's close to the finish line, he repositions, each time driving further, deeper into me.

Since the night we met, I've been resisting this explosion, afraid it would turn our relationship into something temporary. I was wrong. There's no point in denying the fire any longer. We're part of the same flame, burning bright and hot, fueled by the same desire. The connection is strong, more than the sum of parts touching and thrusting. I'm complete with him, even as he tears my body into a million seizing pieces.

The mirror behind me warms, the sweat of my body painting a slippery coat against it. With every thrust, every push of his thighs, I slide further up the glass. In the vacant moments, I'm able to open my eyes. I see the ridges of his back fold and crease, his muscular ass pulling taut with every shift of his hardness.

His cock drives into me again and again. Scars begin to form under the pressure of my firm grip. I hold onto him tight, not because I fear I could fall, but because if I don't, I could be fucked out of this world and into the next.

That time in the grass, he was holding back. There's no other explanation as a second orgasm begins to rise from the bottom of my being, ascending all the way to the edges of my mind. Coursing and pulsing through every miniscule vein, taking its time while circling my heart, then finally wrapping firm around my soul until I'm unable to breathe any longer.

My entire body aches, screaming as I break. A weak cry stifles in my throat and I catch his eyes rested on my own. He sees me through my own pleasure, not breaking focus even as he begins to speed up.

His fingers dig into the curves of my ass, holding me in place as he empties himself inside me. His swollen lips vibrate as he gives himself to me completely. I brush a hand through his slick hair, cradling his head so that it doesn't fall back. I watch as the revelation sinks into his eyes. I wanted to go to the edge with him, but we went further than I ever dreamed. There's completeness in the space between us, filled with nothing but the aftershocks of ecstasy.

The tension in his arms break, the impossibly strong grip he had on me becomes lax, and I slide off his thighs and onto my own two feet. It's as if I'm learning how to ride a bike again—it's a chore to stand on my own after being carried into another world.

I've been freed.

CHAPTER SIXTEEN

We tumble out the backdoor of the attraction. I laugh through the cotton of my shirt as I pull it over my chest. Behind me, I hear Blue fumbling to click his belt buckle together. With my shirt back on, I spin toward him. My shoe slips against the mud and I begin to fall, but my clumsiness is no match for his speed. He steadies me as I chuckle at the physical comedy of it all.

I'm lost in him. Lost in the way he smirks at me with that smile handcrafted by God himself. Lost in those blue eyes that shine like the Milky Way, the neon reflections of the carnival like stars on a clear night.

I mean to speak, but nothing comes out. It's like I want to say something, but the part of my brain that controls my mouth is defending me from myself. If I said a word, I'd ruin this beautiful moment. The galaxy wants this. I want this. There is nothing in the world that could ruin this moment. The moment that I know, with every fiber within me, that I lo—

"That's great."

I hear things now. Blue's lips don't move, but I hear him speak. He's reading my mind. Or I'm reading his. I should probably sit down.

"Really great."

From behind me? I turn around and everything breaks. The big fucking bang.

"How long have you been standing there?" I say to Dylan, whose head shakes sideways, disdain pouring out of his soul.

"Long enough."

I brush Blue's arms off me and step toward him. "Dylan..."

"You know what, Charlie? How about we don't?"

I shake my head. "Don't what?"

"Talk about this," he says, "or about anything ever again."

His eyes emote more than his words. He's not crying. I don't think he could if he tried. Some people are just built strong like that. Or they suffer some disorder where their tear ducts are permanently dry. That's the kind of guy Dylan is, but his eyes are washed in a whirlpool of emotions, and I've never seen him this way before. Not the day I broke up with him and not the day that I stood by his side as we buried his father.

"I'm sorry," I say, trying to comfort him, but that seems to be a chore, and I think that's my fault. Or the Molly's.

"Don't!" he barks at me, his voice one decibel away from breaking. He swats his hand at the air, a gesture I've seen before. He's about to take off. And that's what he does—he turns and hurries from the scene. I ball my hand into a fist, but not out of anger. It's a feeling I can't comprehend. My eyes get heavy and the rain begins to build.

Blue rests his hand on my shoulder, giving me a moment of comfort before I rush away from him and toward Dylan. I'm sluggish as I approach him, the weight of my body fighting against the weight of the world. I'm spinning, but this isn't a carnival ride I can enjoy. Hearts are breaking all around me like thunder, and for the first time, I'm already regretting the Molly. I can't help but feel I'd be better suited to handle this situation if my mind were clear. Never mind the probability that I wouldn't even be in this situation in the first place.

I catch up with Dylan and reach out for him, but he swats my hand away as he spins to face me.

"Didn't I tell you we're not doing this?"

"I don't think that's for you to decide."

"Guess what?" he says, and waves his hands at me. "You don't get to tell me when I'm angry."

"That's not what I'm doing," I say as I finally catch my breath. "I didn't want you to see any of that."

"I'm an adult. I think I can handle *that*."

"Then what are you so angry for?" I ask softly. My gut knows the answer but something inside needs confirmation.

"Because it's you, Charlie. The only girl I've ever been with—the only girl I've ever loved." He's calmer now. His voice comes down to a level that can just barely be heard above the pumping hydraulics of the tea cups behind us.

It's the second time in as many minutes that I've wanted to speak, but I can't force the words to come out. I can feel the frustration in his voice. He's waiting for me to respond. I want to give him the one thing he needs, which, like me, is confirmation.

"I. Loved. You." He places emphasis on the beginning of each word. "And you loved me."

"I did."

"And now you're stumbling out of a carnival attraction, putting your clothes back on after getting fucked inside?" He looks me up and down, sizing me up, but resting on my eyes. "You look like you're on drugs, coke or Molly, and I'm not sure which it is because I obviously don't know you anymore."

"Maybe you don't," I say, deadpan. It's a revelation that's the same for the both of us. "Things change. I've changed."

"Don't I know it." He's still shaking his head, and underneath all these layers of mixed emotions, it's starting to grate me.

"This isn't about me, is it?" I ask him pointedly. "This is about Blue, right?"

"It's about *both* of you. What does he have on you?"

"I think I love him. *That's* what he has on me."

He huffs. "Well, you said you loved me, too, so I guess that doesn't mean a lot."

I feel my tongue roll across my lip. "You have to let me go, Dylan." There's a quiet desperation in my voice, as if I need that more than he does. If he lets me go, then I have nothing else holding me back. Nothing left to leave me so torn.

"I have. Just now. In this moment, I am letting you go."

It sounds like confirmation, but it actually just makes it sting even worse.

"Why don't you go back inside and do another line," he says, dismissing me.

"That's not fair."

"That's great, Charlie. Really. Do you need to be reminded why we're not together?"

Coming from my side, I hear two kids laughing. I remember those days. The two kids cut between Dylan and me, chasing each other with inflated plastic swords. I'm hoping they cut this conversation short because I already know where it's going.

"In case you've forgotten, you left me." He begins to close the distance between us. He's about eight feet away, and I'm beginning to understand claustrophobia. "You said you couldn't do the long distance thing. That you were going to college, and I didn't fit into your perfect little plan."

Everything he says is true.

"When did you know you weren't actually going? Was it after you hooked up with him?"

"No," I say. "Of course not."

"As much as I love you, I was willing to let it go. Willing to let you go and do whatever it was that you needed to do, hoping that someday you would come back to me. But it's become apparent that I've lost you."

"You don't have to lose me," I say tenderly, and then like drums beating, preparing for war, I continue, "but you can't have me."

The world goes silent.

He pinches the bridge of his nose with his fingers, then rolls them into his eyes, wiping away the tears that I've just noticed are actually there. I will forever be the first person to ever make Dylan Parker cry. The punch against my stomach is intolerable.

"Fine," he says, defeated.

"I'm sorry," I say under my breath. It's so quiet that I know he can't hear it.

"Go back to your carnie." He waves me off with his hand. "He's waiting for you."

He walks away, probably for good. And I've never bled as badly than I am in this moment, watching someone I truly care about walking out of my life against the neon-lit background of a carnival painted against an impossibly black sky.

This is what it feels like to lose innocence.

Blue's breath against my skin startles me. I have no idea how long he's been standing there. He's fully dressed now and I'm a blank-faced, emotional mess, yet somehow I still manage to notice the way his shirt sticks to his sweaty chest, outlining every muscle in his upper body. Must be the Molly.

"Are you all right?"

"Yeah..." I trail off. "Let's go somewhere."

His eyes light up. "I know just the place."

* * *

We're lying in the grass beside Blue's Jeep. We're just on this side of the chain-link fence that separates the field from the carnival. Above us, the Ferris wheel cycles perilously close to the fence. A strong wind could topple the six-shot revolver of death onto us. But I'm growing fond of living life on the edge, and it doesn't even feel dangerous anymore.

In slow motion, faded neon colors brush against the cool skin of Blue's face. He's different in this light, and I'm seeing things in him that I've never seen before. Just underneath his beautiful blue eyes, under the right one, is what appears to be a scar hidden by lapses of time. There's a story there and there's nothing I want more than to know what it is.

But how do I bring it up?.

"You're looking at my scar, aren't you?"

I guess that settles it. I answer with a nod.

He rubs his forefinger against his tongue, getting it wet, and then rubs it across the skin surrounding his eye. The scar bleeds into life, and time hasn't really hidden it at all.

"What happened?"

"It's a long story," he says. "One of those *in my past* things."

And I guess it's one of those things I'll have to wait to find out. There seems to be a pattern here.

"It happened during a bar fight."

A soft laugh swells deep in my throat. Of course it did. He's like a bad boy that's not so bad. Not like all those guys you see on television, covered in tattoos with a bike or two stashed in their non-existent garages. Not at all. He has a string of bad decisions under his belt, but who doesn't?

I scoot across the damp grass to get closer to him. He puts his arm under my shoulder, and he cradles me, pulling me close. He kisses the top of my head and I can't wipe the smile off my face. I'm one of those girls who have the best boyfriend in the world. And all the other bitches who think they do are just fooling themselves.

"Tell me more," I say.

"Huh?" he asks, rolling his head toward me.

I look up to his face, his confusion prominent. "About the scar."

"Well," he sighs, "it hurt like a bitch."

"Yeah?"

He nods his head. "Ever had a beer bottle smashed against your face?"

My lips purse. "Nope. Can't say that I have."

He smirks and brushes my hair back out of my face. "That's good. I'd hate to have to kill someone."

Then something passes over his face. I can't pinpoint the emotion, but the smirk fades.

"What's wrong?"

"You're intuitive."

"That's what everyone says."

"It's nothing." He combs his fingers through my hair. He knows I don't believe him, probably because I'm a terrible actress. Being a movie star was never in the cards. "Really, don't worry about it."

"Can I touch it?" I ask. I'm fixated on his scar and desperate to change the conversation from something he doesn't want to talk about to something he already has talked about.

He blinks as he nods his head again.

I reach slowly toward his eye. I'm not sure if it's the effect of the drugs wearing off or just my nature, but I'm being very gentle about the whole affair. Too gentle. My finger connects with the tip of the scar below his eye. It's raised and uneven. It's not the most intimate we've ever been—hello... House of Mirrors—but this feels different. Sure, he's been in me twice now, but this is vulnerability right here.

I trace my finger down, over his eye that is now closed, and rub against the bottom half of the scar. Then it hits me. "You wear makeup," I accuse as I laugh.

He opens his eyes and pushes my hand off him. "Yeah, yeah. Get your laughs in."

"I didn't mean to laugh—"

"I get it," he cuts me off. "It just happens."

"I don't think you should."

"Cover it up?"

"Yeah. It's beautiful."

He slips his arm back underneath me and holds me tight. That word, *beautiful*, is one of the last things most men want to be associated with, but Blue's not like that. Even though it wasn't about aesthetics, something else—something deeper. Something about our histories defining us. Something like that, but it's too complicated to think about in this state, so I think I'm just going to stare at the stars.

Between the glow of the carnival and the dark clouds that long ago settled in the sky, they're not very visible. But in the center of the darkness, there's a cluster of stars, but it takes some squinting to see, and I'm so not in the mood.

"We should stay here," Blue muses out loud. "Forever."

"That's quite a commitment."

"For the first time in my life, I feel like I'm home." His arm shifts under me. "And you're a big part of that."

My cheeks flush, filling with happiness—much cheaper than Botox injections.

"I'm being serious," he continues.

I turn on my side to face him. "What about Vegas?" I question. "We talked about it when we first met."

"I remember." A smile hitches up the side of his mouth. "It's on the to-do list."

"Could you really spend the rest of forever here?"

His turn to roll onto his side. "Happiness is hard to find, so I think that once you find it, you should do everything you can to hang onto it."

"I'm inclined to agree." I pause and think how to say what comes next. "But Lakeview has never seemed like home to me."

His head tilts sideways. "Then why haven't you left?"

"I've always wanted to leave this place behind," I sigh, "but after my parents were divorced, my mom was a complete wreck. I kind of figured I owed it to her to take care of her, after everything she's done for me. Then, out of the Blue," I smile, immediately catching the unintentional pun, "she gets better and she wants me to go to college, and I don't know if that's what I want anymore. And I'm stuck here until I figure it out."

"At least you don't have to be alone," he says. "Because I'll be stuck in the mud right next to you."

* * *

Emptiness. It's devastating. Walking through a fresh-cut field and there's no one around. That's not the emptiness, though. It's something else. My five senses are on overload as they try to absorb anything past the thickness of nothing.

I stand still. The world rotates around me, giving me a panoramic view of everything between the moon and me, but something's missing, and I can't quite put my finger on what.

The sky above me begins to illuminate and my eyes shift upward. The sky is being painted in neon colors. Happiness floods through my veins as if the mural somehow completes me. A face begins to form in the neon swirls.

It's Blue, his face formed with brushes of paint that Photoshop couldn't clone. He reaches out to me, his arm stretching an impossible distance. He grabs me by the hand and lifts me into the sky. Beneath me, the field blurs into a calm sea as I'm pulled into the stars.

Up here, we're nothing but clouds. Blue places his hand beneath my chin and raises it ever so slightly. His eyes are the perfect storm of neon-blue whirlpools.

The colors of the world swirl around us—wrapping us in its beauty, and pushing us closer to each other. Just as we're about to kiss, there's a clap of thunder and everything goes black.

* * *

I was in the clouds, and now I'm looking at them. My legs hang over the side of Blue's Jeep and my body lies against Blue's bare chest. I must have been dreaming when Blue carried me over to the Jeep, and I wonder if he did so as he lifted me into the sky.

I turn into his chest and press myself close to him. My head rests just below his, and I tilt upward and land a kiss on his cheek.

The last thing I see before I drift back off to sleep are the clouds rolling away, revealing a picture-perfect rendering of the starlit sky. Nothing in this world compares to being here, beneath this neon sky. That moment when your reality becomes better than your dreams can't be described. It can only be felt. And I got the feels.

CHAPTER SEVENTEEN

Everybody talks about how great Molly is—the people adventurous enough to try it, anyway—but nobody ever talks about the day after. It's like going to heaven and then being ripped out of a world that isn't ready for you to leave. Once you've been to the sea of Molly dreams, reality has a way of pulling you back to reality. I wonder if I would have done it if Blue had warned me that I would feel like an emotional hurricane the next day.

Probably.

All I want is to lie down, even while knowing full well I couldn't fall asleep again. We turn onto my street and a part of me isn't ready for the night to end. Sure, the sun is well into the sky, but these last twenty-four hours feel like one night divided by artificial definitions of time.

A cool breeze, warmed by the piercing rays of the sun, brushes against my skin. Blue's hair blows in the September wind. He looks so damn sexy in his knock-off Prada glasses. I could spend the rest of forever in this Jeep. Sex is the furthest thing from my mind—looking at him is enough for me to melt.

All my life, I thought I would marry Dylan. Even after we broke up, I could never shake the feeling that my life would come full circle with his. Then there is this boy who never should have been a part of my journey. Some people look at fairs and carnivals as festering grounds for lost souls. I never did. To me, they were magical places full of memories, especially for youth. Many first dates have transpired in these places. I don't know the statistics, but I'm almost positive I'm one of a few who have ever fallen this far for a carnie. If my life leads me to the latest Jerry Springer knockoff, then that's my decision to make.

We pull into the driveway and I rest my head against the seat. The clicking of his seat belt draws my attention to him.

"I had a real good night," he says.

"Me, too." I rub my thumbs against my eyes. "I don't want to walk inside. Can I just stay here in the Jeep?"

He smiles. "You can do whatever you want."

"I should probably go inside. My mom's probably worried."

He brushes my cheek and pushes my hair behind my ears. "Call me crazy, but I think I'm going to love you someday."

"Someday?" I ask with half a smile, almost tired of hearing that word.

"Someday soon."

Releasing my seat belt, I lean across the gear shift. "I think I love you today."

"Like, right now?"

I just nod, unable to pull my eyes away from him.

"I'm cool with that." He leans closer to the point where our noses glide past each other. The only thing that separates us is a thick slice of a breeze. It flows between us like the colors of the wind. "It seems like a good day to fall in love."

"Where did you come from?"

"A carnival. I'm a carnie, remember?"

"I remember."

We both move closer still. His lips brush against mine and I feel as high as when I was on Molly. Excitement. Bliss. Loved. He caresses my lips, taking his time. His lips become softer with every lap. He presses his tongue against my lip and slips into my mouth as he pushes me backward and climbs atop me.

I'm not even worried what the neighbors might think. I'm not worried about anything, because there's nothing left to worry about. My hand slides up his back, running along his smooth skin.

In the last twenty-four hours, I've discovered something with Blue—the elusive thread of truth that we seem so privy to while the rest of the world looks on in utter disbelief that anybody could be this happy living within their own rules.

* * *

The front door is unlocked, which is very unusual. From a very young age, my parents harped on the dangers of unlocked doors, and I spent many hours as a child learning how to properly lock them. Seriously, hours.

I push the door open and quietly shut it behind me. It almost feels like I'm sixteen again, sneaking into the house after an all-night drinking binge. It's a little past noon, so there's probably no reason to be too quiet.

I make my way to the kitchen, ignoring the girl who's sitting on the couch. I pull the door of the refrigerator open and grab a carton of orange juice. As the door closes, I realize there was someone in the living room. I sit the carton on the counter and leave the kitchen.

I backtrack into the living room to see that it's Summer, dressed in jeans and an Ohio State jersey. The game was the previous day, so I'm not sure if she's being a skank or has simply lost track of her days.

"Hey," I say.

"Your mom got called into work. She said it was an emergency or something."

"Okay..." I say confused, about why she's talking about my mom.

"Are you okay?"

"I was up all night, so I'm a little tired."

She stands up, her feet grinding into the floor. "It's okay not to be okay." She steps closer to me. "God knows that I've been through the wringer."

Something's wrong. "Is everything okay with you?"

"Wha— how can you even ask me that? Of course I'm not okay."

I rush to her, embracing her tightly. "What's wrong? Did something happen at college?"

"I'm talking about Dylan."

I step back. "What about him?"

She pinches her face with her palm. "Oh my God," she says, and turns around. "You don't know."

"Know what?" I grab her and turn her around to face me. Her eyes water and for the first time, I notice how incredibly red they are. "Summer! You're scaring me."

Her throat tightens. The color of her skin drains to a pale white. "Dylan died last night."

I shake my head, laughing gently. "He's fine. I saw him at the carnival."

"He was leaving and he was hit by a truck."

"You're wrong." I bite hard into my lip and reach for my phone. I look at a black screen for a good thirty seconds before I remember it was dead all night. I throw it on the couch where it bounces off and rolls onto the ground. I rush into the kitchen and rip the home phone off the counter, and dial Dylan's number from memory. It begins to ring and some stupid country song begins playing.

Summer steps into the kitchen. "Charlie—"

I push a hand up to her. "Stop talking."

"What's up?" Dylan asks through the phone.

"Thank God," I say, running my hand through my hair and glaring at Summer.

"Hold on, I can't hear you."

"Dylan, people think you're dead."

"What?"

"People think yo—"

"Psych!" he yells through the phone. "You've reached the voicemail of Dylan Parker. Leave a message, but I probably won't get back to you."

I hang up and dial again, putting the phone to my ear.

"Charlie..." Summer says and moves closer.

"Stop," I command.

That damn country song drives me insane. There's nothing I need more than to hear Dylan's voice, but it's becoming clear that that's not going to happen.

"The caller you are trying to reach has a full inbox. Please hang up and try again at a later time."

The line goes dead. I hold the phone to my ear, still waiting for him to talk. Staring at nothing, even though I'm not the one who died, I see his entire life flash before my eyes. Everything I ever felt for him, every time we made love, every time we fought... it all comes pouring back to me.

"Charlie, you need to sit down," I hear Summer say. It sounds like she's all the way on the other side of the world. And she might as well be there, because in these seconds of paralyzing sobriety, walls heaven-high spike up around me.

"I'm going to be sick." My voice barely registers a decibel. I feel the weight of Summer push past me, presumably to get a trash can. She's not quick enough. I hunch over, choking on my throat as I vomit on the floor.

With my back to the wall, I slide down and rest on my heels. I dial Dylan's number and weakly put the phone to my ear. I'm waiting for a miracle. Waiting for a change of fate that will never come. "The caller you are trying to reach has a full inbox. Please hang up and try again at a later time."

All I want, all I need is to hear his voice. I guess many others feel the same way, filling his inbox with goodbyes or worried messages. Guilt sweeps over me. What if he tried to call me? How many calls had I received from family and friends? Everyone was hurting while I was on top of the world. I should have been hurting.

Then there's Blue. I had just told him that I loved him. But Dylan wanted me back. He got in his car and drove away last night because of Blue and me. I know it's not right to blame myself, and it's definitely not right blaming Blue. But in these moments, when you find your world burning, it's the only thing that makes any sense.

It takes a while to register Summer's arm wrapped around me. A little longer to realize that she's crying.

"What are we going to do?" I ask behind dry sobs.

"I don't know, but we should probably get you away from this mess."

* * *

The balcony off my bedroom has been my safe place since I was a child. Beautiful French doors stand between it and me. The sunlight taunts me, streaming through the glass. It warms me, emotionally and physically. I'm cold and I need the sun.

Summer's somewhere else, in the kitchen maybe. Or the living room? Maybe she went home. I'm not really sure. I hold the phone tightly clutched in my hand. It rings and my mind jumps, while every part of my body besides my arm holds still. I raise the phone to my ear. "Hello," I say weakly.

"Hello, Mrs. Scott."

"She's not home." My hand drops to my side. From across the world, I hear the front door slam shut.

"Charlie?" Blue yells.

Up here. The words never come out. I figure he'll eventually find me. What difference does it make when?

My bedroom door creaks open and that's when the first tear comes.

"Charlie," he says softly from behind me.

I blink my eyes. A few more tears. I turn to him.

"Are you okay?"

"Everybody asks that." My voice is monotone. "But everybody already knows."

He wants to comfort me—I can sense it. I put my hand up to stop him from moving closer but my hand folds into a fist. My nails dig into the palm of my hand. I can't tell if my hand is damp from the cold sweat or blood. It doesn't matter either way. "I just want to lie down," I say and move toward the bed.

"Do you want me to wait downstairs?"

"No." I sink onto the bed. "Stay."

"Are you sure?"

My shoulders rise and fall. He walks to the bed and the bed sinks down beside me. I push him onto his back and crawl up next to him, resting my head on his chest. He wraps an arm around me and pulls me into his body. I feel a solitary moment of peace before I begin to drift off.

* * *

My hair blows in the wind and my legs cut through tall blades of grass in a meadow. The field bleeds into a sea of trees in the distance and another tree sits alone in the middle. I want to run into the forest but something tells me I should walk to the tree instead.

I stand at the base of the tree. It's short but round and it only takes a moment for me to climb to the top. I lean against the center, my arm grabbing a branch for balance.

"It's beautiful, isn't it?" Dylan says from behind me.

"It's familiar."

"Isn't that the same thing?"

"It shouldn't be."

"Come on," he says. "Jump."

I turn to look at him but he's not there. Rather, he's on the ground holding out his arms as if he's about to catch me.

"No," I say. "It's too far."

"Come on. What are you afraid of?"

"Falling."

"Too late for that." He picks me up off the ground. I cling to his red plaid shirt for a moment. Then he's running through the field, away from me and laughing, but it's not his voice. It's a child's voice.

I give chase to him, running through the field. His unbuttoned shirt waves like a flag in the wind. The grass gets taller, soon too tall and I lose track of him.

"Dylan?" I wait for a reply and grow anxious. "Dylan!?"

He comes from behind me and knocks me to the ground. Brushing my hair back, his eyes duel with mine. "You were always beautiful." Then he rolls off me and onto his back. "Just like the sky."

My attention shoots to the sky.

"That beautiful blue sky."

"Do you have to go?" I ask him.

His face crinkles and he pauses. "That's what everybody says."

"Who's everybody?"

Paying no attention to me, "Do you see that?"

"See what?"

Dylan points to clouds gathering in the sky. "It's a carnival ride."

It takes a beat for me to see the ride floating in the sky. "A Ferris wheel..."

"Your favorite." He laughs.

He's walking away from me now. A deep sadness chills through my bones. "Wait!" I yell. "Will I ever see you again?"

He turns back to me, and I've never seen him more handsome.

"Someday."

* * *

My eyes jolt open and I'm cold. Still wrapped up in my snoring lover's arms. I gently lift Blue's arm off me, trying not to wake him. Rolling over, I give him the softest kiss I've ever given on his forehead. I slide across the wrinkled sheets and gently place my feet on the cushioned floor.

Quietly, I make my way to the balcony doors and pull them open. The sun, now setting, blinds me. Strangely, I'm okay with it. I just want to feel something, whether it's heat, or peace, or pain. And it's a little bit of all three. Collapsing to the ground is a legitimate option but peace seems more appropriate.

It felt like a dream but it haunts me like a nightmare. Maybe those two are closer than they first appear. The town below and around me is quiet. Kids in the distance cackle and laugh. God, if I could be a kid again, but last night was the point of no return. I would never be a kid again. I would never fall asleep ignorant to the cruel grasp of this world again. There are too many things I know now that I couldn't have known then.

Kids love but they don't fall in love. Kids take baby Tylenol, but we've graduated to party drugs. Would I even want to be a kid again? Knowing what I know now? No. Being able to forget it all? Sprinkle me with angel dust.

I peer inside to make sure Blue's still asleep. Even he looks innocent. Then I catch my reflection across the glass on the door. The dying sun reflects across my face and illuminating the two gates to my hollow soul.

CHAPTER EIGHTEEN

I'm still not ready when Blue comes to pick me up for the funeral. How could I ever be ready? I set my priorities and rush into the bathroom to gargle mouthwash. The last thing I want is for everybody to know I've been drinking. My hands clench the edge of the sink as I peer into the mirror.

Who the hell are you?

I'm sure my reflection is asking the same thing. At least we're both on the same page as we spit out recycled Listerine.

I pull my top off and throw it on my bed, atop numerous other outfits that weren't making the cut. I need to look how he'd want me to look. I eye a plaid shirt hanging on my bathroom door. Everybody says you can't wear plaid to a funeral. Yeah, well, nobody's supposed to die when they're eighteen. Rules are fucking broken. I think my infraction is more forgivable than the cruel hand of death.

Blue doesn't knock. He just walks in. He looks gorgeous dressed up and here I am standing in a bra and skirt unable to pick a fucking shirt. Maybe that's the problem. I rush to my closet and grab the nearest dress. It's gray, not black, but I'm pretty fed up with the rules. I press it against my body and turn to Blue.

"How does it look?"

"It looks good."

"Good?" That dress gets thrown on the bed.

He steps close to me. "It doesn't matter what you wear."

"That's the stupidest thing I've ever heard."

"Are you sure you wanna go?"

I throw my hands up. "No. I don't want to go. I shouldn't have to. This whole thing is stupid. It's not fair and it's stupid. He's dead and he can't come back. I want to curl up in bed with a bottle of whiskey but I can't do that. I'm not allowed. I have to mourn, get over it, and move on because that's how it works. But that's not how the world works. He was too young to die. I'm too young to lose him and it hurts. It *fucking hurts*."

Blue guides me to the bed and sits me down. I feel the bed push down beside me as he joins me, embracing me. His rough lips kiss the side of my head. "I love you, baby."

I push him to his back and climb on top of him. With force, I go in for a kiss, separating his lips with my tongue. My hands grab his shirt and push it over his abs as I go down south. I unbuckle his belt and his rough hands grab me. "What are you doing?"

I glance at him and hold my gaze as I pull the belt apart and pull his slacks down just enough so his cock springs free.

He runs his hands over his eyes, through his hair and takes a drawn-out breath. He's apprehensive and I need something to cling to, so I lift my legs up and straddle him. Without care or condom, I lower myself onto him. He sinks away from me, a pained look on his face. This isn't about making love. It's about me needing something and I'm taking it from him.

I maneuver him, bobbing up and down. My hands dig through his shirt, into his chest. His hands find my hips, his knees rise, and he starts driving into me, filling me with the only thing that can make me feel alive.

Without pulling out, he flips me over onto my back. The belt on his slacks clatters against the bed as he fucks me deep into the mattress. There's an animal inside of him with the instinct of a lion. He knows this is exactly what I want even as a tinge of guilt creeps over his face.

His palms clench the sheets, his arms pulling tense as he comes inside me.

And the release was only temporary. I eye the plaid shirt hanging from my closet door.

* * *

Believing in a higher power is often difficult. On days like this, believing in God is especially a chore. Does God cry? My mother used to tell me when I was young that raindrops were the tears of God. If that's true, he doesn't care about Dylan.

My faith was shaken a long time ago but I'm still not ready to commit to a life as a nonbeliever, even if the last thing I want to hear today is that God has a plan. I want nothing to do with His plan. I want Dylan back.

A part of me wishes my mom could be here today, instead of away on a business trip. The other part of me is relieved that she can't be here. I've always been strong—some would argue I've been too strong. Showing weakness isn't a flaw, but there are some people I couldn't stand to see me break.

Our car pulls up to the church and there is already a small crowd gathering. An army of plaid clashes with a sea of suits. Was I the only one worried it would be inappropriate? It doesn't matter, and for the first time since we left the house, I feel a hint of relief.

Blue doesn't pull the Jeep around back with the rest of the cars. Instead, we park on the opposite side of the street. There are only a few reasons a girl would go running out of a church. A bride running from her groom... and me, running anywhere else. It's not like I plan to have a nervous breakdown in between the eulogy and the prayer, but it's a definite possibility. If I need to leave, we can get out without a fuss, and if we stay, we can pull behind the procession of sedans and pick-up trucks.

"You got them?" I ask, staring blankly out the window.

"I do, but I don't think it's a good idea."

"I won't make it through the service without them."

He sighs as he reaches into the armrest and pulls out a bottle. I grab for it but he jerks away and unscrews the lid. He takes out one pill and hands it to me, then stuffs the bottle into his pocket. I don't think he trusts me with them. He should relax and be happy that I'm asking for Xanax and not Molly.

Even though I think it, I can't bring myself to say it. Molly would daze me—that's for certain, but it would also suppress the pain, even if only fleetingly.

Blue checks his watch and pops his door open. Must be time to go in. Without anything to drink, I swallow the pill dry.

* * *

Who decides what music is played during funerals? They should be fired. Each and every funeral director in the world. This isn't the *Titanic*, and this isn't our final moments. I'm not asking for Alanis Morissette or Katy Perry, but damn what just a little bass would do to lighten the mood.

Dylan awaits us at the front of the room, permanently locked inside a closed casket. There is nothing in this world I wouldn't do just to see him again. There's an emptiness present, ironic in a room full of people. The world around us moves at full speed, while those of us here in Lakeview seem to be stuck. I wonder if this is what purgatory feels like.

A light breeze blows in behind us from the open church doors. It's warm, suffocating, and violent. As we make our way to our seats, I spot Cassadee out of the corner of my eye, sobbing into a handkerchief. She barely knew Dylan, and even in a world that has quit making sense, the reason she's here is something I'm unable to grasp.

Summer and Tyson have three seats saved in the third pew with Bibles laid across the bench. Blue leads me into our row. I sit down, placing the Bible into the back of the bench ahead of us. Summer is calm. She looks peaceful and at ease, but when she grabs my hand and squeezes it, I know it's an act. "Did you see Cassadee?" she whispers without facing me.

I nod. "Where's Joey?"

"In the bathroom." I've never heard her be this quiet. "He's drinking."

I guess we're all fucked up, each in our own little way. Summer can hide it better than the rest of us. Tyson's eyes are bloodshot red, matching his wrinkled plaid shirt. I think of Joey, drinking alone in the church bathroom. There's no doubt in my mind that that's exactly what Dylan would have wanted, although maybe not the *alone* part. He wouldn't want us to be trashed, but he would definitely recommend a shot or two to take the edge off. I haven't been invited yet to the inevitable celebration-of-life party, and I'm not sure I'd even want to go. It may be exactly what Dylan would want, but it would still feel wrong. A shot of Jack doesn't sound too bad, though. Maybe I'll join Joey in the bathroom.

Too late.

Blue slides closer to me as Joey scoots into the last seat in the row. He barely cares to hide the bottle of Jack as he scoots it in between his and Blue's hips. The scent of whiskey is as strong as year-old cologne, except it smells better.

Sobs complement the soundtrack of grim tracks. They've always seemed quiet—sobs, I mean—but they begin to drown out everything else. Like a thousand people, all screaming for release. Dylan's mother, Teresa, cries the loudest. It's a terrible sight, and like an accident, I can't look away. Sadness is the most difficult thing to describe. It's so much easier to spot. I want to give her a hug and slip her a Xanax.

I know it's unethical to drug someone without their consent, but I'd be doing her a favor. It's not like the pain is gone, because it's not. You know it's there, but you just can't reach out and grasp it.

I understand that some people need to go through the agony of grief on days like this. I've heard it's part of the healing process, but I'm not strong enough for that. Not today.

The church doors close, and the finality sinks in. The air flow is cut off, and while I've never been claustrophobic, I feel as if I'm about to choke. The walls move in on us, and on the inside, I'm screaming for someone to open the damn doors.

CHAPTER NINETEEN

Joey stands at the front of the church, elevated above us on top of the stage. He leans against the podium. With one hand, he moves to adjust the microphone. An obnoxious, tormenting screech echoes through the silence of the church.

He clears his throat and prepares to speak. He's weak, both his body and his voice, as if his grasp on this world is endangered and he could disappear in mid-sentence. I worry for him and for everyone in attendance. He's always been the least even-tempered one amongst us. Toss in alcohol and he could crash and burn, catching us all up in the blaze.

"I woke up today sick to my stomach. If I didn't have to stand here in front of all of you, I don't think I would have come. Because I've lost something that I can never get back." He shifts his weight to the side, gripping the podium tightly. "We've all lost the same thing in different ways. I lost my best friend, but he was always more than that. He was a brother, and growing up an only child, that's all I ever wanted.

"It would be selfish of me to stand here and not acknowledge everyone else who has lost something.

But if I'm being honest, my reality, the one in which I was the only one to lose someone so precious, was much easier to bear. In that reality, I'm able to pretend."

I've never heard him speak this way before, like there's something else there. A hint of something he's always been able to hide. "But when I stand here, in front of this room, I can't deny it anymore. That it's permanent, that it's tragic, that it's fucking stupid."

The crowd is taken aback, sending ripples of murmurs through the air. You're not supposed to curse in a church, but as life has shown us recently, rules are broken.

"During these things, people always get up here and claim that the deceased was the greatest of us. I guess that helps many forgive and move on, but this is different because Dylan really was special, and he was loving, and he was the greatest man I've ever known. The greatest man I'll ever know.

"None of us will ever know what was going through his mind in those final moments, and to me, that's the most tragic thing of all. The idea that we will never see it coming and that it'll happen to many of us someday on some mundane Tuesday. It won't be sad for the one lost. It'll be sad for those of us left behind. I think about walking down the street and buying an ice cream cone. It's chocolate, my favorite, and I'll never know it's the last thing I'll ever eat, because my life will be over the second a car veers out of control."

Summer sobs into a tissue. Tyson's feet patter against the floor nervously. Blue holds me tightly. And I'm trapped in a theater watching Joey get struck by a car. It's gruesome, but I can't look away. His words have meaning, and it's the saddest thing I've ever heard.

"Dylan wanted something in his final moments, and I wish I knew what it was. Not because it would change anything. It wouldn't, but there's something comforting about knowing, isn't there?" There's a sudden shift in his voice, the break I saw coming. I take in a deep breath and hold it. "So what do we know now? We know that we're all here for the same reason, to mourn the passing of Dylan Parker. Or maybe we're celebrating his existence, and the mark he left on the world. A mark that we all carry. And it was great and it was beautiful, and he was ours, and now he's not." His voice explodes, taking even himself off guard as he pulls back from the mic. His jaw pulls tight. His eyes flicker, trying to trap the tears. He shakes his head, then continues, "I don't know what comes next, what comes in the future, but this mark seems too heavy a burden. When I talk about the concept of knowing, it's all bullshit, because the only thing I know is that I loved him. And now he's gone.

"But there has to be a light, doesn't there? There has to be a silver lining, because without it, all that's left is emptiness. And I suppose the day will come when the hurt begins to fade into a whisper so silent that only I'll be able to hear it. I wish that day was tomorrow, but until then, I'll say this. I love you, Dylan Parker. You were a friend, a brother, a nephew, a son, and there's a hole in the world without you in it."

Everything inside of me is paralyzed, unable to respond in any adult manner. I should cry, but I've been reborn as a machine. I stare blankly ahead as Joey flees the stage with grace that breaks completely once he hits the floor. His lip trembles, holding everything back until he storms past us, past his seat.

The church doors are thrown open, the flash of cool air a relief before the doors slam back shut. I should chase after him, but again, paralysis.

The speech begins to register with me. The first thing I notice is how bitter, angry, and beautiful it was.

The second thing I notice is that I'm about to be the bride running out of the church.

A preacher ascends the steps to the podium, the crowd still silent as the sound of his every step carries throughout the room. When he clears his throat to speak, I'm finally able to move. If I'm forced to sit here and listen to this man give purpose to Dylan's death, there will likely be two coffins sitting up front. I don't need to hear a word about God's plan.

I pat Blue on his leg, grabbing his attention. "Wait here."

* * *

I don't care what the world must think of me as I sweep down the center aisle. The preacher waits to speak, for whatever reason, until I'm out the big oak doors. Joey sits on the concrete steps, his head buried in his knees. I place a hand on him softly and get the reaction I should have known I'd get. He springs to his feet, wiping the corners of his eyes furiously.

"What do you want?" He spins on his feet so that he's both looking at me and away from me.

"I just wanted to make sure you're all right."

"I just needed some air." His eyes pull tight. "I don't know if I can go back in there."

"I think we have to."

He laughs softly. "I don't have to do anything."

"You know what I mean."

He shakes his head. "How are you okay? How can you stand there and act like this isn't a big deal?"

My face pulls tight. "It is."

"Then why doesn't it look hard for you?" The whiskey begins to take effect and his voice rises. He finally turns to face me completely. His eyes are swollen.

"I'm sorry you think that," I say. "To be honest, I don't feel much of anything."

"That figures," he mumbles under his breath.

Excuse me. My nails roll into my palm.

As the church doors are pushed open gently, Tyson glides down the steps, the bottle of Jack in one hand. "I'm taking him home."

"You guys can't leave."

Joey rolls his eyes. Tyson hands Joey the bottle and takes me aside. "I don't want to, but I'm worried what will happen if he stays."

I unroll my fist and pinch the bridge of my nose, ready for the tears, for the release. "You'll never have this chance to say goodbye again."

He shrugs, not because he doesn't care, but because there's nothing else to do. "I already said goodbye the night I drove home alone and saw the lights."

I know that he cares. I know they both do, but it doesn't make sense to me for them to leave. It feels like they're running out on the responsibility and the rest of us can't. Joey's halfway to the car, nursing on the bottle, and I know they've already made up their minds. Tyson leans into me, hugging me so tight that I can feel his pain. "I love you, Charlie," he whispers.

When he's ready to pull away, I latch onto him just a moment longer. We're in this together, like we've always been. The motley crew of Lakeview.

* * *

The hair on my arms stands on end, and I know. The only raindrop in the sky splashes onto my hand, and I know. Thunder rips across the sky, starting with a whimper and ending in a roar, and I know. If He exists, He understands the solemn pain in all of our hearts on this long day that will shape the rest of our lives. I'm ready for the rain to rinse my soul.

Without warning, the gates of heaven open up and it's on. No buildup and no mercy. The temperature drops in seconds, the wind cuts through the cemetery. The crowd begins to dissipate as the rain races toward the ground. The sky dims. I should follow everyone, but this is where I need to be. After everyone is gone, I'm going to need some time, because I honestly don't know if I could ever stand to come back.

Summer touches my shoulder. The nod of my head lets her know it's okay if she goes. Blue wraps his arm around me and I lean into him, resting my head against his shoulder.

"You ready?" he asks me.

"Not yet," I say somberly.

He rubs my arm. "No rush."

Being comforted by my boyfriend at my ex-boyfriend's funeral should be awkward, but the pain is stronger. I love–loved–them both, in different ways, for different reasons. My life could have ended with either one of them, and I believe I would have been happy. Fate, or God, or Nostradamus took that choice from me.

But I've already made a choice between old and new, and I was content with that choice. I don't understand why it's so difficult now. Will I find myself in an annoying, young adult love triangle with Blue and a ghost?

The rain is freezing, but I can't bring myself to care. Our warm breath dances in front of us, putting on a show.

CHAPTER TWENTY

I desperately need sleep, but it's not in the cards. It's past midnight, and whenever I try closing my eyes, I can't fall asleep. My eyelids are sore from forcing them shut. Blue lies behind me, holding me while he sleeps peacefully. His embrace is strong, as if he believes he'll lose me if he lets go. He has no intention of letting go. He breathes slow and shallow, well into a deep sleep.

It takes all my strength to move his arm off me and reposition myself so I'm facing him. He flinches in his sleep, and his arm finds its way back around me, pulling me in tight. A mere inch separates our faces. He's my world now.

When it becomes clear I'll be up all night, I pull away from him and spin my legs off the edge of the bed. He turns to his side, placing a hand under his head.

I walk into the bathroom and flip on the light. My reflection in the oversized mirror above the sink startles me—not out of surprise but because I'm tired of running into her. She's had her soul ripped out, replaced with emptiness. Her eyes tell of a fairytale with the final, happily-ever-after pages ripped out. Her pale face sick with worry and regret. Guilt hangs over her like a cloud, causing the lights above to flicker.

I turn away from her and flip off the light switch. It's easier than punching the mirror into a million shattered pieces.

The water is cold at first, appropriate and pleasant against my skin, waking me up from the sleep I craved but couldn't find. My throat begins to tighten, making it hard to breathe. I reach down and turn the hot water all the way to the right and the temperature races from cold to warm. My breaths become shallow. My hand rests on the knob until I twist the cold knob to the left. With every twist, the temperature spikes.

If we had a normally functioning water heater, I'd probably need emergency care. Steam fills the bathtub and then the entire bathroom. It clears my airways and wakes me up on the inside. For the first time today, I'm able to feel something. My skin burns and my mind races.

I grab a towel and step out of the shower. The bathroom light flickers on. My eyes squint shut, the brightness disorienting me. "Blue?"

"Are you okay? It's like a sauna in here."

My eyes adjust to the light, and I see him standing at the doorway, steam billowing around him. "I'm good. I just needed a shower."

"It's really late," he says, rubbing the sleep from his eyes.

"I know, but I can't stay here. I need to get out."

His palm falls to the frame of the door, and he leans against it. "Where do you wanna go? I'll take you."

* * *

The moonlight bounces off the highway and the headlights shine through the darkness. Blue's too tired to say much. It seems to be a chore for him to stay awake, his eyes blinking a million times a minute. The occasional yawn from him and the tires spinning against the wet pavement break through the deafening silence. I face the window, my eyes transfixed by the forest flying behind us. Every tree passed is another memory coming back to haunt me, like that night Dylan, Tyson, Joey, Summer and I spent the night in the woods playing a never-ending game of flashlight tag.

The blinker flicks on, stealing my attention. There's a hypnotic quality to the beat of the flashing lights as we slow down, making a careful right turn onto Joey's dirt road. The rain hasn't stopped since the funeral, but it's turned into a light sprinkle. Everyone at the party is probably soaked. *Party.* What an obnoxious word in the context of what today was. It fits all the parameters of the word—after all, there are people socializing with a healthy dose of booze. Still, it feels so wrong, and calling this a *celebration of life* doesn't take the sting out of it either.

We pull to the side of the road, parking behind a string of cars, all sitting dangerously close to a foot-deep ditch. The driveway's packed with cars, and I'd bet that nobody's leaving until sunrise. The front of the farmhouse looks void of human life, and all the inside lights are out.

I hop out of the Jeep, almost jumping into the ditch. We cross the slick road, and as we make our way through the maze of parked cars, I hear people for the first time. It's a slight relief that this isn't just another loud party with drunks behaving like juveniles. This will be different. We're not here for the sole purpose of getting trashed and having fun. We are here to remember the young man we've all lost.

Behind the house is a bonfire, burning hot and high. About twenty former classmates stand around the smoldering blaze. Some have beer in their hands, other have Solo cups. Most stand with their hands in their pockets. As we move closer to the crowd, my stomach begins to come unhinged. I thought I wanted a peaceful, somber affair, but I begin to crave a long night that will lead to a total blackout. It's sudden, but I want to bury my grief in a bottle of whiskey. Everybody knows that's the simplest, most efficient way to let it all out. It also brings the bonus perk of not being able to remember.

It's Joey's party, but he's nowhere to be seen. He must be off somewhere else, doing something else. God knows what. Tyson's also absent, probably off in the forest or in the house. Maybe he's with Joey. From across the flames, Summer spots me. She leaves the circle and greets us, the hood of her soaked jacket covering her head.

"I didn't think you were coming," she says.

"I wasn't going to, but I couldn't sleep."

"I know the feeling." She looks over to Blue, and forces a grin. "Hey, fair boy."

A smile forms on my face. It's a fleeting moment of happiness, but for the first time in days, I'm able to do anything besides feel empty.

"Hi," he replies, followed by a yawn that he shakes off. "I'm going to go get a drink. You want one?"

Lying, I shake my head. When the time's right, I'll sneak off and drink on my own. Blue lets go of my hand slowly, until he knows that it's okay, and he walks toward his apartment–the garage.

"Where are Joey and Tyson?" I ask.

Summer looks behind her, then back to me, shrugging her shoulders. "I'm not sure. They were here a minute ago."

"How were they after the funeral?"

"They've been drinking since they left. They're both wasted."

"Are they okay?"

"Tonight? No," she says, and her eyes sink. "Not tomorrow, or next week, but one day they'll wake up and realize it's not healthy to hold onto the past. What about you?"

I'm the furthest thing from being okay. I know that. I'm choking on empty screams, and they're silent, but I understand deep down that in time, I'll be okay. "Give me time," I say somberly.

"I hear you on that," she says. "I already hate that I'm leaving tomorrow. I feel like I need to be here, you know?'

"Where are you going?" I ask blankly.

She cocks an eyebrow. "School."

I had forgotten about it, the fact that she was in school. She's only been gone a few weeks, so her being around these past few days remind me of the way things used to be. It also reminds me of the way things could have been, if I had followed the plan and gone to college. Maybe none of this would have happened. Dylan still would have driven drunk. He did it all the time, but he probably wouldn't have done it that night, at that time. I know I shouldn't blame myself, but I can't turn off the split-screen movie running fervently through my mind, stuck on replay. On one side of the reel is reality, and on the other, an alternate reality where everything isn't so fucked up.

"I really wish I could stay," she says.

I perk up. Maybe it's time for a new reality for myself. "I wish I could go with you."

She places her palm on my shoulder, gripping me just tight enough that it's comforting. "You have no idea how much I would like that." She smiles. "But you've got things here you need to take care of."

She reminds me of what I already know, though something tells me that she's talking more about my mom than Blue. She probably doesn't know my mom is much better, or how quickly the change transpired. Involuntarily, I frown, reflecting on my decisions and the things I have no control over.

"There's always next semester, though. You should really consider it," she says with enthusiasm.

"Consider what?" Blue asks from behind me.

I turn to him. He's holding two beers, one in each hand. That's my Blue, always doing the right thing, even when he's been told not to. "Nothing important." I don't want him to know I'm thinking about leaving just as we're growing closer. Columbus isn't too far from Lakeview, but going away to college, no matter the distance, brings its fair share of complications. Especially for a newer couple, and we have enough complications as it is. In my mind, as it stands, I can have one or the other—Blue or an education.

I grab a beer and take a short sip. It's cool and calming. An arm wraps around my neck, pulling me in for a hug from the back. "Charlie," Joey slurs. The scent of malt overpowers me. He pulls back, looks at Blue, and gives him an unpleasant nod. "I'll be right back."

He walks between Blue and me. I sense his intention is to cut between us with purpose, and he does. Blue rubs his hand across my back. Joey chuckles wickedly, and then spins around on one foot, almost fumbling to the ground. "Could you stop doing that?"

Stop doing what?

"Stop pretending like you're so in love, and if you are in love, stop that, too. It's making me nauseous." He grimaces.

"Joey," I plead softly, hoping he'll leave it alone.

"What, Charlie?" he asks with a mocking tone. "Don't want to hear what everybody's thinking?" His hands wave in the air, a can of beer about to fly across the red sky.

"We're all hurting."

"He's dead, Charlie. Dylan is dead." It's starting to turn into a scene as random heads crane toward us. "Remember him? You used to love him, and now he's just some dead guy you used to know."

Blue steps forward, putting an arm around Joey. "Okay, I think that's enough. Let's go for a walk."

Joey brushes Blue off him, his face distorted. "Don't touch me."

"Come on," Blue says.

Joey ignores him and laughs a little. "Seriously, Charlie? Can you take your boyfriend somewhere else? You're not welcome here."

Fuck you. "You're just drunk," I say, on the verge of tears. He's too drunk to cry. The sadness is gone, lost somewhere in the bottom of a bottle, and all that's left is anger.

"Tell me something I don't know." He stumbles backward. Blue grabs onto his arm, steadying him. Joey glares at him. "Didn't I tell you to leave?"

"Sorry, cousin, I'm not going anywhere."

I go to move toward the testosterone, but Summer holds me back, wrapping an arm around me.

"Is that right?" Joey asks. Blue answers with a nod and receives a quick punch to the face. I race toward Blue as he fumbles backward. I catch him in my arms and shake my head at Joey.

"You might want to have a doctor check that out," Joey says smugly, shaking off his fist. "In other words, leave."

I hold Blue in my arms, still recovering from the punch. He pushes back against me and throws himself toward Joey, tackling him to the ground.

"Blue!" I scream as the boys scrap in the grass.

"Get off me," Joey grunts as Blue pulls his fist back, ready to punch, but it just sits there, floating in the air, shaking in hesitation. He pulls himself off Joey, who scrambles against the ground before taking off. Blue turns to look at me, probably to comfort me, but I'm already gone.

I walk toward the edge of the forest in search of a refuge far from the light of the burning fire. The branches hang high, casting ominous shadows onto the ground below me. Behind me, I hear someone, probably Blue, beginning to give chase and my brisk pace turns into a sprint. At first, I just needed to get away from Joey and Blue, but now I just want to run until I see the sun.

My heart races, skipping a beat as I almost crash into a tree. There's a good chance that I've lost whoever followed me into the woods, so I slide my body against the trunk of the tree. The nothingness is exactly what I need.

CHAPTER TWENTY-ONE

I sit against the tree, not moving and unable to think about anything beyond pondering how long it'll be until the sun rises. My best guess is that I'm at least six hours away from the peace I crave and when the sun will warm me again.

A twig snaps violently in half, and I know I've been found.

"When a girl flees into the forest, that's usually a pretty good sign that she wants to be alone."

"Maybe," Blue replies through the darkness.

"Definitely."

As he draws closer to me, the outline of his body forms against an easel of darkness. Piercing rays sent from the moon shoot holes through his clothing. "You never have to be alone."

"I've been surrounded by the people that I love for days, and I've still never felt more alone, so maybe this is exactly what I need."

"I don't think it is." He moves closer still.

"Please, don't take another step."

"All right." He nods and finds a tree of his own, sliding down the trunk of it and kicking his feet out into the dirt.

My eyes roll. "Please, Blue."

"Sorry," he says. "I'm not leaving. There could be bears out here, or lions, or tigers."

"This isn't a zoo."

"I think it's best to stay on this side of caution."

I push my head back, against the tree. Maybe my silence will bore him.

"I could stay here all night," he muses out loud, and brushes leaves and twigs out from under him. "It's comfortable, quiet, and a little too dark."

"Fine, you want to know what's on my mind?"

"Every scary detail."

"I miss being that smartass, life-loving girl I used to be. It's only been a few days since my world was turned upside down, but I feel like an asteroid losing pieces with every minute that ticks by. I just want to be that girl again, and I have no idea how to get her back."

"The first step is to not worry about it." I can see him look at me through the blackness. "The second step is to just wake up some random day—it'll be the day you're least expecting, but you'll be okay."

"You seem to know a thing or two about it."

"I've been through loss. It sucks." He brings himself to his feet and begins moving toward me, the light of the moon shining upon him. "I know what it's like to want to scream so loud that astronauts can hear you. I know what it's like to be stuck in quicksand, suffocating and drowning, because the world won't let you stand up."

I stand up with the world's permission, as he closes in on me, reaching into my heart while reading all the hurt. "You get it."

He shrugs. "Like you said, I know a thing or two."

This is the worst thing I could possibly say. "I need you to know something, and it's not easy to say. It's probably harder to hear, but I would do anything to have him back. Even if it meant rewinding time and changing everything."

His face goes blank as he processes what I've just said, knowing full well what I meant. I would leave him, even if it meant dooming myself to an ordinary life with Dylan. "I wouldn't blame you," he says.

I shake my head. "How can you be so understanding of that?"

"Because I told you that I love you, and despite my tendency to lie about the little things, I'd never lie about something so big. And it *is* big, because you're my whole world now."

He really is something special.

"And I know that I can't be your whole world right now, but I've got enough patience to last a lifetime."

"Is that so?"

His lips purse. "Well, maybe not that long."

I lean in, pushing my weight against him. Standing on my toes, I kiss him softly, but I want so much more. When I go back in, this time with more passion, he pulls back but holds me at the waist. "I don't want a repeat of earlier."

"What do you mean?"

"If we're going to have sex," he says contemplatively, "I want it to be because you want me, not because you're looking for anything else."

"Most guys would jump at the chance to bang a girl against a tree."

He snickers and brushes his hand through my hair. "I'm not like other guys, remember?"

"How could I forget?" I smile, knowing that there's a light at the end of this road.

"Now, come on. Let's get out of here before we're mauled by a bear."

* * *

We exit the forest after what feels like hours to find a dying fire devoid of life surrounding it. The driveway is almost barren, which means there are a lot of drunk drivers on the road, or there were enough people here with the common sense to refrain from drinking. After what happened to Dylan, I must force myself to have faith that it's the latter.

"Charlie," Tyson calls out. "Come help me."

I search for him and I spot him propping Joey up against the side of the house. Blue and I rush to them. Joey is too intoxicated to stay awake, or even stand. His eyes are heavier than a cloud before a thunderstorm. Blue's stronger than me, obviously, but I don't think it's a good idea for him to assist Tyson in carrying Joey into the house, even if they are cousins.

Tyson and I pick Joey up off the ground, each pulling an arm around our necks. We're a little too efficient for our complete lack of experience as we quickly ascend the steps. Blue holds the door open as we stumble into the house.

"I don't want to carry him up the steps to his bedroom," Tyson says with a light laugh. "I'm too drunk for that."

"Let's just put him on the couch," I reply.

We move to the couch and lay him down gently. He jerks awake before folding his hands under his head and seemingly drifting back off.

"Should we take off his boots?" Blue asks.

I shake my head. "No, he's weird. He likes sleeping in them when he's drunk."

"You're right," he says quietly. "That *is* weird."

By itself, it means nothing, but for the first time, I realize that I know Joey better than his own cousin knows him. I don't have any cousins myself, but I wonder how close we'd be if I did. I have a mom and that's about it as far as family is concerned. Sure, technically, I have a dad too, but... yeah. I now understand why the loss of Dylan hurts so much, besides the obvious, because he was more than just an ex, more than just a friend—he was a part of our family.

Tyson stumbles up the steps, and the real reason he didn't want to carry Joey up there becomes clear. He wanted the bed to himself and I don't blame him. Blue's at the door, waiting for me, but I get lost watching Joey sleep. He's survived the longest, toughest day of his life, and now, at day's end, he's able to find some peace.

"Charlie," he says, his eyes blinking open.

"I'm going to bed, Joey. I'll see you in the morning." I turn to walk away.

"Come here," he mumbles.

A part of me doesn't want to while another part of me, the better part, knows I have to. I wave at Blue, who steps out onto the porch, shutting the screen door behind him.

"What?" I ask Joey as I approach the couch, hoping for an apology but expecting the worst.

"It's about earlier."

"It's okay." I rub his shoulder. "We can talk about it later."

"I meant it."

No apology, then...

"You can't be with Blue."

* * *

Every time I wake up next to Blue, I feel something different. Like I've been a million different people since the day I met him. This time I have no choice but to run. I've been lying here awake for at least an hour, alternating between staring out the window, at the ceiling, and at him. There's a darkness around his right eye that threatens to turn into a bruise before he awakes. Any second now, I'll make my move. If I wait any longer than that, he'll wake up, and I'll never have this choice again.

In many ways, Joey was right. I can't be with Blue with this weight over me. In the brief time I've known him, less than thirty days, I've fallen for him in every way you can fall for someone. I've been to ecstasy and back, but like all the best things in the world, the timing couldn't be worse.

We went to bed in his apartment above his uncle's garage in a quiet understanding. An agreement that we could work everything out if we're just patient with it. Of course, he didn't know what Joey had said to me or what it meant—the idea that my relationship is hurting those I care about.

Gently, I push the white sheets off me and to the side. I grab my jacket off the floor and creep toward the edge of the room. The door is silent as I pull it open. I pass through the frame, and then turn my head over my shoulder. He's so peaceful and happy as he sleeps. Either he's in the midst of a great dream or he's not dreaming at all. It feels like I'm running away from him. More than that, I feel as if I'm leaving him. And it's not because I don't love him. It's because I love him too much. If I can force us to take a break, then maybe we can pick up again right where we left off when I'm able to be that girl that he fell in love with.

I'm too lost, too angry, too bitter, too emotional, and too unstable to be with right now. He deserves better than a girl who changes her mind every other scene.

* * *

The rain must have picked up again, and then promptly ended just a few short hours ago. Puddles are formed in the road. My mom, in her car, comes to a stop beside me. I open the door and hop in with no intention of saying a word.

She steps on the gas, spinning rain against the asphalt. "I wish you would tell me what's wrong."

"Why does anything have to be wrong?" I ask, staring blankly out the window.

"Because I'm picking you up at seven in the morning after just getting home from a flight two hours ago." There's concern in her voice, like she senses the hell I'm going through. "I'm sorry I've been gone these past few days."

"Can you just drive?" I say deadpan.

Her thumbs tap against the wheel. "You're really not going to tell me?"

"No." It's not like I don't want to, because I do. But lying to myself is enough lying for the day. What the hell am I doing, anyway? I should have her drop me back off at Joey's, but we're already back on the main road, and I don't have the energy to tell her to turn around. I'd just change my mind, anyway.

CHAPTER TWENTY-TWO

I'm sitting on the kitchen counter, lost in a daze as I stare at pictures on the refrigerator. There's one picture in particular that I can't take my eyes away from. It was taken about ten years ago at the local park. There's five of us in it—Summer, Tyson, Joey, Dylan, and me. We're all smiling from ear to ear, and it's an innocence that none of us will ever get back. The picture itself is comforting, but the happiness is hidden under layers of pain.

My phone vibrates against the counter, and I don't even need to see who is calling. I know it's Blue. I turn the ringer off and contemplate tossing the phone into a glass of water. Seven missed calls and it's only a quarter past noon. Compared to yesterday, when there were twenty, it's a relief.

Mom walks into the kitchen. "Your phone's ringing," she says as she grabs the coffeepot. She acts as if she's out of the loop, but something tells me she knows what's going on. "Why don't you answer it?"

I shrug. "It's just a bill collector."

She turns to me, coffee in one hand. "You don't have any bills."

Busted. My upper lip sinks into my lower lip and I nod. "Touché."

"I know you think I can't or won't understand," she says and steps closer to me. "But give me a chance." She takes another step, and I'm thinking that if she comes any closer, I might just run.

"You know I don't want to talk about it, so why keep trying?"

"Because you're hurting, and I wish there was something I could do."

"*Nothing* seems like a perfect alternative."

"I can't do that. You're my daughter, and it's killing me to see you this way."

"Then don't," I say. The words come out angry and that's become perfectly normal over the course of the past few days. I've lost control of my emotions and I'm within an inch of a temporary bipolar diagnosis. Maybe it's just a fleeting bout of depression. If I wake up a year from now and still feel this way, I'll seek some sort of help. But right now, I can't help but believe my behavior is as normal as can be for an eighteen-year-old girl who just lost her best friend.

"Being angry at the world won't solve your problems."

"It'll have to do for now," I say and hop off the counter. My feet slam into the floor and I brush past her.

"Charlie," she calls to me.

I ignore her, grab my hooded jacket, and rush out the front door.

"Charlie!" Joey calls out to me. Just my fucking luck. I pivot and put my hand on the doorknob. I don't want to talk to Joey and I don't want sympathy from my mother. It's a tough call.

"What do you want, Joey?" I say with my head down.

"I just wanna talk to you."

A sigh escapes my lips, and I turn around to face him. He has both hands in the pockets of his jeans. "Is that so?"

He just nods his head.

"Got something else you want to get off your chest?"

"Kind of," he says as he pulls his left hand out of his pocket and scratches his head. There's a hesitation in his voice, so I take the lead.

"What is it? Did you leave a few key words out of your drunken truth-bomb rant?"

"It's not like that."

"It's exactly like that, Joey!" I yell as my voice breaks.

"I just wanted to say—"

"For you to question how much I loved him." I jab a finger at him, scolding him like he's a child. "And Blue, you attacked him!"

"I really am sorry."

"That makes it all better. Erases everything. Really, what do you want? A hug?"

He wipes his eye with the corner of his hand. It's not something you see every day, but I've seen it a lot lately. Strong men showing emotion. My stomach turns. I can't do this. I can't be that person who lashes out, hurting others. There's a moment of silence where neither of us says anything. "What happened to us?" I ask with a laugh, but I'm not being funny.

He shrugs. "I don't know. I guess we're all just fucked up."

There's another pause where neither of us says a word.

"Do you think we'll ever get things back to the way they used to be?" he asks. I'm not sure if he really expects an answer, or if it's just some kind of deep thought that he's posing as a question.

I purse my lips. "I don't know. Everything just feels so broken."

"If it makes it any better, I apologized to Blue. Bought him a bottle of whiskey."

Every time I hear his name, I think of him. More than that, I see him—that face, that smile, those beautiful fucking eyes.

"How is he?" I scrape my shoe against the asphalt.

"Blue?" he asks. "Haven't seen him much. He hasn't really been home."

I clench my eyes shut and pinch the bridge of my nose.

"You're not ignoring him because of me, are you?"

"No." I open my eyes. "Maybe. I just need a little space and a little time."

"He really is a good guy."

I nod my head. "Yeah, he is."

He moves toward me and places his palm on my shoulder. "I've gotta go. It's my first day back to work." He pulls his hand back, readying himself to walk away.

I practically lunge at him, wrapping both arms around him, and rest my head against his chest. It takes a moment, but his hands come down and embrace me. I want to cry, but my eyes are dry. Maybe

I am crying, but inside... All I know is that these last seventy-two hours without physical affection have taken a toll on me, and there isn't anywhere else in the world I'd rather be right now than here, being held.

That's a lie. There is one place I'd rather be–in Blue's arms, but I've mucked that up.

"I've gotta go," he says under his breath.

I pull back and his arms slide out from around me.

"Take care," I say.

He nods, then turns to walk away. But I have one more thing to say. "Yes."

Curious, he turns back around, but still walks.

"Yes. I think we'll get things back to the way they were." I force a smile. "Someday."

His eyes trail to the corner, then back toward me. "Yeah. Someday."

I watch him as he walks away. His hands fall back into his pockets.

And then it hits me. He's going back to work at the place he used to spend his days with his best friend. At the garage. I'm not sure how he's going to do it. I know that I couldn't. My eyes dampen and it brings me an odd sense of relief. I wipe away the tears and know that I'm going to be okay. Just not today.

* * *

My life is turning into a Hallmark movie. That's the only explanation I can think of as to why it rains every time I visit this place. Dylan's grave is covered in flowers that are now drowning in a pool of mud. As a temporary headstone, a large toy tractor sits where the mound of dirt meets the grass. That was his favorite toy growing up.

While most of my childhood is a blur, I have vivid memories of the day he brought that tractor in to class for show and tell. I was a childhood cliché and brought a collection of Barbies in to class that Friday afternoon. After class was over, we snuck out of school.

Our parents found us outside on the playground. There's a photo around somewhere to prove it, but it's been long forgotten about by everyone but me. In my memory, and in that picture, we are both crawling on the ground. I hold my prized Barbie on top of his tractor while he pushes it through the grass. Our parents were worried sick about us and had every right to be angry. But they weren't angry. At least we didn't notice if they were. Maybe the childhood bliss that flashed across our faces made them forget our transgression.

I'm soaked, but it's warm enough out for me not to care. The sadness that I felt the last time I was here, the day of Dylan's funeral, is gone. It's been replaced with an odd sense of peace. I read online that some people experience a downtime of depression after taking Molly. For some people, it only lasts a few days, and for others, it can last weeks. I would guess that I'm one of those in the latter category, the after-effects of the drug pulling tight on my already broken heart.

"Hey, Charlie," Blue says quietly from behind me. I don't even need to turn around to know it's him, but his finding me is just my luck.

"Do I have a tracker in my arm or something?" I ask.

"I'm not sure. I haven't seen your medical transcripts lately."

That's just the type of corny joke I love. The fact that I don't laugh is troubling.

"It's just a bad joke."

I turn around. "Really? You mean you weren't serious?"

His hair is tousled and wet, looking like it's grown at least an inch over the past few days. Now I know that's not possible; he just looks different. His eyes are sunken like he hasn't been sleeping. I guess that makes us twins. He's wearing torn jeans, boots, and a tight-fitting plain white tee, the rain outlining every single line of his body. He's starting to look like one of them. And by one of them, I mean Joey and Tyson. And Dylan. You know what they say about women who spend too much time together? That scientific discovery that their periods will actually sync? Well something like that seems to happen to the boys in this town.

"I don't want to sound like *that* guy, but I've really missed you."

I push my hair behind my ear. "I've missed you, too."

He moves toward me like he's about to embrace me or something. It's not a conscious choice, but I lean back. He gets the hint and stops.

"What's wrong?" he asks.

I need a second to think about the answer. It's right on the tip of my tongue, but it's not ready to come out. I look everywhere but at him. "The world."

"That's mysterious," he says with a nod, "but I get it."

My eyes catch his. "Do you?"

"I figured it out about fifteen minutes after I woke up."

"Sorry about that."

"For leaving? Don't be. Like I said, I get it."

I begin playing with my hair. I'm sure it annoys everyone but me when I do it.

He gets closer and this time I don't pull back. "You're hurt. You're scared. You're kind of lost. The world's spinning and you just wanna jump off?"

"Something like that."

"Let me get off with you."

A chuckle escapes my throat. Blue's eyes squint and I can tell he's a little frustrated. "That's not what I meant."

"I know," I say and straighten my face out, back into serious mode. Those two words reminding me how terribly lost I've been.

"What I'm trying to say is that we all get lost sometimes. Just like you're lost now, I was lost when I met you." The rain rolls off the edge of his lips. "I think I'm still kind of lost, like I'm all the way out there on Venus or wherever the hell it is that you girls come from."

"Blue," I interject.

"No. I'm going to finish because I'm not going to take the chance that you're going to say something stupid."

"Stupid?" I ask, offended.

"Please, let me finish."

My hand pats against my jeans. "Fine."

"So I'm out there on Venus, but it's you who always brings me back to Earth. Like you're the Sun and I'm the Moon, and I know that we belong together because, hey, gravity."

Strangely, I get his point. Even if he's getting to said point in a rather contrived fashion. I wonder aloud, "One might think you're on drugs or something with all this *Plato-ing*."

"I want to say that your love is my drug, but I think I'm all cheesed out." He smiles and it's a relief.

"That's probably a good thing." I roll my tongue across my lip. "Now, can I say something stupid?"

"About that, I didn't mean to—"

"Look, I love you and that's not a question, it's a fact. Some days, I wake up and know that I want to spend the rest of my life with you. Other days, it's a neon blur. It's like I don't know who I am anymore."

It's quick and it's gentle, but his palms grab me and hold me by the cheeks. "I know who you are. You're Charlie. Sweet, beautiful, smart as fuck Charlie—the girl that I'm going to spend the rest of my life with. Everybody gets lost at some point, but I'm here to remind you exactly who you are."

His words silence me. His eyes lock with mine like two soldiers about to go to war. My lip trembles and I feel as if I'm about to break.

"Okay," he whispers.

Okay, what? Then his lips are on mine. They're rough, but moist from the rain. It takes me by surprise, but within a second, that wears off and I grab him by the waist, pulling him closer. His hands caress my face, moving to the same rhythm as his tongue. His hands slide into my hair. As I pull back to breathe, I can feel his fingers combing through my locks.

"I love you." His voice is strong, completely devoid of doubt. He's on solid foundation and knows exactly what he wants. I wish I were as sure as he is that this can work out, but I'm sure enough that I kiss him back.

Like the ending of a Hallmark movie, the sun beams through the clouds and the rains subside just as we are locked in a passionate embrace. There's nowhere in the world I'd rather be than here, and I don't mean the cemetery. I mean here in his arms.

CHAPTER TWENTY-THREE

Blue and I walk down the empty Sunday street. There's something unsettling in the air, like somehow our town has turned into a wasteland overnight. It's past five, so everyone must be home with their families, recovering from a hangover, or just being lazy. I don't know, but it's not normal for the streets to be this dead, even in a small town like Lakeview.

It's nice, however, to be walking and nothing else. Just Blue and me enjoying each other's company. The thoughts in my head are settled, and I think it's the first time for as long as I can remember. I never realized how exhausting my overpowering inner monologue was until it's no longer dominating every ounce of me. Not thinking about the world is a nice change of pace, and I never thought I'd say it, but I enjoy the emptiness. The stillness of it all is refreshing.

We turn a corner onto Old Main Street, which is exactly what you would guess. It's the old Main Street. There was a fire when I was young. It spread from shop to shop until the entire block was on fire. They never bothered to rebuild, but it's always eluded me why they never tore all the hollow buildings down. It's nothing but a memorial of tragedy.

There's a man standing in the center of the sidewalk up ahead by about fifty feet. He's not moving, like he's waiting for something. I'm not sure what for, exactly, but it's certainly a dramatic statement.

He's probably on drugs.

The last thing I want to do is talk shit about drug addicts, especially given my recent history, but over the past year, drugs have really begun to rear their ugly head in this town. Drug addiction is sad and it's avoidable. I hope I never get to that point because I don't agree with the *drugs are bad* slogans that are thrown around high school auditoriums across the country. Drug addiction is complex, and I don't think anyone ever sees it coming. It just sort of happens.

A chill runs down my arms as we draw closer to the man. There's something wrong, and I can't put my finger on it. When we're a few feet away from him, he turns around, and he has this mischievous smile on his face. Something is definitely wrong.

Blue squeezes my hand tight and comes to an abrupt halt. I feel as if my bones are about to crack, so I pull my hand away from him. A haunting pale color fills his face and his cheekbones pull tight.

"Blue?" I ask softly. When he doesn't respond, I turn to the man, dressed in dark clothing. His face is rough and unshaven. One of his eyes is pinched, permanently half shut. He's locked into a childish staring war with Blue.

The man raises his eyebrows, and I think he's about to speak.

"Hi, Blue."

"Rake," Blue responds tensely. They know each other, and I can smell the aroma of testosterone in the air. "What are you doing here?"

"I'm just visiting," Rake says. "What about you?"

"That's none of your business."

Rake laughs and it's dramatic, over the top, and completely fake. "You are my business, Blue."

"Get out of here," Blue huffs. I glance at Rake, then at Blue. The man's not moving a muscle, much less his legs. I don't think he has any intention of leaving. "I mean it, Charlie. Go."

Wait. You're talking about me? "Blue?"

"Just go."

"I'm not going anywhere."

"Yeah," the man says, "I think she should stay."

It's silent. Blue scratches his nose with his forefinger, then chuckles. "Yeah, she should stay."

Blue's balls his hand into a fist, and without notice or pause, he strikes the man hard in the face. The man stumbles back. Blue grabs my hand and pulls me away. He picks up the pace and jogging turns into sprinting. I can barely keep up with him. I turn my head to look back, but my hair flies into my face, and I can't see much.

The man stands up and reaches behind him. He pulls a gun.

"He's got a gun!" I scream at Blue.

Blue looks behind us, then rips me sideways. I hear gunfire. This is so not the way I wanted my life to end. The pain is sudden. The skin of my knee burns and my head cracks against the pavement. I pull my hand up to cradle my throbbing head.

Everything's a blur, both sight and sound. Blue is yelling something, but I can't quite make out what. My body rises up off the ground and Blue's face becomes clear. "Are you okay?"

Am I? I take stock of myself. I realize that I wasn't shot, but instead, the pain I feel is from being pulled into an alley by Blue. "I'm good."

"We have to go."

Boots pad against the sidewalk and I know the man is approaching. Blue grabs my hand and we begin to run again. Up ahead at the end of the alley is Third Street. If we can get there, we'll be safe. For now, anyway.

As we exit the alley, I turn around one last time and see the man turning into the alley on the opposite end.

* * *

We're both out of breath as we come to a stop behind a church on Sixth Street. We've lost the man, but something tells me that he's going to keep looking for us. Blue slides down the wall of the church, and comes to rest with his legs kicked out. I'm tired, confused, scared, and a little angry that I was almost shot.

"We need to call the police," I say through ragged breaths.

He pounds his fist against the wall behind him. "We can't do that."

"What?" I shake my head. "Why not?"

"Just trust me on this."

"I don't know how it works on the carnival circuit, but out here in the real world, we call the police when someone tries to shoot us." I wait for a response, but he just rubs his palms against his knees. "You know what? I'm going home."

"You can't."

I scoff. "I'm fairly certain that I can."

He stands up, his back pulling away from the wall. "I don't think you understand how serious this is."

"What are you talking about? Of course I know it's serious, hence my burning need to call the police."

"Do you want to lose me?" he asks, scraping his boot across the ground.

"That's a rather stupid question, don't you think?" And it has nothing to do with this.

"If I told you the truth, could you handle it? If the truth changed everything, would you still love me?"

"Nothing can change the way I feel." I move to him. "But I always need the truth."

"The truth can be worse than ignorance."

"Just tell me what's going on."

He shakes his head. "I don't know if I can."

"I just love it when you act coy," I say. His lips pull tight, and he looks everywhere but at me. "That's sarcasm, by the way."

"I'm trying to protect you," he says and I believe him. I just want to know what he's protecting me from.

"I can handle the truth."

"Fine," he sighs. "You might wanna sit down."

"I'd rather stand."

He thumbs his lip. "The truth is that I've sold drugs for my dad since I was fourteen years old. The man who was chasing us? His name's Rake, and I killed his brother, Trey." There's sorrow in his voice.

"I've changed my mind. I need to sit down." I pass him and take a resting position against the church exterior, preparing for the worst. I'm in love with a murderer. Any sane person would run, but I wouldn't make it out of the church driveway before hitting the pavement. "I can't believe you would keep this from me."

"That's not really fair. What is it that you wanted me to say? It's not exactly a great conversation starter." He reaches out his palm, pretending to meet me for the first time. "Hi, my name's Blue and I'm a carnie. By the way, I killed someone once."

"Point taken."

"Can I continue now?"

I nod, unsure why I haven't started to run.

"There was a mix-up and things got heated. I was selling coke for Trey, two ounces. I had it stored in my dad's camper, and when I went to get it, he said that the camper was broken into and the drugs were stolen. I didn't believe him then, and I don't believe him now."

"That explains that," I interrupt, under my breath, referencing the disdain he has for his dad.

"When Trey came to collect, I tried to explain what had happened. I tried to make a deal, but he pulled a gun on me and Cookie." He shakes his head, his face zoning in on the past. "He was high and he wouldn't listen. I was able to wrestle the gun from his hands, but he pulled a knife and charged me. The gun flew out of my hand. He was about to kill me when Cookie shot him."

I stand up, relieved. "So you didn't kill him."

"Does it matter who pulled the trigger?" he asks with a dazed look. "I took the blame with Trey's family because I knew they wouldn't go to the police. I accepted whatever fate I had resigned myself to and I thought it was over, but I guess I was wrong."

"Have you tried talking to him?"

The *no shit* expression on his face speaks volumes. "Did you see that man? That's not somebody you can easily reason with."

"What about the truth?"

"Point the finger at Cookie?" He bites into his lip. "That's not gonna happen."

"You would lose everything for him?" I ask angrily.

"He saved my life."

I stare down at my hands, my thumbs digging into each other. "Then what are you going to do?"

He lets out an exasperated sigh and pulls against his short hair. "I don't know. The only thing I can think to do is run."

My eyes widen. "I'm not going anywhere."

"If you stay, then I stay, because he knows your face and your name. He's lost everything, with nothing left to lose, and he won't stop until he has blood."

"What does that have to do with me?"

"If you think he won't hurt you to get to me, then you're naive."

"Sorry, I don't have a lot of experience hanging out with psychopaths!"

"You think I wanted this?" he yells. "It's the reason I left the carnival. It wasn't because I hated the job, or the hours, or the traveling. It's because every day I spent there was another day I risked losing myself to the person I used to be. And then I met you." His voice softens. "And I fell for you in ways I didn't know were possible. You gave me the world, a reason to leave everything else behind. A reason to keep the past in the past."

"Let's call the police," I plead. "They'll understand."

"That a man was killed during a drug deal? There are no innocent parties in the eyes of the law."

An urgency to speak rushes over me, thinking if I hesitate, I might not say a word. "Then kill him," I say, deadpan. My mouth drops in shock at my own words.

His head shakes. "I can't do that."

"Why not?" I ask dryly, unable to back down. If Rake is as dangerous as Blue says, then I don't see any other way.

"Because I understand his anger and his pain. And stopping him right now means going down a road I can't go down. You want me to handle him, but I'm telling you that I can't. I will run from him, I will hide. I will beat him into the ground if I have to, but there's already been too much blood."

"I love you, Blue..."

"What do you want to do?"

I throw my hands in the air. "It doesn't matter what I want, does it? You've backed me into a corner with no real options. Either I go with you and leave everything I've ever known behind, or I stay here, spending every minute of every day looking over my shoulder."

"I'm sorry. I didn't want any of this." He stares at the gravel beneath us.

"I know that." I close my eyes tight, hoping the darkness behind them will give me some insight. Nothing comes.

His hand falls onto my shoulder, gently caressing me. "Look at me."

I do as I'm told, staring deep into his eyes.

"There's a way to fix all of this." He rubs his palm against my cheek. I move into his touch. "I just need to figure it out, but until then, I don't think we have any choice but to run."

I laugh lightly, a little because I'm uncomfortable, but mostly because I never saw any of it coming. "I've wanted to leave this town for so long."

A faux smile forms on his face as he tries to make the best out of this impossible situation. "That's a silver lining right there."

"I just never thought it'd be this way."

He caresses my arm, assuring me that everything will eventually be okay. "We'll leave tonight."

I step back. "That's not enough time."

"Just pack a few bags and don't tell anyone where you're going," he says, forming a plan out loud and conveniently ignoring me.

"Where will we go?"

"Wherever the road takes us."

I step back further.

"It's not like I was expecting this."

"Promise me something," I say.

"Anything."

"Promise that we can be happy away from here."

"That's easy." His smile lights up my soul. "You're the only home I've ever had."

"I'm not a house, Blue."

"That's not what home is. Now, I need to pick something up from the carnival. Can you meet me there?"

"Yeah," I say, processing the last five minutes. There's a swelling of energy in my legs, because I'm more than ready to run.

CHAPTER TWENTY-FOUR

Good or bad, everyone will have something to say about your relationship. Your head will certainly have an opinion of its own. Armed with boxing gloves, it'll be ready to knock your heart out in one punch. Your heart can't possibly know what it's talking about, because it lacks the computing power to fully understand the consequences of love. Conversely, the brain thinks too much, and it can never calculate an arbitrary equation as complex as love. The arithmetic simply isn't there.

So, yeah, there's a war brewing deep in my bones. They're going to fight to the death, but something tells me I'm the only one who's going to lose anything. I'm going to lose my future or I'm going to lose Blue. I've already lost too much and I'm going to war to keep them both, armed with nothing but desperation.

I should go with him. I should stay here. Every second I allow my brain to think, I change my mind. It's exhausting. I crank up the music as I drive home, hoping the blaring bass will drown out any more decision-making my brain attempts.

I think of the people I'm leaving behind and have to remind myself that I won't be gone forever. Just long enough for Blue to figure out what he's going to do. And this could be a good thing for me too, getting away from all the pain and bullshit of the past month. I've never been one to run away from my problems, but that's probably because I've never really had actual problems before. I'm new to this adult thing and I don't think I'm cut out for it.

I pull into my driveway and put the car into park. I still have time to change my mind. I get out of the car and gently close the door. My mom will be home in less than an hour.

* * *

It's funny how one thing changes a million other things. I stare at the pictures of my friends and family taped to the corners of my mirror–I'm old-fashioned that way. Born in the wrong decade, I tell you. But that's not the point. The point is that my bedroom feels distant, strange, and unfamiliar, like it's not even my room anymore.

I felt the same way as I ascended the steps. I was walking on foreign carpets. I'm not sure if this is something everyone goes through when they leave home, or if it's a special feeling reserved for those of us fortunate enough to experience a crazy carnival ride at such a young age. I'm part of a special club now.

The duffel bag on my bed is almost full, stuffed to the top with randomly selected clothing. I've barely made a dent in my closet, but it's not like I'm moving out. I'm running away. It's a far cry from the days I used to daydream of leaving for college. My family and friends would be here to send me off in a U-Haul packed with everything in this room and my mom's sofa because it's the most comfortable damn thing I've ever had the privilege to sleep on.

I grab a blank sheet of paper that sits alone in my printer. I'm not sure what to say even as I begin to scribble a note—it's been a while since I've written anything by hand, and it shows. I leave the completed note on my bed, held down by a snow-globe with a picture of me and Summer in it.

I zip up my bag and take one long glance at my room before I gently shut the door. It's really goodbye and it's not until I'm well out the front door that I process the letter I just wrote for my mother. It was meant as a goodbye-for-now letter but reads much more like fiction. In the future, when all the dust has settled, maybe I'll try my hand at being a writer.

Mom,

I wish things could have been different. I wish I could be the perfect daughter. I wish a lot of things these days, but most of all, I wish I had the courage to tell you goodbye.

But I know that you love me unconditionally, and because of that love, you would have convinced me to stay. And you would be right, but that's not what I need right now.

But I love you too. And I'll be home. Someday.

Love, Charlie

I throw my bag into the backseat of the car, and then take another longing glance at the house I grew up in—the house that built me, if you will. The foundation is cracking, and I hope there's still a house standing whenever I decide to come back.

* * *

Tyson sits in the passenger seat. He's quiet, but so am I. He hasn't said much since I told him I was leaving town. I think he's mulling it over in his head, either trying to process it or come up with a reasonable plea to make me stay.

"I like Blue," he says, breaking the silence. "I mean, you have to take the good with the bad."

I turn to him, knowing full well that I should keep my eyes on the road. "Is it too much bad, though?"

"Not if you love him." He shrugs. "I guess."

His words soak in and I nod in agreement.

"Road, Charlie!" he yells and points ahead.

I'm straddling the lanes like a cowgirl. I jerk the wheel to the right to correct myself. "It's not like I'm not coming back," I say. "I am. Someday."

His turn to look at me. This is definitely a safer way to communicate, even if I can feel his judgment, although not vocalized, poking and prodding against the side of my face.

"What's the plan again?" he asks.

"I'm meeting Blue at the carnival, and then I need you to take my car back home."

"Right." There's a smirk on his face.

"Tyson..."

"What? I just wanna take it for a short drive."

Tyson is that unfortunate kid in every town who has those parents who believe their kids must work for their first car. He's been working since he was seventeen, but he spends way too much of his pay on all the stupid things we all spend our own cash on. It's a rough life.

"Just make sure it's in my mom's driveway before noon tomorrow."

He flashes a wide grin. "Sure thing."

We pull into the packed field of the carnival. I drive up and down the aisles of the lot searching for Blue's Jeep. It takes a good few minutes before I see it parked underneath a large tree. I pull in beside it.

Tyson jumps out of the car, opens the door to the backseat, and grabs my bags. A perfect gentleman. He tosses them into the back of the Jeep.

I make my way around the car to find him swaying on his feet, both hands deep in his pockets. "Do you think I'm making a mistake?"

"I don't believe in mistakes."

I nod in newfound agreement. "I wish I could say goodbye to everyone."

"I'll give them the message."

"How angry do you think they're going to be?"

"Pretty pissed." He smiles and caresses the thick air with his hand. "But I'll smooth it over."

"I don't want to make this any harder than it has to be, so I should—"

His arms circle around me, hugging me tight. "Just promise you'll call whenever you get where you're going," he says quietly against my ear.

I pull back, brushing the length of his arms. "I promise."

We give each other knowing looks, the kind that says a less formal, final version of goodbye. With a nod of my head, I turn and begin my journey toward my new life.

"I get it," he says.

I turn around, waiting for the rest of his sentence.

"I know why you're leaving. I'd do the same thing."

I just smile.

"Plus, he's kind of hot..."

I rush toward him, embracing him. If I hold him any tighter, his head would probably pop off. "You were always the best of us."

"I know." He grins. "You should go find Blue."

There are tears in my eyes when I walk away. I don't bother wiping them because it's a relief.

From within, I feel the humanity surging through me, but I know it's fleeting. It'll flicker out soon, and I won't know when it'll hit me again.

As I approach the gate, I take one last glance at Tyson, leaning against the trunk of my car.

CHAPTER TWENTY-FIVE

It's the last day of the carnival and things are in full swing. The crowds have ballooned since the last time I was here—the night Dylan died.

Traditionally, fireworks burst across the sky during the last four hours. Tonight is no exception. It's still early, so there are longer spans between the bangs and the booms. Streams of rockets are launched into the sky, painting willow trees against the backdrop of illuminated clouds.

I tried to call Blue as I hopped the gate, but his phone went straight to voicemail. He has a knack for not charging his phone, which is really unfortunate on a night like this. I have no idea how I'm going to find him, but I guess the best place to start would be the offices toward the back.

The crowd is thick as I push my way through the throngs of carnival-goers. To the left of me is an impossibly long line for the Zipper. But I see a shortcut, so I ditch through the crowds, pass the loading gate, and escape onto the midway that circles around the entirety of the grounds.

I brush my hand through my hair and press forward. I'm in the center of Game Street. Booths line both sides of the midway, thousands of dollars being stolen by unethical carnies scamming for their overlords. There's a girl sitting on a stool preparing to launch darts against under-inflated balloons. The prize for success? A bear that retails for fourteen dollars at a chain department store near you.

I make a left at the end of Game Street and approach the campers that double as offices. One of them is Blue's dad's. Maybe I'll finally get to meet him.

I'm not really thinking as I climb the steps and open the squeaky door without so much as a knock. I lean my head into the camper, and it's empty of human life but full of empty beer bottles that sit on a desk covered in envelopes.

I crane my head to look over my shoulder, making sure nobody sees me as I shut the door and step toward the desk. I have a sudden urge to be nosy. We'll just say that it's natural curiosity, and I'm trying to make a little sense of the situation I've found myself in.

I shuffle through a stack of envelopes and one in particular catches my eye. In thick red markings, Blue's name is scribbled across an empty envelope. I wonder if he's been here already.

Fireworks crackle from outside, followed by a sonic-boom-like explosion.

"Hello."

My body jumps and I spin around to face the intruder. I recognize him as Cookie, Blue's friend.

"I didn't even hear you come in," I say with an innocent smile. "The door's usually kind of squeaky."

"You just have to know how to open it," he says. "What are you doing here?"

I'll skip the snooping part and go straight for the semi-truth. "I'm looking for Blue. Have you seen him?"

He shakes his head. "Not today."

I'm going to be here all night.

"Do you maybe wanna step outside before Big Daddy comes home?"

"Big Daddy?" I ask, though I didn't mean to say it out loud. I walk past him and push the door open. He follows me out and gently shuts the door behind him.

"See?" he says, referencing the silence of the door as it closed. "You just gotta know how to do it."

I smirk. He scans the area then looks at me. "Do you want me to wait with you?"

"I should probably find him." I shrug. "Do you really think he'll come here?"

"If I know him as well as I think I do, then yes."

Hmm.

"I know him very well. He'll show."

"All right." I sit down on the steps of the camper. Cookie joins me. Previously, we had only met for a total of sixty seconds, so we're still in that awkward stage of being complete strangers. But I know him a little more than he knows me. I know his deepest, darkest secret. It's silent as we both stare ahead, waiting for the same man but for different reasons.

He rubs his palms against his jeans.

Do I tell him the truth? That I know everything? That Rake is in town?

Cookie digs into the pocket of his jeans and pulls out a balled-up bag of what I presume is Molly. I don't say anything as he spills the contents of the bag out onto a debit card, then begins to separate the powder into lines. He's quick and efficient. And I'm wanting and craving. My eyes are glued to the drug, like it's the perfect medication to calm my derailing nerves.

It's here, in this moment, when I'm thinking about what it is that I want to do—Molly—that the toll begins to really hit me. All the fear, which is the reason I'm running, and all the doubt, the reason that I'm sitting here instead of being out there in the crowds, searching for him. Everything that made some sort of fucked-up sense just a few hours ago is unraveling. All these little threads of—

"Want some?"

"Huh?"

He pushes the debit card toward my lap. My common sense tells me I need to have a clear head but my fingers are soldiers for the part of my mind that's screaming *Fuck that*. He hands me a rolled-up twenty and I press it against my nose. The Molly burns against the fibers of my nose and shoots down my throat. I pinch my nose with one hand and pass the card back with the other. Swiftly, he snorts up the last line.

"I guess this makes us friends." He nudges me playfully.

"Is that all it takes?"

"I guess I'm just a people person."

"Right," I say. "Irresistible."

"Why you looking for him, anyway?"

"We're running."

"Shocking." He chuckles. "That boy can't stay put anywhere for too long."

"Yeah, well, I don't think he planned on a psychotic drug dealer tracking him down."

His eyes turn to steel. "What are you talking about?"

I shouldn't have said that. "It's nothing." I swallow a chunk of air. My heart beats through my jeans. I become aware of every breath, of every sight and sound. "I have to go." My feet shake, almost like Jell-O, as I stand up quickly.

"I thought you were waiting for Blue."

"I have to find him."

"Maybe you should sit down." He rises and moves to the front of me, grabbing my arms. I can feel my eyes sinking toward the ground. I push him off me and flee.

* * *

My feet are heavy and it's becoming increasingly difficult to walk. This Molly is different from the time before. It's stronger—much more dangerous. My face is flushed, my cheeks clammy. I rub my palm against my forehead, wiping off a layer of sweat. It's a chore to keep my eyes open. It seems all I want to do is close them and sway to the beat of carnival music. And that's what I do. Dancing lights flash against my eyelids, putting on a show in the dark. My head sways to the side.

I open my eyes and shake it off. There are two cops leaning against the back of a concession stand. I can feel their eyes burning holes through me. I turn around with a new resolve to find Blue before the police find me. Everything is heightened—smells, sights, and sounds—like the sound of feet plodding against the ground. I pick up the pace and push myself into a thick crowd clustered together outside a shelter house where a local—and rather shitty—amateur band plays.

Screaming rockets shoot into the sky and explode into golden glitter. I can feel every particle disintegrate. I begin to move again and as I exit the concert crowd, I run into the back of a sharp-dressed man. He turns around, and he's all too familiar. "Hey, Jimmy Clay," I say, my disdain beaming through clenched lips.

"Do I know you?"

"Not exactly." I turn around, leaving him behind.

Ding! Ding! Ding! I fumble to the side, tripping over the carefully placed feet of a clown doing clown things in front of a crowd of children. The clown stares at me as I recover. The parents of the children do the same. Everybody knows I'm fucked up.

Ding! Ding! Ding! A man pulls a hammer up over his shoulder, boasting in sheer pride at the strength of his swing.

"Douchebag," I whisper under my breath.

Or so I thought.

He turns and stares me down. Everybody is staring at me. I cut through the grass and stumble through the line for the tea cups and right into the short line for the Ferris wheel. Of course it's a short line. The majority of people, even in this town, are smart enough to avoid this terrifying death trap.

It wasn't intentional, my landing here, but I figure it's my best chance to find Blue in this suffocating mess. My eyes are racing as I wait for the line to move. When it finally does, I'm about ten feet too slow and have to jog to the gate before it shuts.

A cute carnie—yes, there's more than one—ushers me into my seat. My heart is pounding before the ride even begins. I expect that once it starts, it'll beat right out of my chest. It won't be the way I had always imagined dying on this ride, but it's death, just the same.

Instead of intense terror, I feel peace. The way the cool wind blows softly against my skin comforts me. Up here, the paranoia that the entire world is watching me fades away. Instead, I watch them. Thousands of ants all biting on the same spilled bag of cotton candy. I feel for them, all searching for something they'll never find.

I need to find Blue.

An eruption of red, white, and blue fireworks glows against my face. Always patriotic and almost never the Fourth of July. As the ride cycles closer to the ground, my eyes are drawn to him like magnets that are drawn together in science class.

I've found Blue. He's walking toward the field, probably going to his Jeep. He's ready to leave without me.

"Blue!" I scream, but I'm overpowered by another burst of neon explosions in the sky. He turns his head toward the fireworks and watches them fall back to earth as he continues to walk. I scream for him again, but he turns his head back around.

The six-shot revolver of death comes to a sudden halt. I'm close to the bottom, but not close enough to jump.

"Hey," I yell to the carnie, waving my hands at him.

He looks up to me and tips his hat backward so he can make eye contact. "Need off?"

I nod my head. He smiles at the carnie who operates the ride, and the ride starts up again. I don't have the three minutes this ride will steal from me if I'm forced to go again. I resolve to jump out, but wait until I'm closer to the ground. When that time comes, I stand up and steady myself against the bars, ready to jump. The seat wavers back and forth, and even though I'm only about ten feet from the ground, I can feel the tidal waves in my stomach.

The ride jerks hard and I fall back into my seat. The carnie looks up to me, screaming, "Are you stupid?"

"No," I say and hop over the bar and onto the platform. "I'm in love."

He's not amused and waves me off. "Get outta here!"

And I'm gone.

* * *

I've lost Blue, but I know where he's heading. I squeeze through the impossibly small cracks that separate one person from the next, bumping into countless strangers, and not caring. The fireworks have now come to a stop and there is an excitement in the air. The grand finale is about to start.

Through the sea of blank figures, I see an opening into a clearing. I push through and exit the crowd, immediately heaving in the sudden abundance of air. I see Blue sitting on a park bench in front of an empty horse barn. Miraculously, I was able to catch up to him.

Just a few more deep breaths, and then I will launch myself toward him. I'll jump in his arms, he'll embrace me and—

My eyes shoot toward the sky—a thousand supernovas exploding all at once. The creation of an entire new galaxy emerging before my eyes. The Milky Way has nothing on this new world of neon lights. One after another, the beautiful formation of new worlds.

A hand clasps around my mouth and pulls me backward. I taste gasoline. I punch my elbow backward, connecting with a thick sheet of air. My screams are muffled, not that anyone could hear me over the big bang anyway. I throw another jab and miss again. Please let my assailant have a dick—my next move basically depends on it.

I throw my foot back and upward, kicking my assailant in the groin. His hand falls away from my mouth and I feel him stumble back. I spin around to face him.

It's Rake.

He's got one hand on his dick, the other one firmly ready to knock me in my face. He grimaces. "You're going to pay for that."

"Sorry," I say. "I'm all out of cash."

Not my smartest moment. Typical Charlie behavior, running my mouth when I should be running. *Do the smart thing*.

I remember that Blue is less than a hundred feet away. I pivot and race toward him. Rake gives chase and even with an injured reproductive system, it's clear he's going to catch me.

Somewhere I wonder if someone is recording this. They'll play it to an apathetic high school audience that watches on in horror as I'm brutally murdered by a psychotic drug dealer. In flashing red letters as the scene comes to a close, the screen will say *Drugs Are Bad*.

Real fucking bad. I look behind me and he's within arm's reach. The part of my brain that tells my body to run faster must be fried, because I physically cannot shift up. It's like you're always stuck in second gear? Well try being stuck in first with Scarface on your tail.

If I'm going to get away, I'll need a new strategy. I can't outrun him, but I might be able to hide from him in a faceless crowd. Just have to get there first. Up ahead, there's a crowd gathering around stuntmen on bikes that are set up inside a spherical cage.

I look behind me to gauge the probability of escape. The odds are directly correlated to the distance between us. Two feet? I'm fucked.

Out of nowhere, Rake is bull-rushed to the ground. Blue picks Rake up off the beaten grass, pulls back his elbow, and punches him in the face. Rake falters to the ground again. Blue drops himself onto Rake's chest and begins hitting him with a barrage of fists.

It's not the violence that turns me on, but the idea that I have my own personal superhero. I don't fancy being the damsel in distress, but I could be saved by Blue every day.

In the near distance, crowds begin to part, and I can vaguely make out what appears to be cops hustling toward the scene. I dart to Blue, grabbing his arm as he's about to land another punch. My eyes plead with him to stop. I see the struggle in the canvas of his face. He's not done yet. He's angry. His chest rises and drops. Ragged breaths force their way through his tight lips. He bites into them and nods at me. Rake certainly deserves what's coming to him, but not here and not now.

Blue stands up and steps over Rake's body. It looks like he's about to kick him, but he just rushes to me and takes my hand. I take one last look at Rake, who is lying on the ground, covered in blood. He seems perfectly capable of taking care of himself—so why didn't he fight back?

We exit the parking gate, head straight to Blue's Jeep and drive away. Behind us, a stray firework screams into the sky, exploding in a cloud of white dust.

CHAPTER TWENTY-SIX

We opt to take the back way out of town, avoiding the highway. The headlights on Blue's Jeep illuminate the dark path ahead of us. Dry, cracked pavement zooms past us. I imagine that every crack is another inch away from home. It's exciting. It's terrifying. It's a whole lot of other things, too.

My head is slouched against the seat, turned so that I stare out the window. It's been about two hours since we left the carnival, and I've turned off my phone. By now, my mom probably knows I'm long gone.

The Molly has started to wear off and the after-effects are strong. There's a blankness in my mind. I'm unable to feel or process anything outside basic emotions. It's liberating.

Blue has one hand on the wheel, the other firm on the gearshift. There are no stoplights for miles, but he's always ready to shift.

"There should be a hotel up here soon," he says through a yawn.

I look to him. "Do you want me to drive?"

He chuckles. "Seriously?"

"No," I say with a smile.

If there is a hotel coming up soon, it won't be the Hilton. A Red Roof Inn is probably asking too much on this desolate road that the world has long forgotten. There are no lights lining the edges of the road. It's just trees, cornfields, and our love out here. It's almost perfect.

I lower my head back toward the window. Headlights bounce against the passenger mirror and I snap awake, instantly becoming fully alert.

"Blue," I say, not breaking my focus on the mirror. "Behind us."

He cranes his head over his shoulder. His eyes focus on the speeding lights.

"Do you think—"

"That it's Rake?" He finishes my question. "I don't know."

He reaches across my lap, his elbow brushing against the denim of my jeans. His hand feels for the glove-box and pops it open. He grabs something.

I can feel cool metal rubbing across me as he places a handgun onto his lap. My eyes widen.

"You have a gun?"

"What kind of self-respecting former drug dealer wouldn't?"

Good point.

The car behind us gets closer and closer until the *closer than they appear* lights become blinding in the side mirrors. Blue squints, losing sight of the lines between lanes. His hand lowers to his gun, flipping the safety off.

I shake my head as his hand wraps around the grip of the gun. His fingers follow suit.

Then it's blue and red lights.

"Shit," Blue cries. He's probably worried about the gun on his lap, but something tells me it's more than that. Like he has a trunk full of drugs, perhaps?

Then, the sirens wail. I take in a deep breath, prepared to meet our fate. But the cop car slides from behind, and into the oncoming lane. He speeds past us.

Blue throws his head back into the headrest and lets out a light laugh. So do I. We're two paranoid motherfuckers.

* * *

I lean against the Jeep with my palms pressed against the warm hood. My body glows red from the neon-lit Vacancy sign that sits atop the roof of the two-story motel. It was flashing No Vacancy when we first pulled in, but the light changed a few minutes after Blue had stepped inside the motel office. I told Blue that we should keep driving because they didn't have any rooms. He said that he's seen plenty of available rooms in not-so-available motels in his years on the road. And if there wasn't a room, we could just sleep in the Jeep again.

We've done it before, but things were different then. There wasn't a psychopath chasing us.

I bring my arms up to my chest, hugging myself tight as a cool gust of wind blows past me, tossing my hair into the neon red abyss of the night. In the past ten minutes, I have gone from being too hot to too cold too many times.

A bell rings and Blue pushes through the glass door of the office. He's nonchalant as he opens the door of the Jeep and grabs the gun, placing it in the back of his jeans.

"I told you we'd get a room," he says with a grin, then straightens out his shirt to conceal the gun.

"Whatever," I say playfully.

He steps to the back of the Jeep, pivots on his feet, and tosses me the room key. I'm a klutz so of course it slips through my fingers. I lean down and grab the key. It has a big '21' etched into it, which means I'm going to get lucky. I think.

Blue slings his bag over his shoulder and grabs my bag with his free hand. "Ready?"

* * *

The room is dark, the only light coming from a buzzing fluorescent fixture that hangs over a vanity beside the bathroom door. The room is cold, not the temperature, but a general feeling. It's definitely not home. It doesn't even feel like a stop on the way.

Blue walks ahead of me and tosses our bags onto the bed closest to the door. He dives onto the bed, rustling the twenty-year-old comforter, and pulls a switch on a lamp that sits on a nightstand. I push the door closed with my ass.

I pass a mirror on the way to the second bed and notice that the girl staring back at me has sunken eyes. She's tired. I sink down into the bed, and there's another mirror in front of me.

To my left, Blue unzips a bag and grabs a baggie filled with that magical white stuff. I grin.

"This place is a dump," he says with a mischievous smile. "Wanna have some fun?"

Do I ever. I still haven't come down completely from earlier, but I'm up for trying it again if for no other reason than, here in this closed room I won't be as paranoid.

* * *

My throat runs and it's a familiar feeling. Blue pounds a fist against the air-conditioning unit that sputtered out about ten minutes after we walked in the door. When the motor begins whirring up, Blue leans his face against the blowers, craving the cool air. He immediately clicks the off button. "The damn thing's blowing out heat," he stammers.

Perfect. I grab my plaid shirt off the bed and wipe my face, instantly dampening the fabric. "It has to be at least eighty degrees in here."

"It's about to get hotter." He stands up, pulling his drenched shirt over his head. Sweat rolls down his chest. "It won't shut off."

"We're going to have to switch rooms."

He shakes his head. "I saw a car pull in last time I went outside, and there were only two rooms when we got here."

I throw myself back onto the bed, staring at the ceiling fan that moves in impossibly slow circles. The air is humid, hot, and thick. Above the fan, the ceiling is cracked all the way to the door. What a dump.

The front door swings open. A light tangle of a breeze pushes into the room, but only makes it about a foot in the door before being forced back out. I hop onto my feet and exit the room, meeting Blue against the railing that lines the exterior of the second floor.

He leans coolly against the rail, his hands clasped together in a pondering pose. I can feel the Molly coming over me, impatiently waiting for the release it'll bring me. It's rather odd that every time I do it, it's a wildly different experience. I'd expect some consistency, but it seems to be more a roll of the dice. Sometimes it's fast, sometimes slow.

I lean one elbow against the railing so that I can face him. There's a yearning in his eyes, like he's waiting for something—maybe he's waiting for the Molly, too. There's a sense of loss on the edge of his lips, like he needs to say something—maybe it's *I'm sorry*. But most of all, what I really notice is the way I feel whenever I look at him, like the rest of the world doesn't matter anymore. I don't even want to think about everything I've lost, but it doesn't seem like the worst tradeoff in the world.

"Enjoying the view?" he asks with a light smile.

"What do you mean?"

"You're staring at me."

"Call me shallow, but I'll never get tired of looking at you, wondering what's going on beneath those beautiful blue eyes."

"You're too kind," he says and looks out into the distance, into the forest that sits on the other side of the desolate highway. "I know we didn't leave town under the best of circumstances." He bows his head and twiddles his thumbs. "I'm sorry it had to be this way."

"And I'm sorry I can't enjoy this adventure, whatever it is." I latch onto his shoulder, caressing him. "But I know we can, eventually, be happy because you taught me that home isn't a place. It's an idea, a person," I say softly. "You're my home."

His throat tightens. "Have I ever told you I love you?"

"Once or twice." I shrug with a grin.

"How 'bout a third?" He turns, resting one arm on the railing. "I love you and I want all of you, but I'll settle for all the little pieces until you're happy again."

A tear–a happy one–forms at the corner of my eye. "Have I ever told you that I love you?"

"I think it's slipped out of your beautiful lips a time or two," he says and brushes his palm against my flushed cheeks. "But you don't have to say it because I already know."

I turn and grip the railing with both hands, my wrists tense against the chipped metal. "When I was looking for you at the carnival, I broke into your dad's camper."

He cocks an eyebrow. "Broke in?"

"Walked in," I correct myself. "There were two envelopes—one had your name on it and the other had Rake's."

His eyes roll sideways, confused. "That doesn't make any sense."

"They were empty," I add. "Didn't you say you had to pick something up from the carnival?"

"Yeah." He smiles faintly, as if stating the obvious. "Drugs."

"Seriously?" I ask.

"We have to make money somehow."

My hand rolls into a half fist as I wipe the corner of my eye and force out a yawn.

"You tired?"

"No," I say. "I think the Molly's kicking in."

CHAPTER TWENTY-SEVEN

Blue bites into his lip, his eyes making waves before settling on mine. "I was just about to say the same thing."

I place a hand on his chest, running down the length of his abs and circling just above the edge of his jeans. "You don't think we should talk about the camper?"

"I think we can figure out that mystery later." He picks me up by the waist in quick motion, pulling my legs to the side as he prepares to carry me into the room. It feels like we're on our honeymoon as he pushes his lips against mine, melting into me with his golden kiss.

He steadies his hands on my bottom, making sure he's got me fully supported as he carries me into room twenty-one. One hand pushes the bags off the bed, the other lays me down gently onto the faded white sheets. He hovers above me as all his scents bleed into one. Sweat, musk, Molly, and sex. The weight of his body grinds against me, the friction burning holes in my jeans.

"Close the door," I say, out of breath as his tongue rolls across my neck then nibbles against the rim of my ear.

"Let the whole world watch," he huffs against the side of my face, his breath hotter than a volcano.

I push against his chest, rolling him off me and pointing to the door. He groans as he slides off the bed, stretches his arm out, and slams the door shut. By the time he gets back to the bed, I've moved to the edge, my feet planted on the floor.

His head falls to the side as he peers at me through the corners of his eyes. "Not in the mood?"

"Get over here," I command. I pull my tank over my head and toss it aside.

There's an outline of his hardness pulsing tight in his jeans as he approaches. I pop the first button of his denim, and then pull the rest apart. He's not wearing anything under the jeans, and he lets out a moan of relief as my hands grip his thighs and my lips caress his abdomen. I suck on the smooth skin of his stomach, and then move further down with every lap of my tongue until I'm nuzzled against the thin stubble just above his cock.

My fingers slide into the waistline of his jeans, and I tug them down his hips so that they rest just above his knees. His erect length stares me down and I slide my hand across it, gripping it. His hands come down into my hair, but not forcibly. He brushes his fingers softly through my locks as I kiss the end of his length.

I lick the underside of him, and then roll my tongue around it before taking it in my mouth. He's only the second guy I've ever tasted, and he'll be the last. Most people say sex is the most intimate thing you can do with someone. I disagree. There's nothing more intimate than this right here, and I couldn't do it unless I were in love. So the fact that his dick presses against the back of my throat should be all the proof required in the world that I love him.

"Charlie," he moans.

I raise one hand up and rub the creases of his abs. With my other hand, I stroke his spit-soaked shaft as I pull my mouth off him. I look up to find his eyes locked with mine. My hand strokes his entire length, causing him to gasp with every inch.

I push myself back onto my elbows and he pulls my jeans off in one quick motion. His lips trace a path of kisses up my thigh until he reaches my panties and pulls them down my legs. I push my damp hair back as he climbs on top of me, kicking off his jeans. His belt buckle clatters as they hit the floor.

He grabs a breast in his hand, pulling my bra down so that he can rub me bare. When his teeth nibble against me, I arch my back into the warmth of the bed. "Blue..."

He cranes his head to look at me, his eyes asking *Yeah?*

"Nothing." I shake my head.

A hand travels between my thighs. His fingers glide against the edge of my opening, running circles around my flesh. I pull his head toward me, forcing a passionate kiss. I hiss pleasurably into his mouth as one finger parts me down below. My knees spread at the welcome intrusion, then there's another finger. He draws in and out, stretching and preparing me, making me crave to be filled.

"I love you, Charlie," he breathes into my mouth.

"I love you, too." I take a mental picture of his face so close to mine. Every perfect detail—the way a smile somehow peeks through absolute desire—and every perfect flaw—the story-filled scar below his right eye.

His slick fingers pull out and he rolls over me, nudging my knees wider with his thighs. His steel cock rubs against me, teasing me. "Fuck me," I plead.

He pushes himself up onto his fists, one on each side of my head. His hardness pushes against me, entering me with precision and an unwavering tempo. The further he sinks, the more everything becomes clear. Running is the right thing to do if it means keeping him.

When his pelvis meets mine, he lets out a well-earned moan. My fingers navigate to the muscles on his back, holding on tight as the ride starts. At first, he pulls out slowly, bringing himself all the way to the edge before pushing back in. It's painfully slow, but I know the hydraulics are just getting heated up.

Every thrust quickens while sticking to the same basic beat. He rises to his knees so that his whole body is like a tower peering over me. It's not fair that his body is a landmark not many will ever see. He grabs a small, unopened bag of Molly that sits at the top of the bed and tears it with his mouth. A thin cloud of white powder follows gravity toward my body.

His cock reaches the hilt, and he stays there while he slides my bra off my arms and empties a line of the drug in the fold between my breasts. If I did any more

Molly, I'd probably get lost in some magical world of rainbows and butterflies, unable to ever find my way back. But he's much more experienced than I am.

He pins both my arms against the bed. His tongue rolls against the crease of my breasts, lapping up the line of Molly while he begins to drive into me again. The thrusts are shallower than before, but remain just as effective at making my insides scream.

At the end of the bed, my toes begin to curl. It's funny how they always know that I'm about to explode well before the rest of me is able to catch on. Blue falls back onto his fists, thrusting further into me with every bounce. The only thing that could make this better would be a mirror above the bed so that I could see his miraculous ass while he fucks me senseless.

Sweat drips from his face onto mine. It's the first time since I came into contact with his dick that I'm aware how terribly hot it is in this room. Our entire bodies gleam with a coat of sweat. If Rake managed to find us and walk in that door, he'd be blinded by the light bouncing off us.

The bed begins to creak as he moves faster and harder. He's like a drag racer with a full tank and no speed limits. I fear the bed could break with every thrust. I become aware of the sounds being thrown from my throat. Every time he slams into me, I find myself praying out loud for release.

I almost feel bad for our neighbors in this fully-booked motel. I say *almost* because I'm too lost in a sea of ecstasy to care. The headboard slams against the wall, making sweet music—it's the drums. Blue's grunts are the bass and my moans are the vocals. We have quite the set-up here.

Sweat falls from his face like a tree shedding leaves in October. My hands trail to the swell of his back, pulling him closer to my body.

I've never seen him quite like this. The first time we met, we fucked, but it was quick and distant. Other times, we just fucked. But this is something else. There's an animal in his eyes, like he somehow transforms once he hits the sheets. I'll admit it. I love it. He's so sweet and gentle in mixed company, but when we're alone, he has the power to take me on a trip out of this galaxy.

His blue eyes burn with desire, absorbing every little bit of me there is to see. He fucks me deep into the mattress without saying a word. And there's nothing wrong with that—sometimes you just wanna fuck someone's brains out. And my brains are about to splatter against the headboard.

There are only three things that make me feel alive anymore—sex, Molly, and him. And right now, I have all three. It starts in my toes and then possesses my entire body. I've just died and gone to heaven. My entire body tenses, wrapping tight around both his dick and his ass. My knees rise, locking him in place against me as his thrusts become erratic.

"Fuck," he yells. "I'm gonna come." His hands tangle into the sheets, his chest propped up above me as his entire body quivers. I feel every throb as he empties himself inside me. Every tiny tremor threatens to start up my engine again. He drives into me still, each stroke less deep than the one before. After he's come down from his euphoria and he pulls out completely, I notice he's still hard as steel. He bites into his lip and I know he's not finished yet.

Neither am I.

He grabs my legs and rolls me over and onto my knees. He inserts himself from behind in one sudden slam. My eyes go blind.

* * *

I wake to a cool breeze blowing through a small opening on the side of the window. It's a little past three and far from daylight. It's abnormally quiet, save for the faint blaring of a TV coming from the room behind us.

The ice bucket is empty, so I grab it and step outside. Two simultaneous sounds occur—the clicking of the motel door and the slamming of a car door. My palm wraps around the railing and rides it as I make my way to the ice machine situated halfway down the outdoor walkway.

There's a calmness in the air, betrayed for milliseconds at a time as gusts come and go. My bare feet pad against the concrete, making no sound, as if I'm walking on air. I place the ice bucket under the ice machine and press it back against the handle. Ice grinds against metal, and then shoots out into the bucket. It comes out strong, sending stray chunks of ice against the cement, then rolling toward the railing.

It's not hot out here, but it's warm enough for the ice to melt. It's slow, but puddles begin to form around each escaped cube. I kick the cube closest to me, sending it flying off the edge of the second floor. I make my way to the railing and set the bucket down, then I lean against the railing with my elbows folded, staring out into the nothing of this once-busy highway.

It's difficult to see change in motion. Only when you're looking back do you truly grasp it. With every breath we take, something changes, but it's not until we've breathed a million more breaths that we notice it. I wonder what my life will look like in this moment when I'm thinking back while rocking my chair on a suburban porch at sunset. Will I be able to see that exact moment that everything changed?

The bell attached to the office door rings and a man comes skulking out. His arms are heavy and pulled tight toward the top. He looks like a man on a mission and when he turns around and locks his eyes on me, I know what his mission is.

* * *

Rake races toward the steps and I snap backward, tripping over the bucket of ice. The ice scatters against the concrete and scrapes along my leg. I push myself up with my hands, noticing the clanking on the steps behind me.

It's just like the movies. I'm running from Jason Voorhees and no matter how fast I run, he's right on me. He pivots around the corner, almost slamming into the railing as I finally catch my speed. I sprint to room twenty-one and slide past it once I reach it. My hand twists the knob, thrusting the door open and slamming it shut just as quick.

"Get up!" I scream.

Blue jolts up in bed, throwing off the stray bit of sheet that managed to wrap itself around his right leg. His head and chest are drenched in sweat–so not the point.

"He's here!" I push the deadbolt into place.

"Rake?" he asks very rhetorically. He knows the answer.

He launches himself out of bed. Naked and vulnerable, he practically jumps into his jeans, yanking them up over his legs.

Something thumps against the door. The knob twists and the door pushes open a fraction of an inch before slamming against the deadbolt. Cheap-ass motel door lock.

"Come on, let me in," Rake says through the door, taking a break from beating on it. "I just wanna talk."

His voice is calm and one that could be forgiven for welcoming him with open arms. Not so forgiven? The Good Samaritans dead bodies floating in the bathtub. I back away from the door, opting to not end up in the bathtub. I pace backward, bumping into Blue. He grabs me by the shoulder and pushes me behind him as he buckles his jeans.

"No?" Rake asks.

Blue begins to speak, but pauses.

"Come on, Blue."

"Just give me a minute," Blue says to him.

Rake laughs diabolically. He's insane. And I'm not down with Blue's plan, whatever it is.

"Blue," I whisper, "you're not really going to open that door, are you?"

The look he gives me speaks volumes, whereas he could have just said three simple words... *Are you stupid?*

"I don't got a minute, babyface."

Babyface? I don't say the words—I mouth them—but Blue has an extraordinary ability to read lips. He's not thrilled about it either.

Blue turns his attention back to the psychopath on the other side of the door. "Come on, man. I thought we were past that."

"I don't know, Blue. I think you'll always be Babyface to me."

I've had enough. "All right, seriously, why the hell is he calling you Babyface?" I ask louder than I intended.

Rake laughs. "He didn't tell you?" He clicks his tongue. "Makes you wonder what else he's hiding, huh?"

"All right, where's the gun? I'm going to shoot him," I say. Again, louder than intended.

"That's how we're going to play?"

And then there's a worrying silence. The door that was pinned tight by Rake's body is now quivering against the deadbolt.

Then Rake's body slams against the door.

"Let me the fuck in!" he screams. The full weight of his body is hurled toward the door again.

Blue dives across me, his hand scooping the gun off the bed, cocking it in the same beat. He angles the gun toward the door while looking at me. "You need to go, Charlie. Sneak out the bathroom window and wait by the Jeep," he whispers.

"I'm not leaving you." I shake my head.

"I'll be right behind you."

My eyes bulge. "Don't you know those are the famous last words of every dead person, ever?"

"What are you lovers talking about in there?" Rake asks amusedly through the door.

"Go," Blue commands, then leans in, kissing me. My hand rubs across his soft cheek as I pull away and grab the keys off the table. "I'll be right behind you."

"You better be." I rush into the bathroom and climb over the stained tub. The small window, big enough for me but probably not for Blue, takes force to push open. I pop my head out the window. The ground's not that far down. But for me, someone who is inexplicably terrified of heights, *not that far* is far enough. I don't fancy the idea of jumping. Especially head first.

I turn and stand on my hands, pushing my legs backward through the window. I slowly lower myself against the rough exterior, until all that's left inside the room are my head and my arms glued tightly to the window sill. One more look down and I gauge it's about an eight-foot drop. There's no rational reason this should scare me as much as it does.

I hear the door break open. "Put your gun down!" Blue yells.

I try to pull myself back into the window. God knows why. It's not like I could actually do anything to help Blue. Then there's gunfire and my vision goes black. I lose my grip and drop to the ground, landing squarely on my feet. "Blue!" I scream.

My feet pound against the grass as I circle the back of the motel, racing toward the front. My bare feet press against the cool grating of the metal steps. Once I reach the top of the stairs, I trace my palm against the railing as I carefully pace toward our motel room. I'm half terrified that I'll find Blue dead, equally scared that Rake will be lying on the floor. The two scenarios mean two different things, but both mean that Blue's life has come to an end—either figuratively or literally.

I pass room twenty-four. With every foot closer to our room, the worry in my gut escalates. I'm sure everyone in this motel, out here in the middle of nowhere, heard the gunshot. The police will be here whenever they can manage. My guess is that the nearest police station is at least twenty minutes away. I'm worried about what they'll find almost more than what I will.

Room twenty-three. If there's an argument, a fight, or fists being thrown, I think I'd be able to hear it. But all I hear is silence. It's time to start thinking about best-case scenarios. Otherwise, I might just fold over the railing and puke.

Room twenty-two. The only thing I hear is the buzzing white noise of a tenant tuned into a porn station with a bad signal. That's what you get when you don't pay extra for cable, though I'm pretty sure that's not an advertised amenity.

The edge of room twenty-one. I hesitate, my feet pushed tight against the floor. I search for the deepest of breaths from the furthest reaches of my lungs. My head begins to spin as I lurch forward to the opening of the door.

"Blue!" He's lying face down on the floor with his arms sprawled out above his head. I shift to run toward him, but a rough hand wraps around my mouth.

CHAPTER TWENTY-EIGHT

BLUE

My body's heavy and drenched in sweat as I awake on the warm floor of room twenty-one. I take in my surroundings, briefly wondering how I got here before it all comes flooding back to me. I jump to my feet, catching my reflection in the mirror. I've got two black eyes now. One from my cousin and the other from the man with a death wish.

Can I be that person again? That person I've fought so hard not to be. It doesn't matter, I guess. He's left me with no other options. The only thing left is to put a bullet through his head, similar to the bullet I'd already shot through his heart when I took the blame for Trey's death. Quickly, I scramble for my gun on the floor, slip it into the back of my jeans, and bolt out the door.

Running alongside the rails, I search for Charlie, hoping she found a way to elude Rake. I know the odds that this night ends in any sort of happy ending are slim, but I'll fight until my last breath, even if it means doing the unthinkable.

* * *

Through the glass door of the office, I see the manager on the phone. The same middle-aged man who I'd convinced to give me a room just a few short hours ago. The phone he holds in his hand is an outdated cordless relic from the nineties.

I storm through the door and he fumbles in his seat, pulling back from me as I reach the counter. "He's here," he says quietly into the phone. His face is sunken, a look of terror. "The police are on their way."

"Good," I say through clenched teeth. "Tell them to bring backup."

He stutters, having no idea what's happened. He probably believes I'm the bad guy and maybe he's right. I spot a cell phone on the counter. It's a flip phone so my best guess is that it's the manager's. I scoop it off the counter, and pivot, rushing out the front door.

"He said to bring backup," I hear the man say. "Also, he just took my phone."

I flip the phone open and dial 911, prepared to speak to the police on my own, knowing that even if I manage to save Charlie, I could be hauled to jail in the back of a cruiser right after. She's worth it. She's worth everything, and I'd do anything to save her, the only good thing to ever happen to me. I've let her down, and she probably would've been better off without me.

"Nine-one-one, what's your emergency?"

I spot my keys lying in the gravel. "My girlfriend has been kidnapped." I pop the Jeep door open and hop in, turning the ignition and slamming the gas all in one beat. The tires kick rocks into the sky as I race toward the road. The operator begins to speak, but I cut her off. "Can you track this phone?"

"Yes we can, but, sir—"

"Track it. I'll call you back." I flip the phone shut then open it again, dialing Cookie's number from memory. In all the time I've known him, he's answered his phone in less than three rings. Whether he's working or not, he's got one palm pressed to that damn iPhone at any time. So when the first call goes to his voicemail after just one ring, I grow concerned.

I slam the phone shut. My jaw tenses, my teeth digging into my tongue. "Fuck," I scream and punch the dashboard. There's only one other person I could call—other than Charlie, but I don't have her number memorized. I dial my dad's number, remembering that Charlie said something about sneaking into his camper. Maybe in some fucked-up way he knows what Rake plans to do.

I call about four times before realizing I'm not going to reach him and that I'm out here on my own. The speedometer rises, the pointed line speeding above eighty.

CHAPTER TWENTY-NINE

CHARLIE

I'm about eight years old. It's a sunny morning, closer to the end of the school year than the beginning. I sit at a table in the breakfast nook, my head barely hovering over the top as I play with the letters in my cereal.

"What do you want to be when you grow up?" my dad asks, folding his newspaper against the table.

I just shrug, far more interested in spelling the name of my favorite imaginary friend against the canvas of milk in my bowl.

"Charlie," my mom presses on. "It's When I'm Grown Up day at school today."

My head rises. "I just wanna be happy," I say with a wide, innocent smile. I'm missing my two front teeth, but I'm too young to care.

"Happiness is a given in life," my dad says. "So what do you really want to do when you're older?"

My lips fold against each other, uncertain of an answer. "Why can't I just be happy?"

Mom smiles, glowing with pride and youth. She reaches across the table and grabs my hand. "You can be whatever you want."

"Being happy isn't a job," my dad grumbles. "How about a lawyer?"

I shake my head. "They lie too much."

Mom and Dad both laugh, knowing from experience that it's the complete truth. I laugh along with them, but I still have a childish cackle.

"What about a doctor, then? You could afford anything you want. A nice car and a nice house."

"Dad," I say. "Those things don't make you happy."

"Then I don't know what does." He laughs again and I go along with it, but even at a young age, I know money's not the answer to life–and definitely not happiness.

"The only thing I'll ever need is to be loved," I say, bowing my head toward my cereal, where I've managed to spell the word *someday*.

* * *

The miles fly by with nobody in sight. I'm within elbow's distance of this madman who's kidnapped me and there's nothing within my own power I can do to save myself. I never could have predicted the events of this past month, but what's happening now is ripped straight from the pages of a horror novel. "Did you kill him?" I ask Rake softly, terrified of the answer.

He turns to me, his face haunted with restrained glee. "Uncertainty is a terrible feeling."

I shift in my seat, scooting closer to the door. The farther away from him the better.

"You have any idea how long I waited?" he asks, his eyes now focused intently on the road ahead, seemingly lost in another world. "Not knowing where Trey was, wondering if he was lying dead in some ditch or just out on one of his spontaneous adventures."

"I'm sorry," I whisper. It's true. I empathize with him to a point, but I'm under no illusion that he's anything other than what he is—a villain.

"No, you're not." He shakes his head. "Lying won't save you and it won't save your boyfriend."

I perk up, my body rising up against the torn leather seat. "So he's still alive?"

"Before the end of the night, he'll wish he wasn't."

"What are you going to do to him?"

With one hand glued to the wheel, he cranes toward me with a bent face, lost somewhere between a frown and a sinister smile. "It's not him you should be worried about."

If this were a movie, sinister music would kick in right about now. My hand searches for the door handle. We're going about sixty miles an hour down this back road and I know the odds of survival if I should jump out are not good, but I can't help thinking it'd be a better fate than what Rake has in mind.

His tongue clicks against his cheek. "That door doesn't open from the inside."

* * *

When you're eleven years old, you think you know the world inside out. Like you could grab the universe out of your washer and hang it out to dry. Dylan, his plaid shirt, and I hide behind a thick green bush. The rest of our friends have been found in this hours-long scrimmage of high-stakes hide and seek.

Joey's house is big and the property it sits on is even bigger. A pilgrim probably walked this land once and came to the conclusion that the world is flat. Dylan and I are huddled together, on the verge of a years-long relationship.

He peers through the bush, his eyes searching for our friends, who are looking for us. They're devoted to the cause because once this game's over, we move on to the next—a rousing game of spin the bottle. I'm surprised Dylan hasn't given away our position because I know there's nothing he wants more right now than to kiss me. My hand brushes against his. Not going to lie—it was intentional.

His eyes turn to me. His fingers tangle with mine. "What are we doing?" he whispers.

I sway on my feet, bold enough to make the first move, but not bold enough to say it aloud.

"You like me, huh?"

I shrug, but I can't wipe the smile off my face. I've loved him since I was five, but I've only recently became immune to the paralyzing fear of cooties.

He leans forward, his lips puckered as he pecks me on the lips. My eyes close at his touch, held tight until he pulls away and grabs both my hands. "We should get married," he says.

My feet dig into the dirt, my heels pushing me higher.

"Found you," Joey screams as he dives through the bush, landing squarely on the ground between Dylan and me.

Dylan grabs my hand and drags me away from our attacker. As we run by the line of bushes and toward the barn behind Joey's house, Summer and Tyson spot us immediately giving chase. Dylan pulls me into the barn and grabs the door handle, prepared to push it shut. He grunts, but the door is too heavy for his young body to move by himself, so I give him a helping hand. We push the door shut just as Summer comes within tagging distance. We both lean against the door, out of breath.

"You know they'll get in here soon, right?"

"I know," he breathes heavy. "I just wanted you alone for a few more minutes."

"My own personal hero."

He steps closer, but keeps his hands to himself. "I'll always protect you."

* * *

"Blue's dad tried paying me off. Five thousand blood-soaked dollars. Is that how much Trey's life was worth?" Rake shakes his head viciously. "I took the envelope with my name on it and then saw one with Blue's. You know how much cash was in his?"

I don't nod or reply in any intelligible manner because I don't care. This man has intentions to hurt me or kill me and nothing he says is going to change that. Nothing I say will change that. I'm out of options and I can feel the clock ticking in slow motion. The hour glass has been flipped and I'm running out of time.

"Ten thousand," he continues. "Isn't that something? So I took his, too."

"He let you take the money?"

"Of course not." He grins wickedly, the edges of his lips able to cut through glass. "I killed him."

"Wha—?" I stutter, unable to form complete sentences. My lip trembles at the realization that he's more dangerous—and crazy—than I'd realized.

"Don't cry for him." His voice vibrates, and I can feel his pitch shifting up. "Don't feel sorry for him, Charlie. He was a terrible father," he snarls. I jerk back, away from him, and fumble for the handle again, remembering full well that the door won't open. "Do you ever wonder why Blue is so fucked up? Why he turned out to be the way he is?"

"You're full of shit," I mumble.

"How does a pretty girl like you fall in love with a fugitive, anyway?" He shakes his head. "That doesn't make any sense to me. Sounds more like fiction."

"I don't imagine you're well-read."

"Now I see it." He shifts his focus to me. "You're a smartass, but you're not smart enough to know when to keep your mouth shut. This isn't the place, it isn't the time, and I am not the one, Charlie." His entire face tightens. I've made him very angry. Regret settles in my stomach instantly. "I am not the one you want to fuck with."

"You said 'fugitive'?" I ask, a few minutes late on the uptake, but needing to change the course of the conversation.

"Hmm," he muses aloud. "I think, before I put a bullet through your brain, you should really have a conversation with your boyfriend about honesty."

"I don't believe you."

"What's not to believe, honey? You obviously know what he's done. Otherwise, you wouldn't have left your perfect little life behind."

I turn away, glancing at my reflection against the window.

"Not that I have too much room to talk," he says with a tilt of his head. "I'm a fugitive myself."

"Really? I never would have guessed." What the hell is wrong with me?

"That's sarcasm again." He shakes a finger at me and grins. "Didn't I tell you that I am not the one?"

Out of the corner of my eye, I see him coming but can't pull away quick enough. He backhands me across the cheek, twisting my face so I'm left staring out the window—waiting to be saved or waiting for my life to end. The difference between the two begins to blur.

* * *

Waves rush against my calves as I exit the warm blue waters of the Gulf. I take a seat on a faded beach towel right beside Summer, who is two shots away from a daytime hangover. Out at sea, Joey fumbles for a lost volleyball while screaming, "Wilson!"

"He's such an idiot," Summer huffs. "But he's our idiot and I wouldn't have it any other way."

"I don't know. I think I'd prefer if he were just a little smarter."

She sits up on her towel, pushing her shades to the top of her head. "I've got a theory," she says. "He's kind of like a dumb bimbo who isn't so dumb. It's all an act."

"I wasn't aware you had a degree in psychology."

"Not yet, but I'm well on my way." She lowers herself onto an elbow. "Have you figured out what you're going to do with the rest of your life?"

"Do you have to put it that way? It sounds so terrifying."

She shrugs. "That's the three T's of life; terrifying, traumatizing and..."

"Triumphant?"

"I was going to say terrifying again."

I can't help but chuckle. She's not the biggest pessimist in the world, but she sure sounds like it. "I think I'm just going to file my major as undeclared."

Summer raises herself back onto her ass, probably so that she has more advantage as she hovers above me. "No," she shakes her head. "You absolutely cannot do that. It's a death sentence."

I breathe a heavy sigh. "But I don't know what I want to do for the rest of my life."

"You can just spend the rest of forever with me," Dylan says from behind us. We both turn to face him and see that he's well past drunk. His swimming shorts sag a good few inches beneath his pelvic bone, exposing the mound above his privates. Sunglasses sit on the shelf space at the end of his nose. He bends down to kiss my lips but gets my chin instead. "You know I meant to kiss you on the lips, right?"

I nod.

"I love you, and I don't think you should go to college."

I laugh. "You know I have to."

He throws his head back, and I'm a little concerned his dick might pop out the top of his shorts. "But gas is so expensive," he moans.

Tyson storms past us, cradling a bottle of whiskey in one hand and a beer-bong in the other. He races toward the ocean screaming for Dylan to come join him. Dylan steps a few feet back before he hurdles his body over us, knocking Summer's beer over in the process.

As his strong body fights against the current, I turn to Summer. "I need to tell you something."

She puts a hand to my face, turning her head away from me. "If you're pregnant, I don't want to hear it. I've been telling you to use condoms for years."

I swat at her hand. "If I were pregnant, would I be drinking right now?"

She nods her head. "Good point. Continue."

"I'm breaking up with him."

"The hell you are!" She stands and hunches over me. "If you want to have a mid-mid-life crisis, then so be it. Go get hooked on heroin or buy a fancy car, but I'll be damned if I let you break up this little family we've got going on here."

"Are you done?"

She thinks about it for a second, then says, "Yeah."

"Good." I grab her by the arms and pull her back down. "I love Dylan. He's all I've ever known—"

"You don't get it, Charlie. You're one of the lucky ones. Do you know how many people dream about marrying their high school sweetheart?"

Middle school sweetheart is probably more appropriate. "If I could stay here in paradise forever, then sure, I could stay with Dylan. But we're going home in a few days, and a few months after that, we're leaving for college and he's staying in Lakeview."

"It's only an hour away from State."

"It's not the distance," I say, exasperated. "Whoever I'm going to be, whatever I'm going to do with my life, the one thing I know is that I can't stay in Lakeview. It's never felt like home."

* * *

Rake reaches into a loose pull-string bag that sits underneath the gearshift. He grabs a wrinkled sheet of paper and pushes it into my lap.

"What's this?" I ask weakly, unfolding it to discover it's a wanted poster of Blue. He looks different in the photo—rougher, older, and a lot more dangerous than the man I fell in love with. Whatever Rake's intentions were, showing me this meaningless sheet of paper won't work. He can play chess all he wants, but this queen won't budge. I know—without a sliver of doubt—that the Blue in that picture is not the same Blue I know today.

Something in particular in Rake's bag catches my attention. A fat stack of stolen cash—a third of it his, the rest Blue's. On the offhand chance that I should escape, that money could come in handy. Blue and I could live off it for months until we're able to figure out our next move. If Rake catches me reaching into that bag, he'd probably cut off my hand, and let's be real fucking honest, he'd catch me. I push my back up against the seat and reach into my pocket, searching for a lighter. When I find it, I withdraw it slowly, peering over at Rake to make sure he's not onto me.

He's anywhere else but with me. It's as if he goes in and out of consciousness. I wonder if that's how all sociopaths function, barely able to maintain their grip on this world. I spin the edge of the metal—a spark first and then a flame.

His head snaps toward me as I set the wanted flyer on fire. "What the fuck are you doing?"

I force a smile but in the reflection of the window, it looks far too sincere. "I'm setting the past on fire. Want to know why?" I throw the flaming sheet into the backseat, praying it'll set the car ablaze. "Because it doesn't fucking matter."

He slams on the brakes, pulling the wheel hard to the right. Sparks fly against the passenger side of the vehicle as the car grinds against the metal railing on the edge of the road. We come to a jerking halt as he throws the emergency brake.

He pushes his door open, hopping out onto the asphalt. As he grabs for the back door, I change course. There's no sane reason to grab the money when I should just be running. I lunge across the gearshift while he pushes the flame to the floor, grinding it out with his boot.

My hands reach the surface of the highway. My feet scuttle past the gearshift. If I can make it out of the car, across the highway and into the woods, I'll be safe.

"Where do you think you're going?" Rake asks from above me. When I crane my neck up to look at him, he brings his foot up to kick me in the chest. As my body jumps from the assault, his hands tangle in my hair, pulling me out of the car and onto my feet. "You're pretty, I'll give you that," he grins, holding me by the crown of my hair. "But you are just about the stupidest girl I've ever met."

With his free hand, he draws a gun from his hip and points it directly at my face. The scent of the metal terrifies me more than the sight. I can sense the power, the ability to end a life in the way the cool metal warms my nose. "Pull the trigger," I say, taunting him with false nerves of steel. "Come on, what are you waiting for?"

His fingers tense around the trigger, as if he might just do it. He shakes his head, his teeth sinking into his lips. "I'm waiting for Blue."

* * *

I haven't heard from Blue since we danced in circles for hours. I have the permanent markings on my arm to remind me that I had a date, but I wonder if his have worn off. He's fifteen minutes late, but I don't know him well enough–yet–to know what that means. Does that mean he's not coming? Does it mean he was caught in traffic? You can tell a lot about someone by the amount of time they make you wait.

I glance at my watch and think about all the things that I could have done today—shopping, showing up randomly at Summer's dorm, drinking, or even pleasuring myself.

Blue pulls up to my house in the car of my dreams—a blue Jeep Wrangler. The top's down, and while I've never been the type of girl to melt over a car, I've already lost an inch of my body to the depths of the ground.

He hops out of the Jeep and meets me at the edge of the driveway. He carries his hands behind his back and a smile passes my lips—this girl's getting flowers. "What's behind your back?"

His eyes shift to the side. "Just my hands," he says as he pulls them out from behind.

"Oh," I mumble. "I thought you had something for me."

"I do." He leans toward me and whispers in my ear, "But it's a surprise."

CHAPTER THIRTY

BLUE

I've only passed two cars since I peeled out of the motel parking lot. In that time, I've called Cookie twice more and my dad at least seven more times, but they're both going straight to voicemail now. I'm worried about them, and my mind's creating all these scenarios of what Rake could have done to them. It's probably nothing. That's what I'm forced to tell myself, anyway, while watching all these horror films in my head.

They're right outside of Lakeview, though. Charlie's out here on this highway somewhere. A part of me thinks she can protect herself, but the other part of me is hell-bent on reminding me that Rake isn't just some ordinary guy. He's the reason I fled the carnival, because I was afraid of what he might do. I can't imagine what Charlie must be feeling. If it's worse than the guilt that I feel from within my gut—well, it could bring me to tears.

But I can't cry right now. I'm too overcome with rage. No longer will I hold back. Rake wanted a fight and he's going to get one. There will be a funeral and

I'll attend, because ending his life isn't something I can do with righteous glee, but it's something I'll do just the same.

Up ahead, taillights shine against the slick road. My fingers curl around the gun on my lap. I'm more than prepared to jump out of this Jeep and take matters into my own hands. The closer I get, the more the car looks like something Rake would drive. It's old, beat-up, and the paint is chipped. In the driver's seat, I can make out the hairline of a woman. It's long and dark. Beside her, a tall man with his head relaxed against the seat.

My adrenaline races as I slam on my horn, desperate to gain their attention. The man turns to face me and I tap my brakes, pulling back and away from the harmless old man and the woman I presume is his daughter.

Hopelessness settles in, as if I could spend all night on this highway and never find her. Like I turned right out of the motel parking lot when I should have turned left. I find comfort where I least expect it—in the knowledge that Rake took Charlie for a reason, and that reason involves me. He won't hurt her until I'm able to see it. I have to hold onto that and pray that I'm able to stop him before it's too late.

CHAPTER THIRTY-ONE

CHARLIE

After my attempted escape, Rake put me in the driver's seat. Like any sane person, I thought that was a huge mistake. You don't give your prisoner that kind of power, that kind of control. Then he pointed a gun at me and it all became clear. One miscalculated decision and we're both dead. The scariest part is that he doesn't even seem to care.

I've learned from my time at the movies that you can't reason with a madman. It's a lost cause. You get to a point of diminishing returns once you hit a certain threshold, and that threshold has been breached. This isn't a man with a soul to save or a life to lose. He's the deadliest type of antagonist, with only one thing on his mind. Revenge. Still, I will never go down without a fight. "You don't have to do this. Any of it," I plead through tense lips.

"It's not about needing to do anything. I don't need to kill Blue to find peace. I just wanna take everything away from him because that's just the way I function."

Desperation makes us say the stupidest shit. Like, "Blue didn't kill your brother. It was Cookie."

There's a pause so quiet I can hear the sound of his tongue rolling against his teeth.

"It was an acciden—"

He turns to me, the gun pointed at my head shifting slightly. "Cookie told me everything."

"Then what are you doing?" I cry out. "Just let me go."

"I'm almost sorry you were dragged into this, but it just goes to show that you don't have the best judgment. Falling in love with a murderer."

I turn to him with moist eyes. "He's not a killer."

"He didn't pull the trigger, but he's just as guilty."

"You need to come back down to reality." I shake my head, disturbing a tear that sits on the edge of my eye.

"How about you focus on the road, sweetie?" He wags his gun at the road.

That brings a laugh out of me, but I find nothing funny. "Yeah, well, how about you take some fucking responsibility for your actions." I turn back to him, every vein in my body pulsing.

"Don't test me, girl." He cocks the gun. "I don't care if you're driving this car."

"And I don't care that your brother is dead!" My hands curl tight around the steering wheel. I should say nothing more but the cord between my mouth and my mind has been permanently severed. "Have you ever considered it might be your fault? You got him selling drugs. He learned everything he knew from you, didn't he?"

"Shut up," he demands tersely.

"I bet you wish you could go back and change it all, huh." I continue to taunt him. "Go back and save him by staying out of his life, because if it weren't for you, he'd still be alive today."

"Fuck you," he scoffs.

"No, fuck *you*!" I scream, my voice breaking at the tip of my register.

Headlights beam against the rearview mirror, blinding me. I push a hand above my eyes, squinting so that I can see the vehicle behind me. It's a blue Jeep. A sense of hope runs along the edges of my lips.

"Look what we have here," Rake says, shifting in his seat. He smashes his gun against the window, sending shards of glass rolling onto the highway behind us.

"What are you—"

"Don't worry," he says wickedly. "I'm not aiming for his head."

He pulls the trigger once.

Twice.

Three times. Each shot ricochets off the metal of Blue's Jeep.

"Stop," I cry out. "You're going to kill him."

"That's not the plan," he says and brings his head back into the car. "But anything's possible."

My options are limited, but I have to do something. I have to remember that it's my hands on the wheel, and as much as Rake would hate to admit it, I'm in control. Rake pops his head back out the window, firing another shot. Blue swerves behind us, tapping on his brakes and gaining a little distance between us.

There are only two things I know for certain. The first is that Rake is crazy—rhyme and reason change based on circumstance with him. It seemed like he had a plan. To capture and kill me while Blue watches. But as the seconds pass and the bullets fly, I become certain that his plan doesn't extend past a basic desire to incite chaos.

The second is that I can't lose Blue. Saying goodbye to Dylan was the hardest thing I've ever done. To lose them both in a matter of a week would devastate me. I wouldn't survive the pain. I'm not even sure I've survived the first blow yet.

I pray that Blue has a plan, even if I've come to learn that plans are nothing more than intuitive guesses, and they almost always fall apart. I planned for my life to end different from this, for example.

* * *

Dylan holds my hand as we walk through some stranger's yard. Behind us, the lights of the carnival light the sky. Cars pass by on the road ahead, but they make no noise. It's as if we're in a vacuum where the only thing that exists is the carnival. Everything outside that bubble is meaningless.

"You know it had to be this way," I say to Dylan.

"Sometimes things don't work out." He shrugs.

"So you understand, then?" I ask. "Why I can't be with you."

We both come to a stop where the sidewalk melts against the road. "I get it. Your heart doesn't lie."

"You know I'll always love you, Dylan." I wait for a reply, but he just twists on one foot, his entire body swaying. "You know that, right?"

He brushes his fingers through my hair, smiling. "I know."

"All right." I push my hands into my jeans. "Blue's waiting for me, so I should probably go."

"Have a good time." He kisses me on the cheek, then turns to walk to his truck, parked on the other side of the road.

A violent brush of wind stretches past me. The warmth of the air crackles as the temperature plummets. Something's wrong.

"Dylan!" I scream.

He turns to me, his body halfway into his truck. He slides back out and steps into the road, walking back toward me. The temperature spikes back to normal, and the furious wind subsides. There's a childish grin stretched across the width of Dylan's face.

I let out a sigh of relief.

Then there's an ear-bursting screech. In slow motion, I turn my head toward the explosion of noise. A semi slams on its brakes, the trailer curling sideways.

"I'll see you tomorrow," Dylan calls out, somehow defying the rules of slow motion. I can't move my mouth fast enough to warn him.

The semi slams into him.

I cry out, screaming so loud the world should stop. My pain breaks through the vacuum as the city around me comes back into existence. The truck comes to a halt as I collapse onto the sidewalk.

* * *

I understand it now. It's amazing how everything can become so clear in an instant. Just as I'm in control of my guilt for Dylan's death, I'm in control of this wheel. I'm in control of what happens next for all three of us. Blue, Rake, and me.

My eyelids are heavy, my vision blurred from a welling of tears. There's no way I could survive another loss.The yellow markings in the center of the road become nothing more than abstract paintings. They've lost their meaning, like so many other things lately.

Rake's too occupied with savage glee as he fires the gun out the window to notice the rolling stream of tears overtaking my face.

My fingers fold around the wheel. If I'm going to pull this off, I won't have time to pull my seat belt across my chest. It'll alert him that I'm about to do the stupidest, most reckless thing imaginable. It's just like love—it doesn't make sense and it happens too fast to stop it.

The headlights of Blue's Jeep flash against the rearview mirror, blinding my already blurred vision. Faintly, I can make out Blue's silhouette through the darkness. Somehow, I can see every inch of his body, every inch of his face. I think I've memorized it.

The gun fires, sending blasts of thunder deep into my ears, deafening me. Rake cackles through his mania. This entire ordeal thrills him. It'll take one pull of his finger with his gun aimed at the right place at the wrong time, and Blue could die.

The guilt if that should happen? I couldn't deal. It's so cliché, but my entire life flashes before my eyes. The faces of everyone I've ever loved speaking to me in a montage inside my mind. They smile, they cry, they'll never get the chance to say goodbye.

It's barely a whisper, but I say goodbye to Blue, irrationally hoping he's able to hear me.

I love you.

One deep breath. My grip tightens against the worn leather wheel. My face is heavy, emotion pouring out of me. Rake slides back into his seat. I feel the burn of his gaze against me. "What—"

I cut him off but don't face him, refusing to give him the satisfaction. My tear-stained face probably fills him with twisted glee, but it should fill him with irrevocable fear because his life is about to end. Maybe mine, too.

But I've made peace with myself.

I jerk the wheel to the right.

CHAPTER THIRTY-TWO

BLUE

My foot taps on the brake, hoping to dodge another stray bullet. Rake's gotten erratic, unsure of what exactly he plans to do. That much is obvious. I think he'd settle–at this point–for going out in a blaze of glory where he mistakenly believes he's the hero.

He slides back into the car, into his seat, and I'm thankful for a moment of relief. I step on the gas, hoping to get closer to them while I form a plan. The best idea I've got is to pull up next to them on Rake's side and try to talk some sense into him.

Like that would work.

The other plan is to follow them until they run out of gas. Then I'll rip him out of that car and beat him to death. I'll take a bullet if I have to, but I will never give up on trying to save her.

The trunk of the car pushes up slightly. When I squint, I can make out two things. It's held shut with bungee cords and there's an arm pushing against the trunk. Someone's in there.

The car steers right, veering off the road before hitting the embankment and flipping over. My foot slams the brake through the floor. My Jeep spins out while their car continues to roll into a cornfield.

My Jeep comes to a halt as the back end slams into the base of a road sign with the banner of the Founders Carnival taped across it. I search frantically for my gun, notice it on the floor, and bend down to grab it. When I sit back up, I see smoke rising from the wreckage.

I punch the door open and jump out, immediately sprinting toward the scene of the crash. "Charlie!" I scream as I cock my gun. When I think I can't run any faster, when I feel my heart would beat out of my chest if I did, I push myself harder. I'm running on empty and all that's left is adrenaline.

A flame ignites on the underside of the flipped car. Out here on this deserted highway, there are only three things I hear. My heart racing, emptiness, and someone crying out for help. It's not Charlie's voice. It's a man's voice, but it's muffled.

I reach the overturned car. Rake crawls weakly from the wreckage, his bloody body hovering close to the ground. I extend my arm and point the gun at him. This is it. This is that life-defining moment that nobody ever sees coming. The one choice I didn't wanna want to have to make because I didn't wanna be that person I used to be. He's pushed me to the edge and I have no choice.

I look away as I pull the trigger.

I make my way quickly to the driver's side and dive to the ground. I don't think I've cried since the day my dad informed me that my mother had skipped town, but I can feel the surge rising. I reach through the broken window, my arm scraping across shards of glass.

With force, I drag her from the car and onto the muddy ground. I put an ear against her chest but can't hear a single beat.

"No, no, no..." I mumble and close my eyes tight. When I open them again, everything's a blur. I rub the back of my fist against my eyes, hoping to clear my vision. There's a pounding against the trunk of the car.

I set Charlie's head down gently against the ground and rush to the trunk. Whoever is inside continues to pound their fist against the metal. The flames begin to spread, the smoke filling the interior of the flipped car. Without taking proper aim, I fire a shot at the trunk. It pops open and Cookie rolls out onto the ground. When I reach down to grab him, he screams in pain but I've got to get him away from the car and get back to Charlie.

I drag him away from the wreckage, beyond happy that he's alive and barely noticing the bone that sticks out the bottom half of his leg. He screams again as I drop him onto the ground. I rush back to Charlie, pulling her head into my lap. I push hair out of her face, and I begin to rock her. "You need to wake up, baby."

There are blood-red tear stains scribbled underneath her eyes. I lay her down flat against the ground, frantically searching my mind for an article I read a long time ago. I push my hands against her ribs and breathe into her mouth. I don't remember the exact counts, so I just start pumping away at her chest, taking great care to use restraint so as to not break her ribs. "Come on."

While pinching her nose tight, I press my lips to hers, breathing heavily into her mouth. A tear drips onto her cheek as I plead for her to wake up. "You can't leave me."

The heat of the fire burns against my face. Fearful that the car might explode, I spin to grab her shoulders, dragging her away from the blaze. My foot sinks into a mudhole and I trip, landing hard against the ground. I kick my feet out, digging them further into the mud. "I'm so sorry..."

* * *

I can't bring myself to get any closer. My body leans against the thick trunk of the solitary oak tree. The sky is too blue, too perfect for a day like today. There should be thunder and rain. Lots of rain. There's a gathering of about maybe fifteen people packed densely together at the edge of the freshly-dug grave.

There's a preacher standing before the small crowd, the Good Book spread wide open, resting on the width of his arms as he reads a winding passage. I can't make out a word of what he says, but I know that it doesn't matter. Everything leads back to me.

Loved ones comfort each other through naive tears. They either don't know or don't care how everything spun so far out of control. How a life that once showed promise has now been wasted.

"You know he'll come back someday and make you pay," Cookie says from behind me.

"Maybe," I say somberly, not turning to look at him. He did what he had to do to save me; taking the blame was the least I could do. But since he shot Trey, things have changed, as they tend to do after you take a life. "But maybe it's time for the cycle to end."

"You know Rake better than that. If he doesn't do anything about it, the police will."

I turn to face him. "I don't know what you want me to do."

He shrugs, looking away from me. "I'm sorry I put you in this position."

"Don't be." I curl my palm into a tense fist and swipe my tongue across my lip. "At the end of the season, when we get to Lakeview, I'm done."

He shakes his head. "What will you do?"

"I'll start a new life, leave all this bullshit behind." I put a hand up to the tree, steadying myself as I dream of a future where I can rest my head in the same place every night. "Maybe I'll meet a girl, settle down, and marry her." A mile-wide smile forms on my face, the first time since that life-ending scuffle with Trey.

"That's hilarious," he jokes. "What kind of girl would fall for you?"

"I guess we'll find out."

CHAPTER THIRTY-THREE

CHARLIE

"What is this place?" I ask Dylan as he leads me through a never-ending white space. There's no end in sight in any direction–up or down–it's as if we're walking on clouds.

"We've only got a few minutes, so we need to talk quick." He reaches for my hand and pulls me down as he sits against the emptiness. "You know I've always loved you, right?"

"Dylan..."

"Just answer me."

"I've known since the day we met, and I don't remember anything that far back."

"Then that's all that matters." His tongue rolls across his lips. "It's okay for you to let me go."

I launch myself onto my feet. "What is this?"

He stands up slowly, placing his hand in mind. "Goodbye."

A tear drips from my eye. "I can't lose you again."

"That's the problem," he smiles and goddammit, how I've missed the way his lips curl. "You've never lost me."

"Do dead people have selective memory?" I pull my hand away from his and wipe away the solitary tear.

"Give me your hand." He reaches for my hand and pulls it close to his heart. Then he places his other hand against my heart. "So long as it's beating, I'll be with you forever."

I chuckle through a tightened throat. "This is so cliché."

He ignores me and presses his palm tighter, closer to my heart. "I'll always be a part of you, living inside your heart, because that's where my home is."

"I love you, Dylan," I say softly across quivering lips as a sea of tears rushes down my face.

He places his palms against my cheeks. "Please don't cry. Don't be sad."

I smile. "They're happy tears."

"Wake up!" A desperate cry with the pitch of a scream tears through my ear. My grasp on this alternative world, this white space, shakes. Dylan disappears and I'm pulled out of my body here and into—my body lying in a muddy field beside a blazing fire. My entire body jerks, giving way to a seizure. Cookie's palms are pressed to my chest, and I watch as relief passes across his face. "Thank God," he says through muted breaths.

I raise myself up, taking in my surroundings. There's an entire drum line beating against my skull. The finality of what I witnessed sinks in just as my body is sunk in this mud. Everything's changed. The entire weight of the world lifts off my shoulders. There's a momentary pause of relief where I'm thankful to be alive, knowing I'll never take another breath for granted again. I've survived.

But I look over to see Blue, frozen in place with his legs kicked out against the ground. "Blue..." He doesn't move. His entire body is lost in some sort of catatonic state. "How long was I out?" I ask Cookie.

"I don't know," he pants. "A few minutes."

"And Blue?"

Cookie looks over to Blue, shaking his head slowly. "He was trying to resuscitate you and he just froze."

The heat of the fire touches the skin on my back. I crawl through the mud and place my hands on his shoulders, shaking him. "Wake up, Blue." His beautiful blue eyes are empty, as if there's nothing behind them. I shake him again. "Come on, you have to wake up." My lip trembles. "Blue..."

Cookie groans as he scoots across the ground and I notice a bone sticking out of his leg. My mouth sags and bile rises in my throat. There's a good chance I'll pass out again. While I'm lost, staring at the protrusion in his leg, I hear a slap against flesh. I crane my head to see Blue shaking his head, his cheek cherry red.

"You're welcome," Cookie says as he throws his back against the ground. He's handling the pain much better than I would. It's baffling how I was pulled out of the wreckage without visible injury. I must have hit my head.

Blue's arms wrap around me tightly, scaring the shit out of me, as I didn't see it coming. I hug him back, caressing his back as his head leans against my neck. I think I even hear him sniffle, and trust me, I'd be crying too if my head didn't hurt so badly.

* * *

Blue and I fireman-carry Cookie across the road and into the back of the tattered Jeep. Behind us, the sun begins to crest over the horizon, shining light upon the scene of the dying fire. It's six in the morning and the humidity is already setting in. The thickness of the air surrounds us. Blue hops into the driver's seat and slams the door. I freeze in place, knowing that I've forgotten something but not quite sure what.

I pivot on one foot, turning back to the wreckage. The money. I'm quick on my feet as I run toward the flipped car, throwing myself onto the ground once I get there. It's gone. I stand back up and search the area with my eyes.

The bag's lying upside down in a bush. I grab it and sprint back toward the Jeep, then it hits me—we don't have to run anymore. This nightmare is over. Sirens begin wailing in the near distance and I freeze in place, my feet planted dead center in the middle of the road. None of us thought about this—what would happen if the police came?

I notice Blue's eyes shift toward the incoming sirens. "Get in the car, Charlie," he says dryly, not breaking focus. "Hurry."

It takes a few seconds to shake off the worry, but when I do, I dart to the Jeep in an instant, tossing the bag of cash into the seat beside Blue. "We've only got a few minutes, so I need you to listen to me, all right?"

"Just get in, and we'll talk about whatever it is—"

"I'm not going." The way it comes off my tongue isn't as stern as I intended. Instead, it comes out weak.

Blue shakes his head furiously. "No, I don't accept that."

"You have to." My eyes grow heavy. "I love you, there's no way you could think otherwise—"

"Then get in the car."

"I mean, I flipped a car because I thought it'd save you."

He pops the door open and hops out onto the road. "What about our plan? We were going to leave this all behind."

"It was different then. There was a crazy man chasing after us," I say, processing it all. "I was scared I was going to die."

He brushes a hand through my hair. "I think you kinda did." He laughs through a veil of sadness.

"That shouldn't be funny." But it is—in a fucked-up kind of way.

"All I've ever wanted was a home. And I found it and it was shattered, and then I found it again in that hotel room," he says frantically. "I realized everything was going to be all right because I had you."

My eyes lock with his. "Then stay."

His head shakes. "You know I can't. I'm a wanted man and there's no getting out of this mess."

I grab onto his arm, holding him with a grip of death. "My dad's a lawyer. He can fix this."

"How would we explain a bullet through Rake's brain?"

"We could start with the fact that he's a psycho and build the case from there."

He drags a thumb across his lip. At least I know he's contemplating staying. A long, drawn-out breath and a shrug later, I realize it was false hope. "I'm sorry."

Tears build up in my eyes. "Then get in your Jeep and run."

"Not without you," he says between clenched lips.

I force a smile. This is an impossible decision, but I have to keep a face of resolve. It'll be easier this way. "I'll stay behind and handle everything. And when it's all over, you can come back to Lakeview." There's a good chance he's right, that somehow the police will pin equal blame on all parties involved, but something feels wrong about leaving now. I've only said goodbye to two and a half people. Tyson at the carnival and Dylan in my post-death, pre-resurrection dream. And a half-assed letter to my mother.

"Then I'll be back someday." He grabs both of my hands. "Because a life without you isn't an option."

"You're telling me," I say, relieved, as I wipe my eye with a thumb.

He laces his fingers with mine, holding them tight as he kisses me softly. The touch of his lips brings a million memories to the surface, every single emotion imaginable present in the smoothness of his touch. "I love you," he breathes into my mouth before pulling away.

The sirens grow louder. They are well within a minute's distance. "You should go."

His head bows to the side. "Are you sure you won't come?"

I give him a slight nod, afraid my words would betray me. His fingers slide out of mine slowly, as if he's hoping I'll grab onto him and never let go. Every further micrometer he slips, the strength in my legs grows weaker.

He looks back at me longingly as he slides into his seat. When it sinks in, and he accepts the fact that I'm not going, he turns around and steps on the gas. The wheels turn slowly. I give him one last perfect smile. The steady flow of tears follows instantly.

I don't know if he's driving ten miles an hour or if my world has come to a sudden halt. Blue and red flashing lights spin over a rolling hill less than a half mile away. My head tells me I should step off the road and into the grass but goddamn if my heart doesn't have other plans.

"Blue!" I scream at the top of my lungs, waving my hands like the final girl in a horror film trying to hitchhike a ride after all her friends have been cut into pieces with a chainsaw. Is it just me or are his wheels now turning faster? He must have seen the lights.

I give my entire body a shake and kick my feet against the asphalt beneath me, running faster than I've ever run. "Blue!" I scream again. "Stop!"

He's not slowing down and I'm losing ground while the cops behind me gain it. If they see me in the street, running from the scene, I'll surely spend the rest of my life in prison. "Please stop." I mean to scream again, but it comes out as a whimper. My lungs pull tight, and I throw myself onto the surface of the road in defeat as Blue begins to fade into the distance.

I cry into the cracks of the road, giving myself in to the overwhelming sobs of loss. Then I hear screeching brakes. When I look up, I see Blue's legs running past the red brake lights of his Jeep. My lips quiver on the verge of the revelation that my brief bout of insanity didn't cause me any more grief.

My feet rise before my head, a physical impossibility, but that's the way it feels. I rush toward him, launching myself into his arms.

"You're so stupid," he says, and I know it's the best sort of compliment. "So fucking crazy."

"I know, right?"

"What made you change your mind?"

I kick my legs out from around him and hop onto the ground. "It took me a few seconds too long to figure it out. But if I let you drive away, then all of this would've been for nothing." He nods his head and I assume that he's agreeing with me, but I can't be too sure. "I guess what I'm trying to say is, take me home, Blue."

His lips purse, his head pulls back. This is normally the part where he'd scratch his head. "I thought you just said you wanted to leave."

I shake my head, pursing my own lips along with him. "Have you already forgotten? Home isn't in Lakeview." I grab his hand and place it to my chest. "It's right here. Always here."

"I fucking love you."

He pulls me into a passionate kiss. Every part of him sinks into me, his lips so perfect against mine. It's only been a few long hours since the last time we were so close together, but it feels like a lifetime.

I press against his chest, pulling back, taking a breath, and speaking all at once. "I think we should go."

He nods and pulls me into him again. We melt together, unfazed by the sirens closing in on us. "Yeah, we should probably go."

When he pulls back and grabs my hand, preparing to sprint to the Jeep, I pull him tight against me, needing to taste every bit of him to know that I'm making the right decision.

I am.

The sun rises over the trees as we hop into the Jeep, ready to leave this life behind and start anew somewhere else. We peel out against the asphalt, leaving tracks of evidence behind, but I'm positive Blue couldn't care less. The moment his foot hit the pedal, we all became fugitives. Well, he's already a fugitive, but my point should be clear.

It doesn't matter where we go. We'll never be homesick again.

EPILOGUE

CHARLIE

I lost everything but my heart. It's fragile, always one heartbreak away from shattering, but it is there. I know this because every time Blue touches me—or even looks at me—it skips a beat. All these months later, and everything still feels brand new. Freud would say that's something else entirely, but he's also dead, so what does he know?

The carnival closed about two hours ago and the rest of the crew has long gone to sleep, preparing to rise again in less than seven hours. I should be in bed too, but I've come to understand what Blue meant that night we sat on the porch discussing his troubling sleeping patterns. I'd rather be awake while the rest of the world dreams because, in the stillness of silence, life becomes more vivid than any closed-eye fantasy.

Blue, ever the gentleman, loaded me into the trenches of the Ferris wheel and sent me to the top of the world. Then he shut the power off because it's not exactly within company guidelines to play with the machinery after closing.

A hand folds around the edge of the bucket as Blue pulls himself into the rocking seat and my heart skips a beat. See, I told you. Every damn time. It's peculiar how this particular ride has come to soothe me after years spent dreading the revolver of death.

Blue sits down, hands me a beer, and wraps his arm around me. I rest my head on his shoulder and take a swig. Every Friday night, it seems to be the same thing. Blue and I ascend the heights of the tallest carnival ride, meditating in silent love because we know it's two against the world. Or at least two against the law.

Someday, maybe soon, we'll have to leave the life of the carnival behind. Our past will catch up to us. There was already a close call a few weeks back when a detective came knocking. We're both fugitives of both the law and of our own pasts. We can't change either, but regret isn't an option. That's a dangerous path to go down.

Now, I can't begin to explain the whirlwind. I wouldn't know where to start. The only thing I know is that during these past few months of moving from temporary home to temporary home, one thing has remained consistent—my love for him. It's undying, it's beautiful, and it's everything I never knew I was missing.

The pain fades but the wounds remain. I'm not the same girl that walked into the county fair last August. I'm not the same girl that flipped a car going sixty miles an hour in a reckless bid to save the man I love. I'm always changing. Always evolving. I'll return home someday and pray I'm able to pick up the pieces of my broken life.

For better or worse, Jimmy Clay changed my life— because he's a fucking liar. And I thank him every day because, without him, the chances that I would've met Blue are slim. But the biggest lesson I've learned is that chance isn't the same thing as fate, but it's something more akin to a carnival ride.

Yeah, life is just like a carnival ride.

AMUSEMENT (Carnival #2) coming this fall!
Sign up for the K.B. Nelson Newsletter at
http://eepurl.com/LzHIL

Website:
http://kbnelsonbooks.com/
Twitter:
https://twitter.com/kbnelsonkb
Facebook:
https://www.facebook.com/kbnelsonauthor
Goodreads:
https://www.goodreads.com/author/show/8052332.K_B_Nelson

Reviews are important for all authors. If you enjoyed this book, I'd love for you to share your thoughts on the platform you purchased it from. I love to chat with readers, so feel free to drop me a line on any of the platforms listed above, or through email.

www.ingramcontent.com/pod-product-compliance
Lightning Source LLC
Chambersburg PA
CBHW020232180626
46810CB00006B/2153